CLASSIC RAILWAY
STORIES

More short stories available
from Macmillan Collector's Library

Classic Horror Stories
Classic Stories of the Sea
Classic Fantasy Stories
Classic Love Stories
Classic Christmas Crime Stories
Enchanted Tales & Happily Ever Afters
Standing Her Ground: Classic Short Stories by Trailblazing Women
Sleepily Ever After: Bedtime Stories for Grown Ups
Classic Dog Stories
Classic Cat Stories

CLASSIC RAILWAY STORIES

Selection and introduction by
HARRIET SANDERS

MACMILLAN COLLECTOR'S LIBRARY

This collection first published 2025 by Macmillan Collector's Library
an imprint of Pan Macmillan
The Smithson, 6 Briset Street, London EC1M 5NR
EU representative: Macmillan Publishers Ireland Ltd, 1st Floor,
The Liffey Trust Centre, 117–126 Sheriff Street Upper,
Dublin 1, DO1 YC43
Associated companies throughout the world
www.panmacmillan.com

ISBN 978-1-0350-5495-4

Introduction copyright © Harriet Sanders 2025
Selection and arrangement copyright © Macmillan Publishers International Ltd. 2025

All rights reserved. No part of this publication may be reproduced, stored in a retrieval system, or transmitted, in any form, or by any means (electronic, mechanical, photocopying, recording or otherwise) without the prior written permission of the publisher.

1 3 5 7 9 8 6 4 2

A CIP catalogue record for this book is available from the British Library.

Endpaper pattern by Andrew Davidson
Typeset in Plantin by Jouve (UK), Milton Keynes
Printed and bound in China by Imago

This book is sold subject to the condition that it shall not, by way of trade or otherwise, be lent, hired out, or otherwise circulated without the publisher's prior consent in any form of binding or cover other than that in which it is published and without a similar condition including this condition being imposed on the subsequent purchaser.

Visit **www.panmacmillan.com** to read more
about all our books and to buy them.

Contents

Introduction vii

CONNECTIONS 1

ANTON CHEKHOV 3
A Happy Man

LUCY MAUD MONTGOMERY 13
The Man on the Train

SAKI 27
The Story-Teller

KATHERINE MANSFIELD 37
An Indiscreet Journey

LADY MARGARET MAJENDIE 63
A Railway Journey

DERAILMENTS 83

ARTHUR CONAN DOYLE 85
The Lost Special

V. L. WHITECHURCH 115
The Affair of the Corridor Express

MAURICE LEBLANC 137
The Mysterious Railway-Passenger

ARTHUR CONAN DOYLE 165
The Man with the Watches

AMELIA B. EDWARDS 195
The Four-Fifteen Express

DIVERSIONS 241

SIR ARTHUR QUILLER-COUCH 243
Cuckoo Valley Railway

AMELIA B. EDWARDS 251
The Engineer

O. HENRY 283
Holding Up a Train

MARGARET OLIPHANT 303
A Story of a Wedding Tour

Introduction

Train travel today has lost much of its charm. Trains are expensive, crowded and subject to frequent delays due to all manner of increasingly inventive reasons – 'swans on the line' anyone?

Given today's often disheartening experience, it's worth remembering how much of a dramatic and profound impact the birth of rail travel and its expansion had on life in the nineteenth and early twentieth centuries. Travel became faster, more affordable and more accessible to more people than ever before. Families could visit relatives and enjoy day trips to the seaside, friends could connect and the commute was born. It was a time of unbridled economic growth that created great riches for some and tough labour for others.

Like all social, industrial and economic shifts, the railways in particular had a significant cultural impact on literature, as can be seen in this collection of stories. Indeed, the short story form and early train travel have much in common. Train travel was disruptive, fast and sometimes perilous – all the ingredients too of a good short story. The narrative of a short story needs to move quickly because space is limited, much like hurtling along in a confined railway carriage. Within these confines, strangers and acquaintances are thrown together and, if you miss your stop, you might be in trouble. Then there are the perils of travelling alone to somewhere new, possibly in the dark, when who knows what crimes and mysteries might unfold.

It's no wonder so many authors drew on the new and expanding railways and stations that sprang up around them as the setting for their writing, as well as the labour – both worthy and disreputable – involved in establishing the new railway system.

The stories in this book are divided into three sections: connections, derailments and diversions. In the first section, a wealth of travelling characters find themselves in all kinds of different situations. From the inimitable Saki there's a comedic portrayal of the efforts to control boisterous children, and in Katherine Mansfield's gripping modernist story the narrator risks travelling by train through wartime France in her longing to be reunited with her lover.

Crime and rail travel have always been successful bedfellows and the second section highlights some of the masters of the genre such as Arthur Conan Doyle and Maurice Leblanc as well as lesser-known writers such as train aficionado V. L. Whitechurch.

INTRODUCTION

While the railways represented progress and new opportunities for some, others lamented the loss of the countryside and the threat to rural ways. In his charming story 'Cuckoo Valley Railway', Arthur Quiller-Couch describes the opening of a country railway and the intersection between new technology and traditional country life. By contrast, Amelia B. Edwards' story 'The Engineer' looks outwards and reflects on how this major new industry enabled its workers to take their skills abroad. The engineer of the title works in Egypt, Italy, France and America, but wherever he goes he is tormented by past rivalries and betrayals. And in Margaret Oliphant's dramatic and poignant 'A Story of a Wedding Tour', an unhappy wife, stranded in France, must try to build a new life for herself.

All in all, there is much richness, dramatic opportunity and variety to be found in railway stories, so climb aboard and enjoy!

CONNECTIONS

Anton Chekhov

A Happy Man

The passenger train is just starting from Bologoe, the junction on the Petersburg-Moscow line. In a second-class smoking compartment five passengers sit dozing, shrouded in the twilight of the carriage. They have just had a meal, and now, snugly ensconced in their seats, they are trying to go to sleep. Stillness.

The door opens and in there walks a tall, lanky figure straight as a poker, with a ginger-coloured hat and a smart overcoat, wonderfully suggestive of a journalist in Jules Verne or on the comic stage.

The figure stands still in the middle of the compartment for a long while, breathing heavily, screwing up his eyes and peering at the seats.

"No, wrong again!" he mutters. "What the deuce! It's positively revolting! No, the wrong one again!"

One of the passengers stares at the figure and utters a shout of joy:

"Ivan Alexyevitch! what brings you here? Is it you?"

The poker-like gentleman starts, stares blankly at

the passenger, and recognizing him claps his hands with delight.

"Ha! Pyotr Petrovitch," he says. "How many summers, how many winters! I didn't know you were in this train."

"How are you getting on?"

"I am all right; the only thing is, my dear fellow, I've lost my compartment and I simply can't find it. What an idiot I am! I ought to be thrashed!"

The poker-like gentleman sways a little unsteadily and sniggers.

"Queer things do happen!" he continues. "I stepped out just after the second bell to get a glass of brandy. I got it, of course. Well, I thought, since it's a long way to the next station, it would be as well to have a second glass. While I was thinking about it and drinking it the third bell rang . . . I ran like mad and jumped into the first carriage. I am an idiot! I am the son of a hen!"

"But you seem in very good spirits," observes Pyotr Petrovitch. "Come and sit down! There's room and a welcome."

"No, no . . . I'm off to look for my carriage. Good-bye!"

"You'll fall between the carriages in the dark if you don't look out! Sit down, and when we get to a station you'll find your own compartment. Sit down!"

A HAPPY MAN

Ivan Alexyevitch heaves a sigh and irresolutely sits down facing Pyotr Petrovitch. He is visibly excited, and fidgets as though he were sitting on thorns.

"Where are you travelling to?" Pyotr Petrovitch enquires.

"I? Into space. There is such a turmoil in my head that I couldn't tell where I am going myself. I go where fate takes me. Ha-ha! My dear fellow, have you ever seen a happy fool? No? Well, then, take a look at one. You behold the happiest of mortals! Yes! Don't you see something from my face?"

"Well, one can see you're a bit . . . a tiny bit so-so."

"I dare say I look awfully stupid just now. Ach! it's a pity I haven't a looking-glass. I should like to look at my counting-house. My dear fellow, I feel I am turning into an idiot, honour bright. Ha-ha! Would you believe it, I'm on my honeymoon. Am I not the son of a hen?"

"You? Do you mean to say you are married?"

"To-day, my dear boy. We came away straight after the wedding."

Congratulations and the usual questions follow.

"Well, you are a fellow!" laughs Pyotr Petrovitch. "That's why you are rigged out such a dandy."

"Yes, indeed . . . To complete the illusion, I've

even sprinkled myself with scent. I am over my ears in vanity! No care, no thought, nothing but a sensation of something or other . . . deuce knows what to call it . . . beatitude or something? I've never felt so grand in my life!"

Ivan Alexyevitch shuts his eyes and waggles his head.

"I'm revoltingly happy," he says. "Just think; in a minute I shall go to my compartment. There on the seat near the window is sitting a being who is, so to say, devoted to you with her whole being. A little blonde with a little nose . . . little fingers . . . My little darling! My angel! My little poppet! Phylloxera of my soul! And her little foot! Good God! A little foot not like our beetle-crushers, but something miniature, fairy-like, allegorical. I could pick it up and eat it, that little foot! Oh, but you don't understand! You're a materialist, of course, you begin analyzing at once, and one thing and another. You are cold-hearted bachelors, that's what you are! When you get married you'll think of me. 'Where's Ivan Alexyevitch now?' you'll say. Yes; so in a minute I'm going to my compartment. There she is waiting for me with impatience . . . in joyful anticipation of my appearance. She'll have a smile to greet me. I sit down beside her and take her chin with my two fingers . . ."

Ivan Alexyevitch waggles his head and goes off into a chuckle of delight.

"Then I lay my noddle on her shoulder and put my arm round her waist. Around all is silence, you know . . . poetic twilight. I could embrace the whole world at such a moment. Pyotr Petrovitch, allow me to embrace you!"

"Delighted, I'm sure." The two friends embrace while the passengers laugh in chorus. And the happy bridegroom continues:

"And to complete the idiocy, or, as the novelists say, to complete the illusion, one goes to the refreshment-room and tosses off two or three glasses. And then something happens in your head and your heart, finer than you can read of in a fairy tale. I am a man of no importance, but I feel as though I were limitless: I embrace the whole world!"

The passengers, looking at the tipsy and blissful bridegroom, are infected by his cheerfulness and no longer feel sleepy. Instead of one listener, Ivan Alexyevitch has now an audience of five. He wriggles and splutters, gesticulates, and prattles on without ceasing. He laughs and they all laugh.

"Gentlemen, gentlemen, don't think so much! Damn all this analysis! If you want a drink, drink, no need to philosophize as to whether it's bad for you or not . . . Damn all this philosophy and psychology!"

The guard walks through the compartment.

"My dear fellow," the bridegroom addresses him, "when you pass through the carriage No. 209 look out for a lady in a grey hat with a white bird and tell her I'm here!"

"Yes, sir. Only there isn't a No. 209 in this train; there's 219!"

"Well, 219, then! It's all the same. Tell that lady, then, that her husband is all right!"

Ivan Alexyevitch suddenly clutches his head and groans:

"Husband . . . Lady . . . All in a minute! Husband . . . Ha-ha! I am a puppy that needs thrashing, and here I am a husband! Ach, idiot! But think of her! . . . Yesterday she was a little girl, a midget . . . it's simply incredible!"

"Nowadays it really seems strange to see a happy man," observes one of the passengers; "one as soon expects to see a white elephant."

"Yes, and whose fault is it?" says Ivan Alexyevitch, stretching his long legs and thrusting out his feet with their very pointed toes. "If you are not happy it's your own fault! Yes, what else do you suppose it is? Man is the creator of his own happiness. If you want to be happy you will be, but you don't want to be! You obstinately turn away from happiness."

A HAPPY MAN

"Why, what next! How do you make that out?"

"Very simply. Nature has ordained that at a certain stage in his life man should love. When that time comes you should love like a house on fire, but you won't heed the dictates of nature, you keep waiting for something. What's more, it's laid down by law that the normal man should enter upon matrimony. There's no happiness without marriage. When the propitious moment has come, get married. There's no use in shilly-shallying . . . But you don't get married, you keep waiting for something! Then the Scriptures tell us that 'wine maketh glad the heart of man.' . . . If you feel happy and you want to feel better still, then go to the refreshment bar and have a drink. The great thing is not to be too clever, but to follow the beaten track! The beaten track is a grand thing!"

"You say that man is the creator of his own happiness. How the devil is he the creator of it when a toothache or an ill-natured mother-in-law is enough to scatter his happiness to the winds? Everything depends on chance. If we had an accident at this moment you'd sing a different tune."

"Stuff and nonsense!" retorts the bridegroom. "Railway accidents only happen once a year. I'm not afraid of an accident, for there is no reason for one. Accidents are exceptional! Confound them! I don't want to talk of them! Oh, I believe we're stopping at a station."

"Where are you going now?" asks Pyotr Petrovitch. "To Moscow or somewhere farther south?"

"Why, bless you! How could I go somewhere farther south, when I'm on my way to the north?"

"But Moscow isn't in the north."

"I know that, but we're on our way to Petersburg," says Ivan Alexyevitch.

"We are going to Moscow, mercy on us!"

"To Moscow? What do you mean?" says the bridegroom in amazement.

"It's queer . . . For what station did you take your ticket?"

"For Petersburg."

"In that case I congratulate you. You've got into the wrong train."

There follows a minute of silence. The bridegroom gets up and looks blankly round the company.

"Yes, yes," Pyotr Petrovitch explains. "You must have jumped into the wrong train at Bologoe . . . After your glass of brandy you succeeded in getting into the down-train."

Ivan Alexyevitch turns pale, clutches his head, and begins pacing rapidly about the carriage.

"Ach, idiot that I am!" he says in indignation. "Scoundrel! The devil devour me! Whatever am I to do now? Why, my wife is in that train! She's there all alone, expecting me, consumed by anxiety. Ach, I'm a motley fool!"

The bridegroom falls on the seat and writhes as though someone had trodden on his corns.

"I am un-unhappy man!" he moans. "What am I to do, what am I to do?"

"There, there!" the passengers try to console him. "It's all right . . . You must telegraph to your wife and try to change into the Petersburg express. In that way you'll overtake her."

"The Petersburg express!" weeps the bridegroom, the creator of his own happiness. "And how am I to get a ticket for the Petersburg express? All my money is with my wife."

The passengers, laughing and whispering together, make a collection and furnish the happy man with funds.

Lucy Maud Montgomery

The Man on the Train

When the telegram came from William George, Grandma Sheldon was all alone with Cyrus and Louise. And Cyrus and Louise, aged respectively twelve and eleven, were not very much good, Grandma thought, when it came to advising what was to be done. Grandma was "all in a flutter, dear, oh dear," as she said.

The telegram said that Delia, William George's wife, was seriously ill down at Green Village, and William George wanted Samuel to bring Grandma down immediately. Delia had always thought there was nobody like Grandma when it came to nursing sick folks.

But Samuel and his wife were both away—had been away for two days and intended to be away for five more. They had driven to Sinclair, twenty miles away, to visit with Mrs. Samuel's folks for a week.

"Dear, oh dear, what shall I do?" said Grandma.

"Go right to Green Village on the evening train," said Cyrus briskly.

"Dear, oh dear, and leave you two alone!" cried Grandma.

"Louise and I will do very well until tomorrow," said Cyrus sturdily. "We will send word to Sinclair by today's mail, and Father and Mother will be home by tomorrow night."

"But I never was on the cars in my life," protested Grandma nervously. "I'm—I'm so frightened to start alone. And you never know what kind of people you may meet on the train."

"You'll be all right, Grandma. I'll drive you to the station, get you your ticket, and put you on the train. Then you'll have nothing to do until the train gets to Green Village. I'll send a telegram to Uncle William George to meet you."

"I shall fall and break my neck getting off the train," said Grandma pessimistically. But she was wondering at the same time whether she had better take the black valise or the yellow, and whether William George would be likely to have plenty of flaxseed in the house.

It was six miles to the station, and Cyrus drove Grandma over in time to catch a train that reached Green Village at nine o'clock.

"Dear, oh dear," said Grandma, "what if William George's folks ain't there to meet me? It's all very well, Cyrus, to say that they will be there, but you don't know. And it's all very well to say not to be nervous because everything will be all right. If you were seventy-five years old and had never set foot on the cars in your life you'd be nervous too, and you can't be sure that everything will be all right. You never know what sort of people you'll meet on the train. I may get on the wrong train or lose my ticket or get carried past Green Village or get my pocket picked. Well, no, I won't do that, for not one cent will I carry with me. You shall take back home all the money you don't need to get my ticket. Then I shall be easier in my mind. Dear, oh dear, if it wasn't that Delia is so seriously ill I wouldn't go one step."

"Oh, you'll be all right, Grandma," assured Cyrus.

He got Grandma's ticket for her and Grandma tied it up in the corner of her handkerchief. Then the train came in and Grandma, clinging closely to Cyrus, was put on it. Cyrus found a comfortable seat for her and shook hands cheerily.

"Good-bye, Grandma. Don't be frightened. Here's the *Weekly Argus*. I got it at the store. You may like to look over it."

Then Cyrus was gone, and in a minute the station house and platform began to glide away.

Dear, oh dear, what has happened to it? thought Grandma in dismay. The next moment she exclaimed aloud, "Why, it's us that's moving, not it!"

Some of the passengers smiled pleasantly at

Grandma. She was the variety of old lady at which people do smile pleasantly; a grandma with round, pink cheeks, soft, brown eyes, and lovely snow-white curls is a nice person to look at wherever she is found.

After a while Grandma, to her amazement, discovered that she liked riding on the cars. It was not at all the disagreeable experience she had expected it to be. Why, she was just as comfortable as if she were in her own rocking chair at home! And there was such a lot of people to look at, and many of the ladies had such beautiful dresses and hats. After all, the people you met on a train, thought Grandma, are surprisingly like the people you meet off it. If it had not been for wondering how she would get off at Green Village, Grandma would have enjoyed herself thoroughly.

Four or five stations farther on the train halted at a lonely-looking place consisting of the station house and a barn, surrounded by scrub woods and blueberry barrens. One passenger got on and, finding only one vacant seat in the crowded car, sat right down beside Grandma Sheldon.

Grandma Sheldon held her breath while she looked him over. Was he a pickpocket? He didn't appear like one, but you can never be sure of the people you meet on the train. Grandma remembered with a sigh of thankfulness that she had no money.

Besides, he seemed really very respectable and harmless. He was quietly dressed in a suit of dark-blue serge with a black overcoat. He wore his hat well down on his forehead and was clean shaven. His hair was very black, but his eyes were blue—nice eyes, Grandma thought. She always felt great confidence in a man who had bright, open, blue eyes. Grandpa Sheldon, who had died so long ago, four years after their marriage, had had bright blue eyes.

To be sure, he had fair hair, reflected Grandma. It's real odd to see such black hair with such light blue eyes. Well, he's real nice looking, and I don't believe there's a mite of harm in him.

The early autumn night had now fallen and Grandma could not amuse herself by watching the scenery. She bethought herself of the paper Cyrus had given her and took it out of her basket. It was an old weekly a fortnight back. On the first page was a long account of a murder case with scare heads, and into this Grandma plunged eagerly. Sweet old Grandma Sheldon, who would not have harmed a fly and hated to see even a mousetrap set, simply revelled in the newspaper accounts of murders. And the more shocking and cold-blooded they were, the more eagerly did Grandma read of them.

This murder story was particularly good from Grandma's point of view; it was full of "thrills." A man had been shot down, apparently in cold blood, and his supposed murderer was still at large and had eluded all the efforts of justice to capture him. His name was Mark Hartwell, and he was described as a tall, fair man, with full auburn beard and curly, light hair.

"What a shocking thing!" said Grandma aloud.

Her companion looked at her with a kindly, amused smile.

"What is it?" he asked.

"Why, this murder at Charlotteville," answered Grandma, forgetting, in her excitement, that it was not safe to talk to people you meet on the train. "It just makes my blood run cold to read about it. And to think that the man who did it is still around the country somewhere—plotting other murders, I haven't a doubt. What is the good of the police?"

"They're dull fellows," agreed the dark man.

"But I don't envy that man his conscience," said Grandma solemnly—and somewhat inconsistently, in view of her statement about the other murders that were being plotted. "What must a man feel like who has the blood of a fellow creature on his hands? Depend upon it, his punishment has begun already, caught or not."

"That is true," said the dark man quietly.

"Such a good-looking man too," said Grandma, looking wistfully at the murderer's picture. "It doesn't seem possible that he can have killed anybody. But the paper says there isn't a doubt."

"He is probably guilty," said the dark man, "but nothing is known of his provocation. The affair may not have been so cold-blooded as the accounts state. Those newspaper fellows never err on the side of undercolouring."

"I really think," said Grandma slowly, "that I would like to see a murderer—just one. Whenever I say anything like that, Adelaide—Adelaide is Samuel's wife—looks at me as if she thought there was something wrong about me. And perhaps there is, but I do, all the same. When I was a little girl, there was a man in our settlement who was suspected of poisoning his wife. She died very suddenly. I used to look at him with such interest. But it wasn't satisfactory, because you could never be sure whether he was really guilty or not. I never could believe that he was, because he was such a nice man in some ways and so good and kind to children. I don't believe a man who was bad enough to poison his wife could have any good in him."

"Perhaps not," agreed the dark man. He had absent-mindedly folded up Grandma's old copy of the *Argus* and put it in his pocket. Grandma did not like to ask him for it, although she would have liked to see if there were any more murder stories in it. Besides, just at that moment the conductor came around for tickets.

Grandma looked in the basket for her handkerchief. It was not there. She looked on the floor and on the seat and under the seat. It was not there. She stood up and shook herself—still no handkerchief.

"Dear, oh dear," exclaimed Grandma wildly, "I've lost my ticket—I always knew I would—I told Cyrus I would! Oh, where can it be?"

The conductor scowled unsympathetically. The dark man got up and helped Grandma search, but no ticket was to be found.

"You'll have to pay the money then, and something extra," said the conductor gruffly.

"I can't—I haven't a cent of money," wailed Grandma. "I gave it all to Cyrus because I was afraid my pocket would be picked. Oh, what shall I do?"

"Don't worry. I'll make it all right," said the dark man. He took out his pocketbook and handed the conductor a bill. That functionary grumblingly made the change and marched onward, while Grandma, pale with excitement and relief, sank back into her seat.

"I can't tell you how much I am obliged to you,

sir," she said tremulously. "I don't know what I should have done. Would he have put me off right here in the snow?"

"I hardly think he would have gone to such lengths," said the dark man with a smile. "But he's a cranky, disobliging fellow enough—I know him of old. And you must not feel overly grateful to me. I am glad of the opportunity to help you. I had an old grandmother myself once," he added with a sigh.

"You must give me your name and address, of course," said Grandma, "and my son—Samuel Sheldon of Midverne—will see that the money is returned to you. Well, this is a lesson to me! I'll never trust myself on a train again, and all I wish is that I was safely off this one. This fuss has worked my nerves all up again."

"Don't worry, Grandma. I'll see you safely off the train when we get to Green Village."

"Will you, though? Will you, now?" said Grandma eagerly. "I'll be real easy in my mind, then," she added with a returning smile. "I feel as if I could trust you for anything—and I'm a real suspicious person too."

They had a long talk after that—or, rather, Grandma talked and the dark man listened and smiled. She told him all about William George and Delia and their baby and about Samuel and Adelaide and Cyrus and Louise and the three cats and the parrot. He seemed to enjoy her accounts of them too.

When they reached Green Village station he gathered up Grandma's parcels and helped her tenderly off the train.

"Anybody here to meet Mrs. Sheldon?" he asked of the station master.

The latter shook his head. "Don't think so. Haven't seen anybody here to meet anybody tonight."

"Dear, oh dear," said poor Grandma. "This is just what I expected. They've never got Cyrus's telegram. Well, I might have known it. What shall I do?"

"How far is it to your son's?" asked the dark man.

"Only half a mile—just over the hill there. But I'll never get there alone this dark night."

"Of course not. But I'll go with you. The road is good—we'll do finely."

"But that train won't wait for you," gasped Grandma, half in protest.

"It doesn't matter. The Starmont freight passes here in half an hour and I'll go on her. Come along, Grandma."

"Oh, but you're good," said Grandma. "Some woman is proud to have you for a son."

The man did not answer. He had not answered any of the personal remarks Grandma had made to him in her conversation.

They were not long in reaching William George Sheldon's house, for the village road was good and Grandma was smart on her feet. She was welcomed with eagerness and surprise.

"To think that there was no one to meet you!" exclaimed William George. "But I never dreamed of your coming by train, knowing how you were set against it. Telegram? No, I got no telegram. S'pose Cyrus forgot to send it. I'm most heartily obliged to you, sir, for looking after my mother so kindly."

"It was a pleasure," said the dark man courteously. He had taken off his hat, and they saw a curious scar, shaped like a large, red butterfly, high up on his forehead under his hair. "I am delighted to have been of any assistance to her."

He would not wait for supper—the next train would be in and he must not miss it.

"There are people looking for me," he said with his curious smile. "They will be much disappointed if they do not find me."

He had gone, and the whistle of the Starmont freight had blown before Grandma remembered that he had not given her his name and address.

"Dear, oh dear, how are we ever going to send that money to him?" she exclaimed. "And he so nice and goodhearted!"

Grandma worried over this for a week in the

intervals of looking after Delia. One day William George came in with a large city daily in his hands. He looked curiously at Grandma and then showed her the front-page picture of a man, clean-shaven, with an oddly shaped scar high up on his forehead.

"Did you ever see that man, Mother?" he asked.

"Of course I did," said Grandma excitedly. "Why, it's the man I met on the train. Who is he? What is his name? Now, we'll know where to send—"

"That is Mark Hartwell, who shot Amos Gray at Charlotteville three weeks ago," said William George quietly.

Grandma looked at him blankly for a moment.

"It couldn't be," she gasped at last. "That man a murderer! I'll never believe it!"

"It's true enough, Mother. The whole story is here. He had shaved his beard and dyed his hair and came near getting clear out of the country. They were on his trail the day he came down in the train with you and lost it because of his getting off to bring you here. His disguise was so perfect that there was little fear of his being recognized so long as he hid that scar. But it was seen in Montreal and he was run to earth there. He has made a full confession."

"I don't care," cried Grandma valiantly. "I'll never believe he was all bad—a man who would do what he did for a poor old woman like me, when he was flying for his life too. No, no, there was good in him even if he did kill that man. And I'm sure he must feel terrible over it."

In this view Grandma persisted. She never would say or listen to a word against Mark Hartwell, and she had only pity for him whom everyone else condemned. With her own trembling hands she wrote him a letter to accompany the money Samuel sent before Hartwell was taken to the penitentiary for life. She thanked him again for his kindness to her and assured him that she knew he was sorry for what he had done and that she would pray for him every night of her life. Mark Hartwell had been hard and defiant enough, but the prison officials told that he cried like a child over Grandma Sheldon's little letter.

"There's nobody all bad," says Grandma when she relates the story. "I used to believe a murderer must be, but I know better now. I think of that poor man often and often. He was so kind and gentle to me—he must have been a good boy once. I write him a letter every Christmas and I send him tracts and papers. He's my own little charity. But I've never been on the cars since and I never will be again. You never can tell what will happen to you or what sort of people you'll meet if you trust yourself on a train."

Saki

The Story-Teller

It was a hot afternoon, and the railway carriage was correspondingly sultry, and the next stop was at Templecombe, nearly an hour ahead. The occupants of the carriage were a small girl, and a smaller girl, and a small boy. An aunt belonging to the children occupied one corner seat, and the further corner seat on the opposite side was occupied by a bachelor who was a stranger to their party, but the small girls and the small boy emphatically occupied the compartment. Both the aunt and the children were conversational in a limited, persistent way, reminding one of the attentions of a housefly that refused to be discouraged. Most of the aunt's remarks seemed to begin with "Don't," and nearly all of the children's remarks began with "Why?" The bachelor said nothing out loud.

"Don't, Cyril, don't," exclaimed the aunt, as the small boy began smacking the cushions of the seat, producing a cloud of dust at each blow.

"Come and look out of the window," she added.

The child moved reluctantly to the window. "Why

are those sheep being driven out of that field?" he asked.

"I expect they are being driven to another field where there is more grass," said the aunt weakly.

"But there is lots of grass in that field," protested the boy; "there's nothing else but grass there. Aunt, there's lots of grass in that field."

"Perhaps the grass in the other field is better," suggested the aunt fatuously.

"Why is it better?" came the swift, inevitable question.

"Oh, look at those cows!" exclaimed the aunt. Nearly every field along the line had contained cows or bullocks, but she spoke as though she were drawing attention to a rarity.

"Why is the grass in the other field better?" persisted Cyril.

The frown on the bachelor's face was deepening to a scowl. He was a hard, unsympathetic man, the aunt decided in her mind. She was utterly unable to come to any satisfactory decision about the grass in the other field.

The smaller girl created a diversion by beginning to recite "On the Road to Mandalay." She only knew the first line, but she put her limited knowledge to the fullest possible use. She repeated the line over and over again in a dreamy but resolute and very audible voice; it seemed to the bachelor as though some one had had a bet with her that she could not repeat the line aloud two thousand times without stopping. Whoever it was who had made the wager was likely to lose his bet.

"Come over here and listen to a story," said the aunt, when the bachelor had looked twice at her and once at the communication cord.

The children moved listlessly towards the aunt's end of the carriage. Evidently her reputation as a story-teller did not rank high in their estimation.

In a low, confidential voice, interrupted at frequent intervals by loud, petulant questions from her listeners, she began an unenterprising and deplorably uninteresting story about a little girl who was good, and made friends with every one on account of her goodness, and was finally saved from a mad bull by a number of rescuers who admired her moral character.

"Wouldn't they have saved her if she hadn't been good?" demanded the bigger of the small girls. It was exactly the question that the bachelor had wanted to ask.

"Well, yes," admitted the aunt lamely, "but I don't think they would have run quite so fast to her help if they had not liked her so much."

"It's the stupidest story I've ever heard," said the bigger of the small girls, with immense conviction.

"I didn't listen after the first bit, it was so stupid," said Cyril.

The smaller girl made no actual comment on the story, but she had long ago recommenced a murmured repetition of her favourite line.

"You don't seem to be a success as a story-teller," said the bachelor suddenly from his corner.

The aunt bristled in instant defence at this unexpected attack.

"It's a very difficult thing to tell stories that children can both understand and appreciate," she said stiffly.

"I don't agree with you," said the bachelor.

"Perhaps *you* would like to tell them a story," was the aunt's retort.

"Tell us a story," demanded the bigger of the small girls.

"Once upon a time," began the bachelor, "there was a little girl called Bertha, who was extraordinarily good."

The children's momentarily-aroused interest began at once to flicker; all stories seemed dreadfully alike, no matter who told them.

"She did all that she was told, she was always truthful, she kept her clothes clean, ate milk puddings as though they were jam tarts, learned her lessons perfectly, and was polite in her manners."

"Was she pretty?" asked the bigger of the small girls.

"Not as pretty as any of you," said the bachelor, "but she was horribly good."

There was a wave of reaction in favour of the story; the word horrible in connection with goodness was a novelty that commended itself. It seemed to introduce a ring of truth that was absent from the aunt's tales of infant life.

"She was so good," continued the bachelor, "that she won several medals for goodness, which she always wore, pinned on to her dress. There was a medal for obedience, another medal for punctuality, and a third for good behaviour. They were large metal medals and they clicked against one another as she walked. No other child in the town where she lived had as many as three medals, so everybody knew that she must be an extra good child."

"Horribly good," quoted Cyril.

"Everybody talked about her goodness, and the Prince of the country got to hear about it, and he said that as she was so very good she might be allowed once a week to walk in his park, which was just outside the town. It was a beautiful park, and no children were ever allowed in it, so it was a great honour for Bertha to be allowed to go there."

"Were there any sheep in the park?" demanded Cyril.

"No," said the bachelor, "there were no sheep."

"Why weren't there any sheep?" came the inevitable question arising out of that answer.

The aunt permitted herself a smile, which might almost have been described as a grin.

"There were no sheep in the park," said the bachelor, "because the Prince's mother had once had a dream that her son would either be killed by a sheep or else by a clock falling on him. For that reason the Prince never kept a sheep in his park or a clock in his palace."

The aunt suppressed a gasp of admiration.

"Was the Prince killed by a sheep or by a clock?" asked Cyril.

"He is still alive, so we can't tell whether the dream will come true," said the bachelor unconcernedly; "anyway, there were no sheep in the park, but there were lots of little pigs running all over the place."

"What colour were they?"

"Black with white faces, white with black spots, black all over, grey with white patches, and some were white all over."

The story-teller paused to let a full idea of the park's treasures sink into the children's imaginations; then he resumed:

"Bertha was rather sorry to find that there were no flowers in the park. She had promised her aunts, with tears in her eyes, that she would not pick any of the kind Prince's flowers, and she had meant to keep her promise, so of course it made her feel silly to find that there were no flowers to pick."

"Why weren't there any flowers?"

"Because the pigs had eaten them all," said the bachelor promptly. "The gardeners had told the Prince that you couldn't have pigs and flowers, so he decided to have pigs and no flowers."

There was a murmur of approval at the excellence of the Prince's decision; so many people would have decided the other way.

"There were lots of other delightful things in the park. There were ponds with gold and blue and green fish in them, and trees with beautiful parrots that said clever things at a moment's notice, and humming birds that hummed all the popular tunes of the day. Bertha walked up and down and enjoyed herself immensely, and thought to herself: 'If I were not so extraordinarily good I should not have been allowed to come into this beautiful park and enjoy all that there is to be seen in it,' and her three medals clinked against one another as she walked and helped to remind her how very good she really was. Just then an enormous wolf came prowling into the park to see if it could catch a fat little pig for its supper."

"What colour was it?" asked the children, amid an immediate quickening of interest.

"Mud-colour all over, with a black tongue and pale grey eyes that gleamed with unspeakable ferocity. The first thing that it saw in the park was Bertha; her pinafore was so spotlessly white and clean that it could be seen from a great distance. Bertha saw the wolf and saw that it was stealing towards her, and she began to wish that she had never been allowed to come into the park. She ran as hard as she could, and the wolf came after her with huge leaps and bounds. She managed to reach a shrubbery of myrtle bushes and she hid herself in one of the thickest of the bushes. The wolf came sniffing among the branches, its black tongue lolling out of its mouth and its pale grey eyes glaring with rage. Bertha was terribly frightened, and thought to herself: 'If I had not been so extraordinarily good I should have been safe in the town at this moment.' However, the scent of the myrtle was so strong that the wolf could not sniff out where Bertha was hiding, and the bushes were so thick that he might have hunted about in them for a long time without catching sight of her, so he thought he might as well go off and catch a little pig instead. Bertha was trembling very much at having the wolf prowling and sniffing so near her, and as she trembled the medal for obedience clinked against the medals for good conduct and punctuality. The wolf was just moving away when he heard the sound of the medals clinking and stopped to listen; they clinked again in a bush quite near him. He dashed into the bush, his pale grey eyes gleaming with ferocity and triumph, and dragged Bertha out and devoured her to the last morsel. All that was left of her were her shoes, bits of clothing, and the three medals for goodness."

"Were any of the little pigs killed?"

"No, they all escaped."

"The story began badly," said the smaller of the small girls, "but it had a beautiful ending."

"It is the most beautiful story that I ever heard," said the bigger of the small girls, with immense decision.

"It is the *only* beautiful story I have ever heard," said Cyril.

A dissentient opinion came from the aunt.

"A most improper story to tell to young children! You have undermined the effect of years of careful teaching."

"At any rate," said the bachelor, collecting his belongings preparatory to leaving the carriage, "I kept them quiet for ten minutes, which was more than you were able to do."

"Unhappy woman!" he observed to himself as he walked down the platform of Templecombe station; "for the next six months or so those children will assail her in public with demands for an improper story!"

KATHERINE MANSFIELD

An Indiscreet Journey

I

She is like St Anne. Yes, the concierge is the image of St Anne, with that black cloth over her head, the wisps of grey hair hanging, and the tiny smoking lamp in her hand. Really very beautiful, I thought, smiling at St Anne, who said severely: 'Six o'clock. You have only just got time. There is a bowl of milk on the writing-table.' I jumped out of my pyjamas and into a basin of cold water like any English lady in any French novel. The concierge, persuaded that I was on my way to prison cells and death by bayonets, opened the shutters and the cold clear light came through. A little steamer hooted on the river; a cart with two horses at a gallop flung past. The rapid swirling water; the tall black trees on the far side, grouped together like negroes conversing. Sinister, very, I thought, as I buttoned on my age-old Burberry. (That Burberry was very significant. It did not belong to me. I had borrowed it from a friend. My eye lighted upon it hanging in her little dark hall. The very thing! The perfect and adequate disguise—an old Burberry. Lions have been faced in a Burberry. Ladies have been rescued from open boats in mountainous seas wrapped in nothing else. An old Burberry seems to me the sign and the token of the undisputed venerable traveller, I decided, leaving my purple peg-top with the real seal collar and cuffs in exchange.)

'You will never get there,' said the concierge, watching me turn up the collar. 'Never! Never!' I ran down the echoing stairs—strange they sounded, like a piano flicked by a sleepy housemaid—and on to the Quai. 'Why so fast, *ma mignonne?*' said a lovely little boy in coloured socks, dancing in front of the electric lotus buds that curve over the entrance to the Métro. Alas! there was not even time to blow him a kiss. When I arrived at the big station I had only four minutes to spare, and the platform entrance was crowded and packed with soldiers, their yellow papers in one hand and big untidy bundles. The Commissaire of Police stood on one side, a Nameless Official on the other. Will he let me pass? Will he? He was an old man with a fat swollen face covered with big warts. Horn-rimmed spectacles squatted on his nose. Trembling, I made an effort. I conjured up my sweetest early-morning smile and handed it with the papers. But the delicate thing fluttered against the horn spectacles and fell. Nevertheless, he let me pass, and I ran, ran in and out among the soldiers and up the high steps into the yellow-painted carriage.

'Does one go direct to X?' I asked the collector who dug at my ticket with a pair of forceps and handed it back again. 'No, Mademoiselle, you must change at X.Y.Z.'

'At—?'

'X.Y.Z.'

Again I had not heard. 'At what time do we arrive there, if you please?'

'One o'clock.' But that was no good to me. I hadn't a watch. Oh, well—later.

Ah! the train had begun to move. The train was on my side. It swung out of the station, and soon we were passing the vegetable gardens, passing the tall, blind houses to let, passing the servants beating carpets. Up already and walking in the fields, rosy from the rivers and the red-fringed pools, the sun lighted upon the swinging train and stroked my muff and told me to take that Burberry. I was not alone in the carriage. An old woman sat opposite, her skirt turned back over her knees, a bonnet of black lace on her head. In her fat hands, adorned with a wedding and two mourning rings, she held a letter. Slowly, slowly she sipped a sentence, and then looked up and out of the window, her lips trembling a little, and then another sentence, and again the old face turned to the light, tasting it . . . Two soldiers leaned out of the window, their heads nearly touching—one of them was whistling, the other had his coat fastened with some rusty safety-pins. And now there were soldiers everywhere working on the railway line, leaning against trucks or standing hands on hips, eyes fixed on the train as though they expected at least one camera at every window. And now we were passing big wooden sheds like rigged-up dancing halls or seaside pavilions, each flying a flag. In and out of them walked the Red Cross men; the wounded sat against the walls sunning themselves. At all the bridges, the crossings, the stations, a *petit soldat*, all boots and bayonet. Forlorn and desolate he looked, like a little comic picture waiting for the joke to be written underneath. Is there really such a thing as war? Are all these laughing voices really going to the war? These dark woods lighted so mysteriously by the white stems of the birch and the ash—these watery fields with the big birds flying over—these rivers green and blue in the light—have battles been fought in places like these?

What beautiful cemeteries we are passing! They flash gay in the sun. They seem to be full of cornflowers and poppies and daisies. How can there be so many flowers at this time of the year? But they are not flowers at all. They are bunches of ribbons tied on to the soldiers' graves.

I glanced up and caught the old woman's eye. She smiled and folded the letter. 'It is from my son—the first we have had since October. I am taking it to my daughter-in-law.'

'. . . ?'

'Yes, very good,' said the old woman, shaking down her skirt and putting her arm through the handle of her basket. 'He wants me to send him some handkerchiefs and a piece of stout string.'

What is the name of the station where I have to change? Perhaps I shall never know. I got up and leaned my arms across the window rail, my feet crossed. One cheek burned as in infancy on the way to the seaside. When the war is over I shall have a barge and drift along these rivers with a white cat and a pot of mignonette to bear me company.

Down the side of the hill filed the troops, winking red and blue in the light. Far away, but plainly to be seen, some more flew by on bicycles. But really, *ma France adorée*, this uniform is ridiculous. Your soldiers are stamped upon your bosom like bright irreverent transfers.

The train slowed down, stopped . . . Everybody was getting out except me. A big boy, his sabots tied to his back with a piece of string, the inside of his tin wine cup stained a lovely impossible pink, looked very friendly. Does one change here perhaps for X? Another whose képi had come out of a wet paper cracker swung my suitcase to earth. What darlings soldiers are! '*Merci bien, Monsieur, vous êtes tout à fait aimable . . .*' 'Not this way,' said a bayonet. 'Nor this,' said another. So I followed the crowd. 'Your passport, Mademoiselle . . .' '*We, Sir Edward Grey . . .*' I ran through the muddy square and into the buffet.

A green room with a stove jutting out and tables on each side. On the counter, beautiful with coloured bottles, a woman leans, her breasts in her folded arms. Through an open door I can see a kitchen, and the cook in a white coat breaking eggs into a bowl and tossing the shells into a corner. The blue and red coats of the men who are eating hang upon the walls. Their short swords and belts are piled upon chairs. Heavens! what a noise. The sunny air seemed all broken up and trembling with it. A little boy, very pale, swung from table to table, taking the orders, and poured me out a glass of purple coffee. *Ssssh*, came from the eggs. They were in a pan. The woman rushed from behind the counter and began to help the boy. *Toute de suite, tout' suite!* she chirruped to the loud impatient voices. There came a clatter of plates and the pop-pop of corks being drawn.

Suddenly in the doorway I saw someone with a pail of fish—brown speckled fish, like the fish one sees in a glass case, swimming through forests of beautiful pressed sea-weed. He was an old man in a tattered jacket, standing humbly, waiting for someone to attend to him. A thin beard fell over his chest, his eyes under the tufted eyebrows were bent on the pail he carried. He looked as though he had escaped from some holy picture, and was entreating the soldiers' pardon for being there at all . . .

But what could I have done? I could not arrive at X. with two fishes hanging on a straw; and I am sure it is a penal offence in France to throw fish out of railway-carriage windows, I thought, miserably climbing into a smaller, shabbier train. Perhaps I might have taken them to—*ah, mon Dieu*—I had forgotten the name of my uncle and aunt again! Buffard, Buffon—what was it? Again I read the unfamiliar letter in the familiar handwriting.

> 'MY DEAR NIECE,
>
> Now that the weather is more settled, your uncle and I would be charmed if you would pay us a little visit. Telegraph me when you are coming. I shall meet you outside the station if I am free. Otherwise our good friend, Madame Grinçon, who lives in the little toll-house by the bridge, *juste en*

face de la gare, will conduct you to our home. *Je vous embrasse bien tendrement.*

JULIE BOIFFARD.'

A visiting card was enclosed: *M. Paul Boiffard.* Boiffard—of course that was the name. *Ma tante Julie et mon oncle Paul*—suddenly they were there with me, more real, more solid than any relations I had ever known. I saw *tante Julie* bridling, with the soup-tureen in her hands, and *oncle Paul* sitting at the table with a red and white napkin tied round his neck. Boiffard—Boiffard—I must remember the name. Supposing the Commissaire Militaire should ask me who the relations were I was going to and I muddled the name—Oh, how fatal! Buffard—no, Boiffard. And then for the first time, folding Aunt Julie's letter, I saw scrawled in a corner of the empty back page: *Venez vite, vite*. Strange impulsive woman! My heart began to beat . . .

'Ah, we are not far off now,' said the lady opposite. 'You are going to X, Mademoiselle?'

'*Oui, Madame.*'

'I also . . . You have been there before?'

'No, Madame. This is the first time.'

'Really, it is a strange time for a visit.'

I smiled faintly, and tried to keep my eyes off her hat. She was quite an ordinary little woman, but she wore a black velvet toque, with an incredibly surprised looking sea-gull camped on the very top of it. Its round eyes, fixed on me so inquiringly, were almost too much to bear. I had a dreadful impulse to shoo it away, or to lean forward and inform her of its presence . . .

'*Excusez-moi, Madame*, but perhaps you have not remarked there is an *espèce de* sea-gull *couché sur votre chapeau*.'

Could the bird be there on purpose? I must not laugh I must not laugh. Had she ever looked at herself in a glass with that bird on her head?

'It is very difficult to get into X at present, to pass the station,' she said, and she shook her head with the sea-gull at me. 'Ah, such an affair. One must sign one's name and state one's business.'

'Really, is it as bad as all that?'

'But naturally. You see the whole place is in the hands of the military, and'—she shrugged—'they have to be strict. Many people do not get beyond the station at all. They arrive. They are put in the waiting-room, and there they remain.'

Did I or did I not detect in her voice a strange, insulting relish?

'I suppose such strictness is absolutely necessary,' I said coldly stroking my muff.

'Necessary,' she cried. 'I should think so. Why,

Mademoiselle, you cannot imagine what it would be like otherwise! You know what women are like about soldiers'—she raised a final hand—'mad, completely mad. But—' and she gave a little laugh of triumph—'they could not get into X. *Mon Dieu*, no! There is no question about that.'

'I don't suppose they even try,' said I.

'Don't you?' said the sea-gull.

Madame said nothing for a moment. 'Of course the authorities are very hard on the men. It means instant imprisonment, and then—off to the firing-line without a word.'

'What are *you* going to X for?' said the sea-gull. 'What on earth are *you* doing here?'

'Are you making a long stay in X, Mademoiselle?'

She had won, she had won. I was terrified. A lamp-post swam past the train with the fatal name upon it. I could hardly breathe—the train had stopped. I smiled gaily at Madame and danced down the steps to the platform.

It was a hot little room, completely furnished, with two colonels seated at two tables. They were large grey-whiskered men with a touch of burnt red on their cheeks. Sumptuous and omnipotent they looked. One smoked what ladies love to call a heavy Egyptian cigarette, with a long creamy ash, the other toyed with a gilded pen. Their heads rolled on their tight collars, like big over-ripe fruits. I had a terrible feeling, as I handed my passport and ticket, that a soldier would step forward and tell me to kneel. I would have knelt without question.

'What's this?' said God I, querulously. He did not like my passport at all. The very sight of it seemed to annoy him. He waved a dissenting hand at it, with a '*Non, je ne peux pas manger ça,*' air.

'But it won't do. It won't do at all, you know. Look,—read for yourself,' and he glanced with extreme distaste at my photograph, and then with even greater distaste his pebble eyes looked at me.

'Of course the photograph is deplorable,' I said, scarcely breathing with terror, 'but it has been viséd and viséd.'

He raised his big bulk and went to over to God II.

'Courage!' I said to my muff and held it firmly, 'Courage!'

God II held up a finger to me, and I produced Aunt Julie's letter and her card. But he did not seem to feel the slightest interest in her. He stamped my passport idly, scribbled a word on my ticket, and I was on the platform again.

'That way—you pass out that way.'

★

Terribly pale, with a faint smile on his lips, his hand at salute, stood the little corporal. I gave no sign, I am sure I gave no sign. He stepped behind me.

'And then follow me as though you do not see me,' I heard him half whisper, half sing.

How fast he went, through the slippery mud towards a bridge. He had a postman's bag on his back, a paper parcel and the *Matin* in his hand. We seemed to dodge through a maze of policemen, and I could not keep up at all with the little corporal who began to whistle. From the toll-house 'our good friend, Madame Grinçon', her hands wrapped in a shawl, watched our coming, and against the toll-house there leaned a tiny faded cab. *Montez vite, vite!* said the little corporal, hurling my suitcase, the postman's bag, the paper parcel and the *Matin* on to the floor.

'A-ie! A-ie! Do not be so mad. Do not ride yourself. You will be seen,' wailed 'our good friend, Madame Grinçon.'

'*Ah, je m'en f . . .*' said the little corporal.

The driver jerked into activity. He lashed the bony horse and away we flew, both doors, which were the complete sides of the cab, flapping and banging.

'*Bon jour, mon amie.*'

'*Bon jour, mon ami.*'

And then we swooped down and clutched at the banging doors. They would not keep shut. They were fools of doors.

'Lean back, let me do it!' I cried. 'Policemen are as thick as violets everywhere.'

At the barracks the horse reared up and stopped. A crowd of laughing faces blotted the window.

'*Prends ça, mon vieux*,' said the little corporal, handing the paper parcel.

'It's all right,' called someone.

We waved, we were off again. By a river, down a strange white street, with the little houses on either side, gay in the late sunlight.

'Jump out as soon as he stops again. The door will be open. Run straight inside. I will follow. The man is already paid. I know you will like the house. It is quite white. And the room is white too, and the people are—'

'White as snow.'

We looked at each other. We began to laugh. 'Now,' said the little corporal.

Out I flew and in at the door. There stood, presumably, my Aunt Julie. There in the background hovered, I supposed, my Uncle Paul.

'*Bon jour, Madame!*' '*Bon jour, Monsieur!*'

'It is all right, you are safe,' said my Aunt Julie. Heavens, how I loved her! And she opened the door of the white room and shut it upon us. Down went the suitcase, the postman's bag, the *Matin*. I threw my passport up into the air, and the little corporal caught it.

II

What an extraordinary thing. We had been there to lunch and to dinner each day; but now in the dusk and alone I could not find it. I clop-clopped in my borrowed *sabots* through the greasy mud, right to the end of the village, and there was not a sign of it. I could not even remember what it looked like, or if there was a name painted on the outside, or any bottles or tables showing at the window. Already the village houses were sealed for the night behind big wooden shutters. Strange and mysterious they looked in the ragged drifting light and thin rain, like a company of beggars perched on the hill-side, their bosoms full of rich unlawful gold. There was nobody about but the soldiers. A group of wounded stood under a lamp-post, petting a mangy, shivering dog. Up the street came four big boys singing:

'*Dodo, mon homme, fais vit' dodo . . .*'

and swung off down the hill to their sheds behind the railway station. They seemed to take the last breath of the day with them. I began to walk slowly back.

'It must have been one of these houses. I remember it stood far back from the road—and there were no steps, not even a porch—one seemed to walk right through the window.' And then quite suddenly the waiting-boy came out of just such a place. He saw me and grinned cheerfully, and began to whistle through his teeth.

'*Bon soir, mon petit.*'

'*Bon soir, Madame.*' And he followed me up the café to our special table, right at the far end by the window, and marked by a bunch of violets that I had left in a glass there yesterday.

'You are two?' asked the waiting-boy, flicking the table with a red and white cloth. His long swinging steps echoed over the bare floor. He disappeared into the kitchen and came back to light the lamp that hung from the ceiling under a spreading shade, like a haymaker's hat. Warm light shone on the empty place that was really a barn, set out with dilapidated tables and chairs. Into the middle of the room a black stove jutted. At one side of it there was a table with a row of bottles on it, behind which Madame sat and took the money and made entries in a red book. Opposite her desk a door led into the kitchen. The walls were covered with creamy paper patterned all over with green and swollen trees—hundreds and hundreds of trees reared their mushroom heads to the ceiling. I began to wonder who had chosen the paper and why. Did Madame think it was beautiful, or that it was a gay and lovely thing to eat one's dinner at all seasons in the middle of a forest . . . On either side of the clock there hung a picture: one, a young gentleman in black tights wooing a pear-shaped lady in yellow over the back of a garden seat. *Premier Rencontre*; two, the black and yellow in amorous confusion, *Triomphe d'Amour*.

The clock ticked to a soothing lilt, *C'est ça, c'est ça*. In the kitchen the waiting-boy was washing up. I heard the ghostly chatter of the dishes.

And years passed. Perhaps the war is long since over—there is no village outside at all—the streets are quiet under the grass. I have an idea this is the sort of thing one will do on the very last day of all—sit in an empty café and listen to a clock ticking until—

Madame came through the kitchen door, nodded to me and took her seat behind the table, her plump hands folded on the red book. *Ping* went the door. A handful of soldiers came in, took off their coats and began to play cards, chaffing and poking fun at the pretty waiting-boy, who threw up his little round head, rubbed his thick fringe out of his eyes and cheeked them back in his broken voice. Sometimes his voice boomed up from his throat, deep and harsh, and then in the middle of a sentence it broke and scattered in a funny squeaking. He seemed to enjoy it himself. You would not have been surprised if he had walked into the kitchen on his hands and brought back your dinner turning a catherine-wheel.

Ping went the door again. Two more men came in. They sat at the table nearest Madame, and she leaned to them with a birdlike movement, her head on one side. Oh, they had a grievance! The Lieutenant was a fool—nosing about—springing out at them—and they'd only been sewing on buttons. Yes, that was all—sewing on buttons, and up comes this young spark. 'Now then, what are you up to?' They mimicked the idiotic voice. Madame drew down her mouth, nodding sympathy. The waiting-boy served them with glasses. He took a bottle of some orange-stuff and put it on the table edge. A shout from the card-players made him turn sharply, and crash! over went the bottle, spilling on the table, the floor—smash! to tinkling atoms. An amazed silence. Through it the drip-drip of the wine from the table on to the floor. It looked very strange dropping so slowly, as though the table were crying. Then there came a roar from the card-players. 'You'll catch it, my lad! That's the style! Now you've done it! . . . *Sept, huit, neuf.*' They started playing again. The waiting-boy never said a word. He stood, his head bent, his hands spread out, and then he knelt and gathered up the glass, piece by piece, and soaked the wine up with a cloth. Only when Madame cried cheerfully, 'You wait until *he* finds out,' did he raise his head.

'He can't say anything, if I pay for it,' he muttered, his face jerking, and he marched off into the kitchen with the soaking cloth.

'*Il pleure de colère*,' said Madame delightedly, patting her hair with her plump hands.

The café slowly filled. It grew very warm. Blue smoke mounted from the tables and hung about the haymaker's hat in misty wreaths. There was a suffocating smell of onion soup and boots and damp cloth. In the din the door sounded again. It opened to let in a weed of a fellow, who stood with his back against it, one hand shading his eyes.

'Hullo! you've got the bandage off?'

'How does it feel, *mon vieux*?'

'Let's have a look at them.'

But he made no reply. He shrugged and walked unsteadily to a table, sat down and leant against the wall. Slowly his hand fell. In his white face his eyes showed, pink as a rabbit's. They brimmed and spilled, brimmed and spilled. He dragged a white cloth out of his pocket and wiped them.

'It's the smoke,' said someone. 'It's the smoke tickles them up for you.'

His comrades watched him a bit, watched his eyes fill again, again brim over. The water ran down his face, off his chin on to the table. He rubbed the place with his coat-sleeve, and then, as though forgetful, went on rubbing, rubbing with his hand across the table, staring in front of him. And then he started shaking his head to the movement of his hand. He gave a loud strange groan and dragged out the cloth again.

'*Huit, neuf, dix,*' said the card-players.

'*P'tit*, some more bread.'

'Two coffees.'

'*Un Picon!*'

The waiting-boy, quite recovered, but with scarlet cheeks, ran to and fro. A tremendous quarrel flared up among the card-players, raged for two minutes, and died in flickering laughter. 'Ooof!' groaned the man with the eyes, rocking and mopping. But nobody paid any attention to him except Madame. She made a little grimace at her two soldiers.

'*Mais vous savez, c'est un peu dégoûtant, ça,*' she said severely.

'*Ah, oui, Madame,*' answered the soldiers, watching her bent head and pretty hands, as she arranged for the hundredth time a frill of lace on her lifted bosom.

'*V'là, Monsieur!*' cawed the waiting-boy over his shoulder to me. For some silly reason I pretended not to hear, and I leaned over the table smelling the violets, until the little corporal's hand closed over mine.

'Shall we have *un peu de charcuterie* to begin with?' he asked tenderly.

III

'In England,' said the blue-eyed soldier, 'you drink whisky with your meals. *N'est-ce pas, Mademoiselle?* A little glass of whisky neat before eating. Whisky and soda with your *bifteks*, and after, more whisky with hot water and lemon.'

'Is it true that?' asked his great friend who sat opposite, a big red-faced chap with a black beard and large moist eyes and hair that looked as though it had been cut with a sewing-machine.

'Well, not quite true,' said I.

'*Si, si,*' cried the blue-eyed soldier. 'I ought to know. I'm in business. English travellers come to my place, and it's always the same thing.'

'Bah, I can't stand whisky,' said the little corporal.

'It's too disgusting the morning after. Do you remember, *ma fille*, the whisky in that little bar at Montmartre?'

'*Souvenir tendre*,' sighed Blackbeard, putting two fingers in the breast of his coat and letting his head fall. He was very drunk.

'But I know something that you've never tasted,' said the blue-eyed soldier, pointing a finger at me; 'something really good.' *Cluck* he went with his tongue. '*E-patant!* And the curious thing is that you'd hardly know it from whisky except that it's'—he felt with his hand for the word—'finer, sweeter perhaps, not so sharp, and it leaves you feeling gay as a rabbit next morning.'

'What is it called?'

'Mirabelle!' He rolled the word round his mouth, under his tongue. 'Ah-ha, that's the stuff.'

'I could eat another mushroom,' said Blackbeard. 'I would like another mushroom very much. I am sure I could eat another mushroom if Mademoiselle gave it to me out of her hand.'

'You ought to try it,' said the blue-eyed soldier, leaning both hands on the table and speaking so seriously that I began to wonder how much more sober he was than Blackbeard. 'You ought to try it, and tonight. I would like you to tell me if you don't think it's like whisky.'

'Perhaps they've got it here,' said the little corporal, and he called the waiting-boy. '*P'tit!*'

'*Non, Monsieur,*' said the boy, who never stopped smiling. He served us with dessert plates painted with blue parrots and horned beetles.

'What is the name for this in English?' said Blackbeard, pointing. I told him 'Parrot.'

'Ah, *mon Dieu!* . . . Pair-rot . . .' He put his arms round his plate. 'I love you, *ma petite* pair-rot. You are sweet, you are blonde, you are English. You do not know the difference between whisky and mirabelle.'

The little corporal and I looked at each other, laughing. He squeezed up his eyes when he laughed, so that you saw nothing but the long curly lashes.

'Well, I know a place where they do keep it,' said the blue-eyed soldier. '*Café des Amis.* We'll go there—I'll pay—I'll pay for the whole lot of us.' His gesture embraced thousands of pounds.

But with a loud whirring noise the clock on the wall struck half-past eight; and no soldier is allowed in a café after eight o'clock at night.

'It is fast,' said the blue-eyed soldier. The little corporal's watch said the same. So did the immense turnip that Blackbeard produced and carefully deposited on the head of one of the horned beetles.

'Ah, well, we'll take the risk,' said the blue-eyed soldier, and he thrust his arms into the cardboard coat. 'It's worth it,' he said. 'It's worth it. Just you wait.'

Outside, stars shone between wispy clouds and the moon fluttered like a candle flame over a pointed spire. The shadows of the dark plume-like trees waved on the white houses. Not a soul to be seen. No sound to be heard but the *Hsh! Hsh!* of a far-away train, like a big beast shuffling in its sleep.

'You are cold,' whispered the little corporal. 'You are cold, *ma fille*.'

'No, really not.'

'But you are trembling.'

'Yes, but I'm not cold.'

'What are the women like in England?' asked Blackbeard. 'After the war is over I shall go to England. I shall find a little English woman and marry—and her pair-rot.' He gave a loud choking laugh.

'Fool!' said the blue-eyed soldier, shaking him; and he leant over to me. 'It is only after the second glass that you really taste it,' he whispered. 'The second little glass and then—ah!—then you know.'

Café des Amis gleamed in the moonlight. We glanced quickly up and down the road. We ran up the four wooden steps, and opened the ringing glass door into a low room lighted with a hanging lamp, where about ten people were dining. They were seated on two benches at a narrow table.

'Soldiers!' screamed a woman, leaping up from behind a white soup-tureen—a scrag of a woman in a black shawl. 'Soldiers! At this hour! Look at that clock, look at it.' And she pointed to the clock with the dripping ladle.

'It's fast,' said the blue-eyed soldier. 'It's fast, Madame. And don't make so much noise, I beg of you. We will drink and we will go.'

'Will you?' she cried, running round the table and planting herself in front of us. 'That's just what you won't do. Coming into an honest woman's house this hour of the night—making a scene—getting the police after you. Ah, no! Ah, no! It's a disgrace, that's what it is.'

'Sh!' said the little corporal, holding up his hand. Dead silence. In the silence we heard steps passing.

'The police,' whispered Blackbeard, winking at a pretty girl with rings in her ears, who smiled back at him, saucy. 'Sh!'

The faces lifted, listening. 'How beautiful they are!' I thought. 'They are like a family party having supper in the New Testament . . .' The steps died away.

'Serve you very well right if you had been caught,' scolded the angry woman. 'I'm sorry on your account that the police didn't come. You deserve it—you deserve it.'

'A little glass of mirabelle and we will go,' persisted the blue-eyed soldier.

Still scolding and muttering she took four glasses from the cupboard and a big bottle. 'But you're not going to drink in here. Don't you believe it.' The little corporal ran into the kitchen. 'Not there! Not there! Idiot!' she cried. 'Can't you see there's a window there, and a wall opposite where the police come every evening to . . .'

'Sh!' Another scare.

'You are mad and you will end in prison,—all four of you,' said the woman. She flounced out of the room. We tiptoed after her into a dark smelling scullery, full of pans of greasy water, of salad leaves and meat-bones.

'There now,' she said, putting down the glasses. 'Drink and go!'

'Ah, at last!' The blue-eyed soldier's happy voice trickled through the dark. 'What do you think? Isn't it just as I said? Hasn't it got a taste of excellent—*excellent* whisky?'

Lady Margaret Majendie

A Railway Journey

A close cab laden with luggage drove up to Euston Station in time for the 7.30 A.M. train for the north. While the porters surrounded the boxes, the occupants of the cab passed straight through on to the platform, looking rather nervously about them. They were two — a very pretty girl in a most fascinating travelling costume of blue serge and fur, and an elderly woman, who, from her appearance, might have been her nurse.

"Sit here, and don't move, Miss Edith, while I take your ticket: now, mind you don't stir;" and she deposited her on a bench.

"Are you the young lady as has ordered a through carriage reserved?" asked a guard, with official abruptness.

"Yes."

"Then come along of me, miss."

"No, no; I must wait," and Edith, who was quite unused to travelling, grasped her bag and did not move. The guard looked astonished, but only shrugged his shoulders and walked off. Presently he came back.

"You'll be late, miss," he said, not encouragingly. "Train 'ill be off in another minute." Edith looked at him in despair. Should she leave her post? Would Jenkins never come back? A loud aggressive bell began to ring. Edith started up; she seized all the things Jenkins had put under her charge—rugs, carpet-bag, umbrella-case, loose shawl, and provision-basket—and was trying to stagger away under the load, when Jenkins came back very hot and flurried, seized half the packages, and hurried her to the train. The guard unlocked the special carriage and put her in.

"No hurry, ma'am," he said; "four minutes still."

"I don't at all like it, now it has come to the point, Jenkins," said Edith, leaning out of the window.

"Nor I, miss; and how your mamma could let you go all alone like this, passes me; but I have spoken to the guard and written to the station-master, and you've a good bit to eat, and not a blessed soul to get into the carriage from end to end; so don't be afraid, my dear, and I make no doubt that your dear uncle will meet you at the other end."

"I have no doubt that one of my uncles will—I hope Uncle John, as I have never seen Uncle George."

"Everything you want, miss?" said an extra

porter. "I have put in all the rugs and a hot-water tin, and the luggage is all right in the van just behind."

"All right, all right!" said Mrs Jenkins.

"Thank you, ma'am," said the porter, pocketing a shining half-crown.

A gentleman suddenly came running on to the platform; the train was just about to start. "Here, porter, take my portmanteau; quick—smoking carriage!"

"All full, sir! quick, sir, please!"

"It's Mr George!" cried Jenkins, suddenly. Edith started forward. "Oh!"

The gentleman caught sight of Jenkins. "Here, guard, guard! put me in here!"

"Can't sir—special."

"Quick; let me in! it's—it's my niece!"

The train began to move.

"Confound you, be quick!"

The door was opened just in time, and Edith, as excited as Mr George, seized him with both hands by the coat-sleeves, and pulled him in with all her might into the carriage. They were off.

Mr George sat down opposite to Edith with a sigh of relief.

"I am so glad to see you, Uncle George," said Edith, timidly; "for though I am generally bold enough, I was rather afraid of this long journey."

"I will take care of you," said the uncle. "I am very glad to make your acquaintance, my dear." The "my dear" sounded a little strained, as though it were not a common expression on Uncle George's lips, and Edith looked up at him. She had not expected her uncle to be so young in appearance; but she had often heard her mother say that he was the youngest-looking man of his age she had ever known; and now she quite agreed,—for though she knew him to be really about fifty-eight years of age, he might from his appearance be taken for five-and-twenty, or even less. He was remarkably good-looking—more so than she had expected—and his eyes looked very young, and frank, and blue. There was a twinkle in them also; she was sure that he was fond of fun. Edith felt quite fond of her uncle; she was not one bit afraid of him— his face was so open, and good, and kindly.

"Now we must make ourselves comfortable," said Uncle George, and he proceeded to set to work. He put the rugs and baskets into the nets, he pushed the carpet-bag and portmanteau under the seat, took off his hat, put on a very becoming Turkish fez, extracted newspapers from his pocket, spread a shawl over Edith's knees, and then wriggled himself comfortably into a corner seat.

"How well old Jenkins wears!" he said. "She looks like a young dairy-maid."

"Oh!" said Edith, a little shocked at his irreverence.

"I remember how she used to feed me with dried fruit and macaroons out of the store-room."

"Really! surely she is not old enough for that?"

"Oh, ah! I forget her age; but the fact was, I wasn't of course a boy."

"Of course not. Why, I think mamma said that you and Jenkins were born the same day—or was she the eldest?"

"Oh, I was the eldest."

"No, you were not; I remember she was three weeks older than you, and it was because she was your foster-sister that she always was so fond of you. Indeed, mamma said that she wanted to leave her to go to you and Aunt Maria when your eldest children were born, even out to India."

"My eldest children! what do you mean? Oh! by the by, yes; they are dead."

"Dead! my cousin George dead?"

"Yes, yes, my dear."

"Poor little Addie? was it true that George never got over her loss?"

"Don't!" said Uncle George, abruptly; and he held up a newspaper upside down.

Edith touched his arm very gently.

"I am so sorry, Uncle George," she said, sweetly.

"If I had known that you had lost them both, I would not have said anything; please forgive me. And poor Aunt Maria, too! Oh, I beg your pardon."

Uncle George threw down his paper and looked smilingly at her.

"Does your mamma ever speak of me?"

"Constantly, perpetually," said Edith, her voice still a little choked.

"And what does she say of me?"

"She says that you are the dearest, kindest, warmest-hearted, most sweet-dispositioned old gentleman existing; she says you have been a gallant officer, and a loyal, true-hearted soldier." Edith's eyes kindled. "And I have heard how you distinguished yourself in India, and I—I am very glad to see you, Uncle George."

"Yes, yes, he is all that," said he, with enthusiasm.

"What? who?" asked Edith, confused.

"My father—I—I—I mean my son."

"Poor George! he was a most distinguished soldier also. I wish I had known him. No, Uncle George, I won't speak so—I do not want to pain you."

"I like to hear all you tell me about him, my dear."

"I have only heard how good a soldier he was, and that he was so handsome and so good."

"And had he faults and defects?"

Edith looked surprised.

"I used to hear that he was conceited."

"No, no," said Uncle George, hastily; "he never was that. He was proud, I grant—perhaps too proud—but never conceited."

"Poor George!" sighed Edith; "I had so looked forward to knowing him."

"Had you really?"

"Yes; I never had a companion of my own age. Do tell me, shall I like my cousins at Hatton?"

"I think so, some of them: do you mean Uncle John's daughters, or his step-children?"

"Both."

"I think you will like Mary, tolerate Susan, abhor Agatha, admire Jane, and adore Alice."

"Alice is the adorable one, is she?" said Edith, laughing; "and is she the one they say is so pretty?"

"Oh no; poor Alice is deformed, and can never leave the sofa; but she has the sweetness of an angel and the courage of a martyr: she is not in the least pretty."

"Oh, what a trial! always on the sofa!"

"What a sweet little thing this is!" thought Uncle George, but he said nothing.

"How comes it that you know none of your cousins?" said he, suddenly.

"Why do you want me to tell you what you know so much better than I do, Uncle George?"

"Yes, yes, of course; but naturally I want to know your side of the story. Have you never been at Hatton?"

"Never; and I thought it so very kind of you to induce Uncle John to persuade mamma to let me go."

"Yes; I thought, you know, that a few companions of your own age would do you good. How old are you?"

"Did you not get mamma's letter, in which she told you that I was to be eighteen to-morrow?"

"No; it must have been late. I never heard of it."

"How very unfortunate! Then no one will know I am coming. She asked you to tell Uncle John about the trains and things."

"Oh, ah! *that* letter! oh, of course, that is all right. I don't—I—I sometimes don't read letters through."

Edith laughed.

"I will tell you one version of my story. Mamma being papa's widow, and papa having been the eldest son, had to leave Hatton when I was born and turned out to be a stupid little girl; and she went abroad because she was so delicate, and became a Roman Catholic."

"Holloa!"

"What is it, Uncle George?"

"You are not one, I hope?"

Edith looked rather indignant. "It is *very* odd of you to say that," she said, "when you know as well as I do all that you did about it; indeed I shall never forget your kindness. I was very unhappy when mamma wanted me to change; and Uncle John's letters and all Aunt Maria wrote made it worse than ever, only your letters made all smooth; and mamma was so much touched by the one you wrote to her about papa's trust in her, and my not being hers only, and all that, that, indeed, I have always loved you—you have seemed to me like my own dear father."

"I am very glad, my dear child, and I hope that in future you will be guided by my advice."

"I hope I shall see a great deal of you, Uncle George, for I know how fond I shall be of you, for my mother loves you dearly."

"It is very kind of her."

"And do you know, since we came to live in England, I have never paid a single visit, or been for one week away from home. Oh, it is such fun going to Hatton! Do my cousins ride?"

"Yes, a great deal; are you fond of it?"

"I love it; there is nothing in the world to me like a good gallop. Ah, it was the greatest trial of all my life when Queen Mab was sold!"

"When was that?"

"Mamma made me give up riding, or rather I gave it up of myself, because it made her so nervous."

"What else do you care for?—dancing?"

"Oh, I love it; but I have never been to a ball in my life."

"There are to be two at Hatton next week, and you must promise me the first valse at each."

"Do *you* valse?"

"Oh yes. You see I am not such an old fogy as you expected."

"No; nobody would believe you to be fifty-eight, except for one thing."

"What is that?"

But Edith blushed and would not answer.

"You need not mind, child—I never was at all sensitive; and alas! now my memory is not what it was."

"That's it," said Edith, eagerly; "only I did not like to say it. Here we are at a station."

It was now ten o'clock; Uncle George bought the 'Times' and 'Daily News,' and they both began to read. About twelve o'clock the pangs of hunger began to assail Edith, and she exclaimed—

"Uncle George, it is only twelve o'clock, and I must eat to live."

"I have been existing merely for the last hour

with the greatest difficulty, but I have got nothing wherewith to refresh exhausted nature; I calculated on a bun at Carlisle."

"Hours hence! No, I am amply provided. Will you have beef or chicken sandwiches, or cold partridge, or what?"

They made a very good lunch, and uncle and niece grew hourly better acquainted.

"I believe we ought to look out of the window," said he, presently. "My father said that the country about here was quite beautiful."

"That must have been before the days of railways," said Edith, gravely. "Those coaching days must have been quite delightful."

"They were."

"Mamma has told me about that extraordinary adventure you and papa had on the Aberdeen coach."

"It was extraordinary."

"Papa caught the branch of a tree, did he not?"

"Yes; and do you remember what I did?"

"You jumped out just as the coach upset, and sat on all the horses' heads."

"And a most uneasy seat it must have been; and did Uncle Arthur—I mean your papa—remain suspended in mid-air?"

"No, he swung into the tree. I have often heard

of your climbing exploits, and that when you were young you could climb any tree."

"I have not lost the power," said Uncle George, stretching himself. "Holloa!"

"What is the matter?" said Edith, startled.

"Nothing—nothing—sit still!"

But she followed the direction of his eyes. The train (a very long one) was going round a sharp curve, they were in one of the last carriages, and to her horror and terror, she saw, about a hundred yards in front of the train, a whole herd of cows on and off the line—two or three frantically galloping.

All heads were stretched out of the windows, clamouring tongues and even cries resounded from the other carriages, but neither Edith nor George uttered a sound, only she put back her hand and caught his; he seized it very tightly in the suspense, knowing well that a terrible accident might be impending. It was hardly a second, but it seemed a lifetime. The frantic cattle rushed off the line in a body, all but one unfortunate beast. The guards put on the very heaviest brakes, but the impetus was so great that the slackening was hardly perceptible. It may have been fortunate that it was so, for instead of upsetting the train, the cow was tossed off the line utterly destroyed, and the engine rushed on in safety.

George and Edith sat down opposite to each other; both were very pale.

"Thank God!" said Edith, and she covered her face with one hand. George did not speak, but he took off his cap and looked out of the window for one minute.

"Now I shall give you some sherry," he said, suddenly. "You are the pluckiest little brick I ever came across. Any other girl would have screamed."

"I never scream," said Edith, indignantly; "and I don't want any sherry."

"I am your uncle, and I say you are to have some—drink it up."

"I hate wine," she said, giving back the flask.

"There, good child, to do as you are told."

At the next station a perfect crowd of passengers was waiting for the up train. A great *fête* was going on in the next town for the visit of some royal personage, and the train was filled to overflowing. Presently the civil guard came up to the special carriage and said most deprecatingly that there was one gentleman who couldn't find a place anywhere; and as he was only going to the next station, would they admit him just for that twenty minutes? Uncle George consented very discontentedly, and very grudgingly moved his long legs to admit of the entry of a very stout old gentleman, who sat heavily down, and received into his ample lap a perfect pile of packages and baskets, and a brace of hares and a rabbit tied by the legs which he had dexterously suspended by a string round his neck.

"Not worth while, indeed, my dear madam," he said, as Edith began to make room for his things. "Only twenty minutes—no inconvenience, I assure you."

The heavily-weighted train moved off. The old gentleman now began a series of playful bows which made the hares and rabbit dance up and down.

"It really was too good of you to admit an old fogy like me," he said, blandly; "for of course with half an eye I can see the tender situation."

A deep growl from Uncle George. He gave a little start and went on to himself—

"Sweet young couple! just wedded, eh?"

Edith felt half choked with laughter, but she managed to say convulsively—

"Will you give me my book, Uncle George?"

The old gentleman started, cocked his head as a blackbird does when he perceives a very fat worm, and muttered—

"Impossible!"

Edith and George were wrapped in their respective novels. The old gentleman fidgeted, sighed, and arranged his features into a most sanctimonious expression. There was dead silence till he reached his station, where he descended. The departure bell was ringing, when his head suddenly reappeared at the window, the hares and rabbit streaming wildly from the back of his neck.

"My children," he said, "take my advice—go back to your friends. This——" A little shriek ended his discourse; the train was going on; and he, being borne along on the step involuntarily, two stout porters rushed to the rescue and lifted him off. Edith and George laughed till the tears ran down their cheeks.

"I could eat again, with a little persuasion," said George, presently.

"Why, what o'clock is it?"

"Just five, and we shall not get in till eight-thirty. Remember that we had our luncheon at twelve."

"Very well." And they proceeded to eat.

The sun had gone down, and the whole sky was gorgeous with gold and crimson light, on which great black clouds floated prophetically.

"What a grand sky!" said Edith.

"Magnificent! Nowhere does one see such clouds as in England."

"Were you very fond of India?"

"Of course I am; my work lies there, my hopes, my future."

Edith looked astonished. "I should have thought," she said, "that *now* you would have been content to rest at home; but I admire you for loving work. Shall you go out again?"

"That depends very much upon circumstances. It would be a great grief to me to give up my profession."

"It is very odd, but I certainly thought that mamma told me you had given up your profession."

"She was mistaken," said Uncle George, shortly.

"I have often longed to go to India," cried Edith.

"Have you?" said George, very eagerly.

"Oh yes, beyond anything; life there gives everybody a chance. I mean, heroic men and great characters are formed in India, and men have great responsibilities and development for quite a different class of most desirable qualities there."

"That is quite true; and you are just the sort of woman to help a man to do anything."

"I am so glad you think so, Uncle George," she said, laughing and blushing.

At seven o'clock they reached a very large station, where the train had half an hour to wait. They got a cup of tea, and then, both being rather cold, they began to walk vigorously up and down to the very end of the terminus. It was quite dark at the far end, and they stood side by side, looking up into the mouth of the great station with its mighty arch. Trains rushed past, or heavily moved away with a harsh, discordant whistle. Great red lamps loomed out of the darkness like dragons' eyes. George drew Edith hastily on one side that she might not be struck by the chain of a huge carthorse which passed close by them, on its way to bring up a coal-truck. It was very cold, and they stamped up and down, and George enjoyed a fragrant cigar.

"Take your seats!" shouted the porter. "Take your seats!" And they resumed their places.

"Them's a bride and bridegroom," said a stout country-woman to a friend; and the loud guttural "Lor!" with which the news was received reached the ears of the travellers.

A blazing lamp was in the carriage, and under its yellow light Edith tried to read.

"Don't read, Edith," said the young uncle, suddenly. "Talk instead."

She shut up her book.

"To tell you the truth, Uncle George," she said, "we are getting so near that I am beginning to feel ridiculously nervous."

He looked at his watch, and suddenly started.

"So late," he said. "We shall be there in ten minutes."

"Oh!"

"And the fact is," he began, restlessly fidgeting; "the fact is—a—a—I have got a confession to make to you."

"To me! oh, Uncle George!"

"D—n Uncle George!"

Edith looked startled beyond measure.

"The fact is, Edith, I am not my father."

"What do you mean?"

"I mean I am my son."

"But he is dead."

"No, no; only, what was a fellow to say when you pressed me so hard? I am your cousin George!"

"Oh!"

"And we have been such friends, you won't be angry? Are you vexed, Edith?" and he took both her hands.

"No; only astonished. I think—on the whole, I am rather—glad."

"That's all right; for, do you know, Edith, I seem to have known you for years! You have shown to-day every good quality a woman can possibly possess."

"Don't spoil me by such sayings."

"And Edith, dear Edith, do you know—confound it! here we are!—only this, I should like to go on travelling with you, like this, for ever and ever—and——"

Hatton! Hatton! tickets, please. Hatton!

A RAILWAY JOURNEY

"Here, Jones! take Miss Edith's bag. Is the carriage up?"

"Yes, sir."

"And a cart? there is a heap of luggage."

"All right sir."

"Come along, Edith? here we are, and my father is in the carriage."

DERAILMENTS

Arthur Conan Doyle

The Lost Special

The confession of Herbert de Lernac, now lying under sentence of death at Marseilles, has thrown a light upon one of the most inexplicable crimes of the century—an incident which is, I believe, absolutely unprecedented in the criminal annals of any country. Although there is a reluctance to discuss the matter in official circles, and little information has been given to the Press, there are still indications that the statement of this arch-criminal is corroborated by the facts, and that we have at last found a solution for a most astounding business. As the matter is eight years old, and as its importance was somewhat obscured by a political crisis which was engaging the public attention at the time, it may be as well to state the facts as far as we have been able to ascertain them. They are collated from the Liverpool papers of that date, from the proceedings at the inquest upon John Slater, the engine-driver, and from the records of the London and West Coast Railway Company, which have been courteously put at my disposal. Briefly, they are as follows.

On the 3rd of June, 1890, a gentleman, who gave

his name as Monsieur Louis Caratal, desired an interview with Mr. James Bland, the superintendent of the London and West Coast Central Station in Liverpool. He was a small man, middle-aged and dark, with a stoop which was so marked that it suggested some deformity of the spine. He was accompanied by a friend, a man of imposing physique, whose deferential manner and constant attention showed that his position was one of dependence. This friend or companion, whose name did not transpire, was certainly a foreigner, and probably, from his swarthy complexion, either a Spaniard or a South American. One peculiarity was observed in him. He carried in his left hand a small black leather dispatch-box, and it was noticed by a sharp-eyed clerk in the Central office that this box was fastened to his wrist by a strap. No importance was attached to the fact at the time, but subsequent events endowed it with some significance. Monsieur Caratal was shown up to Mr. Bland's office, while his companion remained outside.

Monsieur Caratal's business was quickly dispatched. He had arrived that afternoon from Central America. Affairs of the utmost importance demanded that he should be in Paris without the loss of an unnecessary hour. He had missed the London express. A special must be provided. Money was of no importance. Time was everything. If the company would speed him on his way, they might make their own terms.

Mr. Bland struck the electric bell, summoned Mr. Potter Hood, the traffic manager, and had the matter arranged in five minutes. The train would start in three-quarters of an hour. It would take that time to insure that the line should be clear. The powerful engine called Rochdale (No. 247 on the company's register) was attached to two carriages, with a guard's van behind. The first carriage was solely for the purpose of decreasing the inconvenience arising from the oscillation. The second was divided, as usual, into four compartments, a first-class, a first-class smoking, a second-class, and a second-class smoking. The first compartment, which was nearest to the engine, was the one allotted to the travellers. The other three were empty. The guard of the special train was James McPherson, who had been some years in the service of the company. The stoker, William Smith, was a new hand.

Monsieur Caratal, upon leaving the superintendent's office, rejoined his companion, and both of them manifested extreme impatience to be off. Having paid the money asked, which amounted to fifty pounds five shillings, at the usual special rate of five shillings a mile, they demanded to be shown the carriage, and at once took their seats in it, although they were assured that the better part of an hour must elapse before the line could be cleared. In the meantime a singular coincidence had occurred in the office which Monsieur Caratal had just quitted.

A request for a special is not a very uncommon circumstance in a rich commercial centre, but that two should be required upon the same afternoon was most unusual. It so happened, however, that Mr. Bland had hardly dismissed the first traveller before a second entered with a similar request. This was a Mr. Horace Moore, a gentlemanly man of military appearance, who alleged that the sudden serious illness of his wife in London made it absolutely imperative that he should not lose an instant in starting upon the journey. His distress and anxiety were so evident that Mr. Bland did all that was possible to meet his wishes. A second special was out of the question, as the ordinary local service was already somewhat deranged by the first. There was the alternative, however, that Mr. Moore should share the expense of Monsieur Caratal's train, and should travel in the other empty first-class compartment, if Monsieur Caratal objected to having him in the one which he occupied. It was difficult to see any objection to such an arrangement, and yet Monsieur Caratal, upon the suggestion being made to him by

Mr. Potter Hood, absolutely refused to consider it for an instant. The train was his, he said, and he would insist upon the exclusive use of it. All argument failed to overcome his ungracious objections, and finally the plan had to be abandoned. Mr. Horace Moore left the station in great distress, after learning that his only course was to take the ordinary slow train which leaves Liverpool at six o'clock. At four thirty-one exactly by the station clock the special train, containing the crippled Monsieur Caratal and his gigantic companion, steamed out of the Liverpool station. The line was at that time clear, and there should have been no stoppage before Manchester.

The trains of the London and West Coast Railway run over the lines of another company as far as this town, which should have been reached by the special rather before six o'clock. At a quarter after six considerable surprise and some consternation were caused amongst the officials at Liverpool by the receipt of a telegram from Manchester to say that it had not yet arrived. An inquiry directed to St. Helens, which is a third of the way between the two cities, elicited the following reply:—

"To James Bland, Superintendent, Central L. & W. C., Liverpool.—Special passed here at 4.52, well up to time.—Dowser, St. Helens."

This telegram was received at 6.40. At 6.50 a second message was received from Manchester:—

"No sign of special as advised by you."

And then ten minutes later a third, more bewildering:—

"Presume some mistake as to proposed running of special. Local train from St. Helens timed to follow it has just arrived and has seen nothing of it. Kindly wire advices.—Manchester."

The matter was assuming a most amazing aspect, although in some respects the last telegram was a relief to the authorities at Liverpool. If an accident had occurred to the special, it seemed hardly possible that the local train could have passed down the same line without observing it. And yet, what was the alternative? Where could the train be? Had it possibly been side-tracked for some reason in order to allow the slower train to go past? Such an explanation was possible if some small repair had to be effected. A telegram was dispatched to each of the stations between St. Helens and Manchester, and the superintendent and traffic manager waited in the utmost suspense at the instrument for the series of replies which would enable them to say for certain what had become of the missing train. The answers came back in the order of questions, which was the order of the stations beginning at the St. Helens end:—

"Special passed here five o'clock.—Collins Green."

"Special passed here six past five.—Earlestown."

"Special passed here 5.10.—Newton."

"Special passed here 5.20.—Kenyon Junction."

"No special train has passed here.—Barton Moss."

The two officials stared at each other in amazement.

"This is unique in my thirty years of experience," said Mr. Bland.

"Absolutely unprecedented and inexplicable, sir. The special has gone wrong between Kenyon Junction and Barton Moss."

"And yet there is no siding, so far as my memory serves me, between the two stations. The special must have run off the metals."

"But how could the four-fifty parliamentary pass over the same line without observing it?"

"There's no alternative, Mr. Hood. It *must* be so. Possibly the local train may have observed something which may throw some light upon the matter. We will wire to Manchester for more information, and to Kenyon Junction with instructions that the line be examined instantly as far as Barton Moss."

The answer from Manchester came within a few minutes.

"No news of missing special. Driver and guard of slow train positive no accident between Kenyon Junction and Barton Moss. Line quite clear, and no sign of anything unusual.—Manchester."

"That driver and guard will have to go," said Mr. Bland, grimly. "There has been a wreck and they have missed it. The special has obviously run off the metals without disturbing the line—how it could have done so passes my comprehension—but so it must be, and we shall have a wire from Kenyon or Barton Moss presently to say that they have found her at the bottom of an embankment."

But Mr. Bland's prophecy was not destined to be fulfilled. Half an hour passed, and then there arrived the following message from the station-master of Kenyon Junction:—

"There are no traces of the missing special. It is quite certain that she passed here, and that she did not arrive at Barton Moss. We have detached engine from goods train, and I have myself ridden down the line, but all is clear, and there is no sign of any accident."

Mr. Bland tore his hair in his perplexity.

"This is rank lunacy, Hood!" he cried. "Does a train vanish into thin air in England in broad daylight? The thing is preposterous. An engine, a tender, two carriages, a van, five human beings—and all lost on a straight line of railway! Unless we get something positive within the next hour I'll take Inspector Collins, and go down myself."

And then at last something positive did occur. It took the shape of another telegram from Kenyon Junction.

"Regret to report that the dead body of John Slater, driver of the special train, has just been found among the gorse bushes at a point two and a quarter miles from the Junction. Had fallen from his engine, pitched down the embankment, and rolled among bushes. Injuries to his head, from the fall, appear to be cause of death. Ground has now been carefully examined, and there is no trace of the missing train."

The country was, as has already been stated, in the throes of a political crisis, and the attention of the public was further distracted by the important and sensational developments in Paris, where a huge scandal threatened to destroy the Government and to wreck the reputations of many of the leading men in France. The papers were full of these events, and the singular disappearance of the special train attracted less attention than would have been the case in more peaceful times. The grotesque nature of the event helped to detract from its importance, for the papers were disinclined to believe the facts as reported to them. More than one of the London journals treated the matter as an ingenious hoax, until the coroner's inquest upon the unfortunate driver (an inquest which elicited nothing of importance) convinced them of the tragedy of the incident.

Mr. Bland, accompanied by Inspector Collins, the senior detective officer in the service of the company, went down to Kenyon Junction the same evening, and their research lasted throughout the following day, but was attended with purely negative results. Not only was no trace found of the missing train, but no conjecture could be put forward which could possibly explain the facts. At the same time, Inspector Collins's official report (which lies before me as I write) served to show that the possibilities were more numerous than might have been expected.

"In the stretch of railway between these two points," said he, "the country is dotted with ironworks and collieries. Of these, some are being worked and some have been abandoned. There are no fewer than twelve which have small gauge lines which run trolly-cars down to the main line. These can, of course, be disregarded. Besides these, however, there are seven which have or have had, proper lines running down and connecting with points to the main line, so as to convey their produce from the mouth of the mine to the great centres of distribution. In every case these lines are only a few miles in length. Out of the seven, four belong to collieries which are worked out, or at least to shafts which are no longer used. These are the Redgauntlet, Hero, Slough of Despond, and Heartsease mines, the latter having ten years ago been one of the principal mines in Lancashire. These four side lines may be eliminated from our inquiry, for, to prevent possible accidents, the rails nearest to the main line have been taken up, and there is no longer any connection. There remain three other side lines leading—

(*a*) To the Carnstock Iron Works;
(*b*) To the Big Ben Colliery;
(*c*) To the Perseverance Colliery.

"Of these the Big Ben line is not more than a quarter of a mile long, and ends at a dead wall of coal waiting removal from the mouth of the mine. Nothing had been seen or heard there of any special. The Carnstock Iron Works line was blocked all day upon the 3rd of June by sixteen truckloads of hematite. It is a single line, and nothing could have passed. As to the Perseverance line, it is a large double line, which does a considerable traffic, for the output of the mine is very large. On the 3rd of

June this traffic proceeded as usual; hundreds of men, including a gang of railway platelayers, were working along the two miles and a quarter which constitute the total length of the line, and it is inconceivable that an unexpected train could have come down there without attracting universal attention. It may be remarked in conclusion that this branch line is nearer to St. Helens than the point at which the engine-driver was discovered, so that we have every reason to believe that the train was past that point before misfortune overtook her.

"As to John Slater, there is no clue to be gathered from his appearance or injuries. We can only say that, so far as we can see, he met his end by falling off his engine, though why he fell, or what became of the engine after his fall, is a question upon which I do not feel qualified to offer an opinion." In conclusion, the inspector offered his resignation to the Board, being much nettled by an accusation of incompetence in the London papers.

A month elapsed, during which both the police and the company prosecuted their inquiries without the slightest success. A reward was offered and a pardon promised in case of crime, but they were both unclaimed. Every day the public opened their papers with the conviction that so grotesque a mystery would at last be solved, but week after week passed by, and a solution remained as far off as ever. In broad daylight, upon a June afternoon in the most thickly inhabited portion of England, a train with its occupants had disappeared as completely as if some master of subtle chemistry had volatilized it into gas. Indeed, among the various conjectures which were put forward in the public Press there were some which seriously asserted that supernatural, or, at least, preternatural, agencies had been at work, and that the deformed Monsieur Caratal was probably a person who was better known under a less polite name. Others fixed upon his swarthy companion as being the author of the mischief, but what it was exactly which he had done could never be clearly formulated in words.

Amongst the many suggestions put forward by various newspapers or private individuals, there were one or two which were feasible enough to attract the attention of the public. One which appeared in the *Times*, over the signature of an amateur reasoner of some celebrity at that date, attempted to deal with the matter in a critical and semi-scientific manner. An extract must suffice, although the curious can see the whole letter in the issue of the 3rd of July.

"It is one of the elementary principles of practical reasoning," he remarked, "that when the impossible has been eliminated the residuum, *however improbable*, must contain the truth. It is certain that the train left Kenyon Junction. It is certain that it did not reach Barton Moss. It is in the highest degree unlikely, but still possible, that it may have taken one of the seven available side lines. It is obviously impossible for a train to run where there are no rails, and, therefore, we may reduce our improbables to the three open lines, namely, the Carnstock Iron Works, the Big Ben, and the Perseverance. Is there a secret society of colliers, an English *camorra*, which is capable of destroying both train and passengers? It is improbable, but it is not impossible. I confess that I am unable to suggest any other solution. I should certainly advise the company to direct all their energies towards the observation of those three lines, and of the workmen at the end of them. A careful supervision of the pawnbrokers' shops of the district might possibly bring some suggestive facts to light."

The suggestion coming from a recognized authority upon such matters created considerable interest, and a fierce opposition from those who considered such a statement to be a preposterous libel upon an honest and deserving set of men. The only answer to this criticism was a challenge to the objectors to lay any more feasible explanation before the public. In reply to this two others were forthcoming (*Times*, July 7th and 9th). The first suggested that the train might have run off the metals and be lying submerged in the Lancashire and Staffordshire Canal, which runs parallel to the railway for some hundreds of yards. This suggestion was thrown out of court by the published depth of the canal, which was entirely insufficient to conceal so large an object. The second correspondent wrote calling attention to the bag which appeared to be the sole luggage which the travellers had brought with them, and suggesting that some novel explosive of immense and pulverizing power might have been concealed in it. The obvious absurdity, however, of supposing that the whole train might be blown to dust while the metals remained uninjured reduced any such explanation to a farce. The investigation had drifted into this hopeless position when a new and most unexpected incident occurred.

This was nothing less than the receipt by Mrs. McPherson of a letter from her husband, James McPherson, who had been the guard of the missing train. The letter, which was dated July 5th, 1890, was posted from New York, and came to hand upon July 14th. Some doubts were expressed as to its genuine character, but Mrs. McPherson was positive as to the writing, and the fact that it contained a remittance of a hundred dollars in five-dollar notes was enough in itself to discount the idea of a hoax. No address was given in the letter, which ran in this way:—

> "MY DEAR WIFE,—
>
> "I have been thinking a great deal, and I find it very hard to give you up. The same with Lizzie. I try to fight against it, but it will always come back to me. I send you some money which will change into twenty English pounds. This should be enough to bring both Lizzie and you across the Atlantic, and you will find the Hamburg boats which stop at Southampton very good boats, and cheaper than Liverpool. If you could come here and stop at the Johnston House I would try and send you word how to meet, but things are very difficult with me at present, and I am not very happy, finding it hard to give you both up. So no more at present, from your loving husband,
>
> "JAMES MCPHERSON."

For a time it was confidently anticipated that this letter would lead to the clearing up of the whole matter, the more so as it was ascertained that a passenger who bore a close resemblance to the missing guard had travelled from Southampton under the name of Summers in the Hamburg and New York liner *Vistula*, which started upon the 7th of June. Mrs. McPherson and her sister Lizzie Dolton went across to New York as directed, and stayed for three weeks at the Johnston House, without hearing anything from the missing man. It is probable that some injudicious comments in the Press may have warned him that the police were using them as a bait. However this may be, it is certain that he neither wrote nor came, and the women were eventually compelled to return to Liverpool.

And so the matter stood, and has continued to stand up to the present year of 1898. Incredible as it may seem, nothing has transpired during these eight years which has shed the least light upon the extraordinary disappearance of the special train which contained Monsieur Caratal and his companion. Careful inquiries into the antecedents of the two travellers have only established the fact that Monsieur Caratal was well known as a financier and political agent in Central America, and that during his voyage to Europe he had betrayed extraordinary anxiety to reach Paris. His companion, whose name was entered upon the passenger lists as Eduardo Gomez, was a man whose record was a violent one, and whose reputation was that of a bravo and a bully. There was evidence to show, however, that he was honestly devoted to the interests of Monsieur Caratal, and that the latter, being a man of puny physique, employed the other as a guard and protector. It may be added that no information came from Paris as to what the objects of Monsieur Caratal's hurried journey may have been. This comprises all the facts of the case up to the publication in the Marseilles papers of the recent confession of Herbert de Lernac, now under sentence of death for the murder of a merchant named Bonvalot. This statement may be literally translated as follows:—

"It is not out of mere pride or boasting that I give this information, for, if that were my object, I could tell a dozen actions of mine which are quite as splendid; but I do it in order that certain gentlemen in Paris may understand that I, who am able here to tell about the fate of Monsieur Caratal, can also tell in whose interest and at whose request the deed was done, unless the reprieve which I am awaiting comes to me very quickly. Take warning, messieurs, before it is too late! You know Herbert de Lernac, and you are aware that his deeds are as ready as his words. Hasten then, or you are lost!

"At present I shall mention no names—if you only heard the names, what would you not think!—but I shall merely tell you how cleverly I did it. I was true to my employers then, and no doubt they will be true to me now. I hope so, and until I am convinced that they have betrayed me, these names, which would convulse Europe, shall not be divulged. But on that day . . . well, I say no more!

"In a word, then, there was a famous trial in Paris, in the year 1890, in connection with a monstrous scandal in politics and finance. How monstrous that scandal was can never be known save by such confidential agents as myself. The honour and careers of many of the chief men in France were at stake. You have seen a group of nine-pins standing, all so rigid, and prim, and unbending. Then there comes the ball from far away and pop, pop, pop—there are your nine-pins on the floor. Well, imagine some of the greatest men in France as these nine-pins, and then this Monsieur Caratal was the ball which could be seen coming from far away. If he arrived, then it was pop, pop, pop for all of them. It was determined that he should not arrive.

"I do not accuse them all of being conscious of what was to happen. There were, as I have said, great financial as well as political interests at stake, and a syndicate was formed to manage the business. Some subscribed to the syndicate who hardly understood what were its objects. But others understood very well, and they can rely upon it that I have not forgotten their names. They had ample warning that

Monsieur Caratal was coming long before he left South America, and they knew that the evidence which he held would certainly mean ruin to all of them. The syndicate had the command of an unlimited amount of money—absolutely unlimited, you understand. They looked round for an agent who was capable of wielding this gigantic power. The man chosen must be inventive, resolute, adaptive—a man in a million. They chose Herbert de Lernac, and I admit that they were right.

"My duties were to choose my subordinates, to use freely the power which money gives, and to make certain that Monsieur Caratal should never arrive in Paris. With characteristic energy I set about my commission within an hour of receiving my instructions, and the steps which I took were the very best for the purpose which could possibly be devised.

"A man whom I could trust was dispatched instantly to South America to travel home with Monsieur Caratal. Had he arrived in time the ship would never have reached Liverpool; but, alas! it had already started before my agent could reach it. I fitted out a small armed brig to intercept it, but again I was unfortunate. Like all great organizers I was, however, prepared for failure, and had a series of alternatives prepared, one or the other of which must succeed. You must not underrate the difficulties of my undertaking, or imagine that a mere commonplace assassination would meet the case. We must destroy not only Monsieur Caratal, but Monsieur Caratal's documents, and Monsieur Caratal's companions also, if we had reason to believe that he had communicated his secrets to them. And you must remember that they were on the alert, and keenly suspicious of any such attempt. It was a task which was in every way worthy of me, for I am always most masterful where another would be appalled.

"I was all ready for Monsieur Caratal's reception in Liverpool, and I was the more eager because I had reason to believe that he had made arrangements by which he would have a considerable guard from the moment that he arrived in London. Anything which was to be done must be done between the moment of his setting foot upon the Liverpool quay and that of his arrival at the London and West Coast terminus in London. We prepared six plans, each more elaborate than the last; which plan would be used would depend upon his own movements. Do what he would, we were ready for him. If he had stayed in Liverpool, we were ready. If he took an ordinary train, an express, or a special, all was ready. Everything had been foreseen and provided for.

"You may imagine that I could not do all this myself. What could I know of the English railway lines? But money can procure willing agents all the world over, and I soon had one of the acutest brains in England to assist me. I will mention no names, but it would be unjust to claim all the credit for myself. My English ally was worthy of such an alliance. He knew the London and West Coast line thoroughly, and he had the command of a band of workers who were trustworthy and intelligent. The idea was his, and my own judgment was only required in the details. We bought over several officials, amongst whom the most important was James McPherson, whom we had ascertained to be the guard most likely to be employed upon a special train. Smith, the stoker, was also in our employ. John Slater, the engine-driver, had been approached, but had been found to be obstinate and dangerous, so we desisted. We had no certainty that Monsieur Caratal would take a special, but we thought it very probable, for it was of the utmost importance to him that he should reach Paris without delay. It was for this contingency, therefore, that we made special preparations—preparations which were complete down to the last detail long before his steamer had sighted the shores of England. You will be amused to learn that there was one of my agents in the pilot-boat which brought that steamer to its moorings.

"The moment that Caratal arrived in Liverpool

we knew that he suspected danger and was on his guard. He had brought with him as an escort a dangerous fellow, named Gomez, a man who carried weapons, and was prepared to use them. This fellow carried Caratal's confidential papers for him, and was ready to protect either them or his master. The probability was that Caratal had taken him into his counsels, and that to remove Caratal without removing Gomez would be a mere waste of energy. It was necessary that they should be involved in a common fate, and our plans to that end were much facilitated by their request for a special train. On that special train you will understand that two out of the three servants of the company were really in our employ, at a price which would make them independent for a lifetime. I do not go so far as to say that the English are more honest than any other nation, but I have found them more expensive to buy.

"I have already spoken of my English agent—who is a man with a considerable future before him, unless some complaint of the throat carries him off before his time. He had charge of all arrangements at Liverpool, whilst I was stationed at the inn at Kenyon, where I awaited a cipher signal to act. When the special was arranged for, my agent instantly telegraphed to me and warned me how soon I should have everything ready. He himself under the name of Horace Moore applied immediately for a special also, in the hope that he would be sent down with Monsieur Caratal, which might under certain circumstances have been helpful to us. If, for example, our great *coup* had failed, it would then have become the duty of my agent to have shot them both and destroyed their papers. Caratal was on his guard, however, and refused to admit any other traveller. My agent then left the station, returned by another entrance, entered the guard's van on the side farthest from the platform, and travelled down with McPherson the guard.

"In the meantime you will be interested to know what my movements were. Everything had been prepared for days before, and only the finishing touches were needed. The side line which we had chosen had once joined the main line, but it had been disconnected. We had only to replace a few rails to connect it once more. These rails had been laid down as far as could be done without danger of attracting attention, and now it was merely a case of completing a juncture with the line, and arranging the points as they had been before. The sleepers had never been removed, and the rails, fish-plates, and rivets were all ready, for we had taken them from a siding on the abandoned portion of the line. With my small but competent band of workers, we had everything ready long before the special arrived. When it did arrive, it ran off upon the small side line so easily that the jolting of the points appears to have been entirely unnoticed by the two travellers.

"Our plan had been that Smith the stoker should chloroform John Slater the driver, so that he should vanish with the others. In this respect, and in this respect only, our plans miscarried—I except the criminal folly of McPherson in writing home to his wife. Our stoker did his business so clumsily that Slater in his struggles fell off the engine, and though fortune was with us so far that he broke his neck in the fall, still he remained as a blot upon that which would otherwise have been one of those complete masterpieces which are only to be contemplated in silent admiration. The criminal expert will find in John Slater the one flaw in all our admirable combinations. A man who has had as many triumphs as I can afford to be frank, and I therefore lay my finger upon John Slater, and I proclaim him to be a flaw.

"But now I have got our special train upon the small line two kilomètres, or rather more than one mile, in length, which leads, or rather used to lead, to the abandoned Heartsease mine, once one of the largest coal mines in England. You will ask how it is that no one saw the train upon this unused line. I answer that along its entire length it runs through a deep cutting, and that, unless some one had been on the edge of that cutting, he could not have seen it. There *was* some one on the edge of that cutting. I was there. And now I will tell you what I saw.

"My assistant had remained at the points in order that he might superintend the switching off of the train. He had four armed men with him, so that if the train ran off the line—we thought it probable, because the points were very rusty—we might still have resources to fall back upon. Having once seen it safely on the side line, he handed over the responsibility to me. I was waiting at a point which overlooks the mouth of the mine, and I was also armed, as were my two companions. Come what might, you see, I was always ready.

"The moment that the train was fairly on the side line, Smith, the stoker, slowed-down the engine, and then, having turned it on to the fullest speed again, he and McPherson, with my English lieutenant, sprang off before it was too late. It may be that it was this slowing-down which first attracted the attention of the travellers, but the train was running at full speed again before their heads appeared at the open window. It makes me smile to think how bewildered they must have been. Picture to yourself your own feelings if, on looking out of your luxurious carriage, you suddenly perceived that the lines upon which you ran were rusted and corroded, red and yellow with disuse and decay! What a catch must have come in their breath as in a second it flashed upon them that it was not Manchester but Death which was waiting for them at the end of that sinister line. But the train was running with frantic speed, rolling and rocking over the rotten line, while the wheels made a frightful screaming sound upon the rusted surface. I was close to them, and could see their faces. Caratal was praying, I think—there was something like a rosary dangling out of his hand. The other roared like a bull who smells the blood of the slaughter-house. He saw us standing on the bank, and he beckoned to us like a madman. Then he tore at his wrist and threw his dispatch-box out of the window in our direction. Of course, his meaning was obvious. Here was the evidence, and they would promise to be silent if their lives were spared. It would have been very agreeable if we could have done so, but business is business. Besides, the train was now as much beyond our control as theirs.

"He ceased howling when the train rattled round the curve and they saw the black mouth of the mine yawning before them. We had removed the boards which had covered it, and we had cleared the square entrance. The rails had formerly run very close to the shaft for the convenience of loading the coal, and we had only to add two or three lengths of rail in order to lead to the very brink of the shaft. In fact, as the lengths would not quite fit, our line projected about three feet over the edge. We saw the two heads at the window: Caratal below, Gomez above; but they had both been struck silent by what they saw. And yet they could not withdraw their heads. The sight seemed to have paralyzed them.

"I had wondered how the train running at a great speed would take the pit into which I had guided it, and I was much interested in watching it. One of my colleagues thought that it would actually jump it, and indeed it was not very far from doing so. Fortunately, however, it fell short, and the buffers of the engine struck the other lip of the shaft with a tremendous crash. The funnel flew off into the air. The tender, carriages, and van were all smashed up into one jumble, which, with the remains of the engine, choked for a minute or so the mouth of the pit. Then something gave way in the middle, and the whole mass of green iron, smoking coals, brass fittings, wheels, woodwork, and cushions all crumbled together and crashed down into the mine. We heard the rattle, rattle, rattle, as the *débris* struck against the walls, and then quite a long time afterwards there came a deep roar as the remains of the train struck the bottom. The boiler may have burst, for a sharp crash came after the roar, and then a dense cloud of steam and smoke swirled up out of the black depths, falling in a spray as thick as rain all round us. Then the vapour shredded off into thin wisps, which floated away in the summer sunshine, and all was quiet again in the Heartsease mine.

"And now, having carried out our plans so successfully, it only remained to leave no trace behind us. Our little band of workers at the other end had already ripped up the rails and disconnected the side line, replacing everything as it had been before. We were equally busy at the mine. The funnel and other fragments were thrown in, the shaft was planked over as it used to be, and the lines which led to it were torn up and taken away. Then, without flurry, but without delay, we all made our way out of the country, most of us to Paris, my English colleague to Manchester, and McPherson to Southampton, whence he emigrated to America. Let the English papers of that date tell how thoroughly we had done our work, and how completely we had thrown the cleverest of their detectives off our track.

"You will remember that Gomez threw his bag of papers out of the window, and I need not say that I secured that bag and brought them to my employers. It may interest my employers now, however, to learn that out of that bag I took one or two little papers as a souvenir of the occasion. I have no wish to publish these papers; but, still, it is every man for himself in this world, and what else can I do if my friends will not come to my aid when I want them? Messieurs, you may believe that Herbert de Lernac is quite as formidable when he is against you as when he is with you, and that he is not a man to go to the guillotine until he has seen that every one of you is *en route* for New Caledonia. For your own sake, if not for mine, make haste, Monsieur de——, and General——, and Baron——(you can fill up the blanks for yourselves as you read this). I promise you that in the next edition there will be no blanks to fill.

"P.S.—As I look over my statement there is only one omission which I can see. It concerns the unfortunate man McPherson, who was foolish enough to write to his wife and to make an appointment with her in New York. It can be imagined that when interests like ours were at stake, we could not leave them to the chance of whether a man in that class of life would or would not give away his secrets to a woman. Having once broken his oath by writing to his wife, we could not trust him any more. We took steps therefore to insure that he should not see his wife. I have sometimes thought that it would be a kindness to write to her and to assure her that there is no impediment to her marrying again."

V. L. Whitechurch

The Affair of the Corridor Express

Thorpe Hazell stood in his study in his London flat. On the opposite wall he had pinned a bit of paper, about an inch square, at the height of his eye, and was now going through the most extraordinary contortions.

With his eyes fixed on the paper he was craning his neck as far as it would reach and twisting his head about in all directions. This necessitated a fearful rolling of the eyes in order to keep them on the paper, and was supposed to be a means of strengthening the muscles of the eye for angular sight.

Presently there came a tap at the door.

"Come in!" cried Hazell, still whirling his head round.

"A gentleman wishes to see you at once, sir!" said the servant, handing him a card.

Hazell paused in his exercises, took it from the tray, and read:

"Mr. F. W. Wingrave, M.A., B.Sc."

"Oh, show him in," said Hazell, rather impatiently, for he hated to be interrupted when he was doing his "eye gymnastics."

There entered a young man of about five-and-twenty, with a look of keen anxiety on his face.

"You are Mr. Thorpe Hazell?" he asked.

"I am."

"You will have seen my name on my card—I am one of the masters at Shillington School—I had heard your name, and they told me at the station that it might be well to consult you—I hope you don't mind—I know you're not an ordinary detective, but——"

"Sit down, Mr. Wingrave," said Hazell, interrupting his nervous flow of language. "You look quite ill and tired."

"I have just been through a very trying experience," replied Wingrave, sinking into a seat. "A boy I was in charge of has just mysteriously disappeared, and I want you to find him for me, and I want to ask your opinion. They say you know all about railways, but——"

"Now, look here, my dear sir, you just have some hot toast and water before you say another word. I conclude you want to consult me on some railway matter. I'll do what I can, but I won't hear you till you've had some refreshment. Perhaps you prefer whiskey—though I don't advise it."

Wingrave, however, chose the whiskey, and Hazell poured him out some, adding soda-water.

THE AFFAIR OF THE CORRIDOR EXPRESS

"Thank you," he said. "I hope you'll be able to give me advice. I am afraid the poor boy must be killed; the whole thing is a mystery, and I——"

"Stop a bit, Mr. Wingrave. I must ask you to tell me the story from the very beginning. That's the best way."

"Quite right. The worry of it has made me incoherent, I fear. But I'll try and do what you propose. First of all, do you know the name of Carr-Mathers?"

"Yes, I think so. Very rich, is he not?"

"A millionaire. He has only one child, a boy of about ten, whose mother died at his birth. He is a small boy for his age, and idolised by his father. About three months ago this young Horace Carr-Mathers was sent to our school—Cragsbury House, just outside Shillington. It is not a very large school, but exceedingly select, and the headmaster, Dr. Spring, is well known in high-class circles. I may tell you that we have the sons of some of the leading nobility preparing for the public schools. You will readily understand that in such an establishment as ours the most scrupulous care is exercised over the boys, not only as regards their moral and intellectual training, but also to guard against any outside influences."

"Kidnapping, for example," interposed Hazell.

"Exactly. There have been such cases known, and Dr. Spring has a very high reputation to maintain. The slightest rumour against the school would go ill with him—and with all of us masters.

"Well, this morning the headmaster received a telegram about Horace Carr-Mathers, requesting that he should be sent up to town."

"Do you know the exact wording?" asked Hazell.

"I have it with me," replied Wingrave, drawing it from his pocket.

Hazell took it from him, and read as follows:

"*Please grant Horace leave of absence for two days. Send him to London by 5.45 express from Shillington, in first-class carriage, giving guard instructions to look after him. We will meet train in town.—Carr-Mathers.*"

"Um," grunted Hazell, as he handed it back. "Well, he can afford long telegrams."

"Oh, he's always wiring about something or other," replied Wingrave; "he seldom writes a letter. Well, when the doctor received this he called me into his study.

"'I suppose I must let the boy go,' he said, 'but I'm not at all inclined to allow him to travel by himself. If anything should happen to him his father would hold us responsible as well as the railway company. So you had better take him up to town, Mr. Wingrave.'

"'Yes, sir.'

"'You need do no more than deliver him to his father. If Mr. Carr-Mathers is not at the terminus to meet him, take him with you in a cab to his house in Portland Place. You'll probably be able to catch the last train home, but, if not, you can get a bed at an hotel.'

"'Very good, sir.'

"So, shortly after half-past five, I found myself standing on the platform at Shillington, waiting for the London express."

"Now, stop a moment," interrupted Hazell, sipping a glass of filtered water which he had poured out for himself. "I want to get a clear notion of this journey of yours from the beginning, for, I presume, you will shortly be telling me that something strange happened during it. Was there anything to be noticed before the train started?"

"Nothing at the time. But I remembered afterwards that two men seemed to be watching me rather closely when I took the tickets, and I heard one of them say 'Confound,' beneath his breath. But my suspicions were not aroused at the moment."

"I see. If there is anything in this it was probably because he was disconcerted when he saw you were going to travel with the boy. Did these two men get into the train?"

"I'm coming to that. The train was in sharp to time, and we took our seats in a first-class compartment."

"Please describe the exact position."

"Our carriage was the third from the front. It was a corridor train, with access from carriage to carriage all the way through. Horace and myself were in a compartment alone. I had bought him some illustrated papers for the journey, and for some time he sat quietly enough, looking through them. After a bit he grew fidgety, as you know boys will."

"Wait a minute. I want to know if the corridor of your carriage was on the left or on the right—supposing you to be seated facing the engine?"

"On the left."

"Very well, go on."

"The door leading into the corridor stood open. It was still daylight, but dusk was setting in fast—I should say it was about half-past six, or a little more. Horace had been looking out of the window on the right side of the train when I drew his attention to Rutherham Castle, which we were passing. It stands, as you know, on the left side of the line. In order to get a better view of it he went out into the corridor and stood there. I retained my seat on the right side of the compartment, glancing at him from time to time. He seemed interested in the corridor itself,

THE AFFAIR OF THE CORRIDOR EXPRESS

looking about him, and once or twice shutting and opening the door of our compartment. I can see now that I ought to have kept a sharper eye on him, but I never dreamed that any accident could happen. I was reading a paper myself, and became rather interested in a paragraph. It may have been seven or eight minutes before I looked up. When I did so, Horace had disappeared.

"I didn't think anything of it at first, but only concluded that he had taken a walk along the corridor."

"You don't know which way he went?" inquired Hazell.

"No. I couldn't say. I waited a minute or two, and then rose and looked out into the corridor. There was no one there. Still my suspicions were not aroused. It was possible that he had gone to the lavatory. So I sat down again, and waited. Then I began to get a little anxious, and determined to have a look for him. I walked to either end of the corridor, and searched the lavatories, but they were both empty. Then I looked in all the other compartments of the carriage, and asked their occupants if they had seen him go by, but none of them had noticed him."

"Do you remember how these compartments were occupied?"

"Yes. In the first, which was reserved for ladies,

there were five ladies. The next was a smoker with three gentlemen in it. Ours came next. Then, going towards the front of the train, were the two men I had noticed at Shillington; the last compartment had a gentleman and lady and their three children."

"Ah! how about those two men—what were they doing?"

"One of them was reading a book, and the other appeared to be asleep."

"Tell me. Was the door leading to the corridor from their compartment shut?"

"Yes, it was."

"Go on."

"Well, I was in a most terrible fright, and I went back to my compartment and pulled the electric communicator. In a few seconds the front guard came along the corridor and asked me what I wanted. I told him I had lost my charge. He suggested that the boy had walked through to another carriage, and I asked him if he would mind my making a thorough search of the train with him. To this he readily agreed. We went back to the first carriage and began to do so. We examined every compartment from end to end of the train; we looked under every seat, in spite of the protestations of some of the passengers; we searched all the lavatories—every corner of the train—and we found absolutely no trace of Horace Carr-Mathers. No one had seen the boy anywhere."

"Had the train stopped?"

"Not for a second. It was going at full speed all the time. It only slowed down after we had finished the search—but it never quite stopped."

"Ah! We'll come to that presently. I want to ask you some questions first. Was it still daylight?"

"Dusk, but quite light enough to see plainly—besides which, the train lamps were lit."

"Exactly. Those two men, now, in the next compartment to yours—tell me precisely what happened when you visited them the second time with the guard."

"They asked a lot of questions—like many of the other passengers—and seemed very surprised."

"You looked underneath their seats?"

"Certainly."

"On the luggage-racks? A small boy like that could be rolled up in a rug and put on the rack."

"We examined every rack on the train."

Thorpe Hazell lit a cigarette and smoked furiously, motioning to his companion to keep quiet. He was thinking out the situation. Suddenly he said:

"How about the window in those two men's compartment?"

"It was shut—I particularly noticed it."

"You are *quite sure* you searched the whole of the train?"

"Absolutely certain; so was the guard."

"Ah!" remarked Hazell, "even guards are mistaken sometimes. It—er—was only the inside of the train you searched, eh?"

"Of course."

"Very well," replied Hazell, "now, before we go any further, I want to ask you this. Would it have been to anyone's interest to have murdered the boy?"

"I don't think so—from what I know. I don't see how it could be."

"Very well. We will take it as a pure case of kidnapping, and presume that he is alive and well. This ought to console you to begin with."

"Do you think you can help me?"

"I don't know yet. But go on and tell me all that happened."

"Well, after we had searched the train I was at my wits' end—and so was the guard. We both agreed, however, that nothing more could be done till we reached London. Somehow, my strongest suspicions concerning those two men were aroused, and I travelled in their compartment for the rest of the journey."

"Oh! Did anything happen?"

"Nothing. They both wished me good-night, hoped I'd find the boy, got out, and drove off in a hansom."

"And then?"

"I looked about for Mr. Carr-Mathers, but he was nowhere to be seen. Then I saw an inspector, and put the case before him. He promised to make inquiries and to have the line searched on the part where I missed Horace. I took a hansom to Portland Place, only to discover that Mr. Carr-Mathers is on the Continent and not expected home for a week. Then I came on to you—the inspector had advised me to do so. And that's the whole story. It's a terrible thing for me, Mr. Hazell. What do you think of it?"

"Well," replied Hazell, "of course it's very clear that there is a distinct plot. Someone sent that telegram, knowing Mr. Carr-Mathers' proclivities. The object was to kidnap the boy. It sounds absurd to talk of brigands and ransoms in this country, but the thing is done over and over again for all that. It is obvious that the boy was expected to travel alone, and that the train was the place chosen for the kidnapping. Hence the elaborate directions. I think you were quite right in suspecting those two men, and it might have been better if you had followed them up without coming to me."

"But they went off alone!"

"Exactly. It's my belief they had originally intended doing so after disposing of Horace, and that they carried out their original intentions."

"But what became of the boy?—how did they——"

"Stop a bit. I'm not at all clear in my own mind. But you mentioned that while you were concluding your search with the guard the train slackened speed?"

"Yes. It almost came to a stop—and then went very slowly for a minute or so. I asked the guard why, but I didn't understand his reply."

"What was it?"

"He said it was a P.W. operation."

Hazell laughed.

"P.W. stands for permanent way," he explained, "I know exactly what you mean now. There is a big job going on near Longmoor—they are raising the level of the line, and the up-trains are running on temporary rails. So they have to proceed very slowly. Now it was after this that you went back to the two men whom you suspected?"

"Yes."

"Very well. Now let me think the thing over. Have some more whiskey? You might also like to glance at the contents of my book-case. If you know anything of first editions and bindings they will interest you."

Wingrave, it is to be feared, paid but small heed to the books, but watched Hazell anxiously as the latter smoked cigarette after cigarette, his brows knit in deep thought. After a bit he said slowly:

"You will understand that I am going to work upon the theory that the boy has been kidnapped and that the original intention has been carried out, in spite of the accident of your presence in the train. How the boy was disposed of meanwhile is what baffles me; but that is a detail—though it will be interesting to know how it was done. Now, I don't want to raise any false hopes, because I may very likely be wrong, but we are going to take action upon a very feasible assumption, and if I am at all correct, I hope to put you definitely on the track. Mind, I don't promise to do so, and, at best, I don't promise to do *more* than put you on a track. Let me see—it's just after nine. We have plenty of time. We'll drive first to Scotland Yard, for it will be as well to have a detective with us."

He filled a flask with milk, put some plasmon biscuits and a banana into a sandwich case, and then ordered his servant to hail a cab.

An hour later, Hazell, Wingrave, and a man from Scotland Yard were closeted together in one of the private offices of the Mid-Eastern Railway with one of the chief officials of the line. The latter was listening attentively to Hazell.

"But I can't understand the boy not being anywhere in the train, Mr. Hazell," he said.

"I can—partly," replied Hazell, "but first let me see if my theory is correct."

"By all means. There's a down-train in a few minutes. I'll go with you, for the matter is very interesting. Come along, gentlemen."

He walked forward to the engine and gave a few instructions to the driver, and then they took their seats in the train. After a run of half an hour or so they passed a station.

"That's Longmoor," said the official, "now we shall soon be on the spot. It's about a mile down that the line is being raised."

Hazell put his head out of the window. Presently an ominous red light showed itself. The train came almost to a stop, and then proceeded slowly, the man who had shown the red light changing it to green. They could see him as they passed, standing close to a little temporary hut. It was his duty to warn all approaching drivers, and for this purpose he was stationed some three hundred yards in front of the bit of line that was being operated upon. Very soon they were passing this bit. Naphtha lamps shed a weird light over a busy scene, for the work was being continued night and day. A score or so of sturdy navvies were shovelling and picking along the track.

Once more into the darkness. On the other side of the scene of operations, at the same distance, was another little hut, with a guardian for the uptrain. Instead of increasing the speed in passing this hut, which would have been usual, the driver brought the train almost to a standstill. As he did so the four men got out of the carriage, jumping from the footboard to the ground. On went the train, leaving them on the left side of the down track, just opposite the little hut. They could see the man standing outside, his back partly turned to them. There was a fire in a brazier close by that dimly outlined his figure.

He started suddenly, as they crossed the line towards him.

"What are you doing here?" he cried. "You've no business here—you're trespassing."

He was a big, strong-looking man, and he backed a little towards his hut as he spoke.

"I am Mr. Mills, the assistant-superintendent of the line," replied the official, coming forward.

"Beg pardon, sir; but how was I to know that?" growled the man.

"Quite right. It's your duty to warn off strangers. How long have you been stationed here?"

"I came on at five o'clock; I'm regular night-watchman, sir."

"Ah! Pretty comfortable, eh?"

"Yes, thank you, sir," replied the man, wondering why the question was asked, but thinking, not unnaturally, that the assistant-superintendent had come down with a party of engineers to inspect things.

"Got the hut to yourself?"

"Yes, sir."

Without another word, Mr. Mills walked to the door of the hut. The man, his face suddenly growing pale, moved, and stood with his back to it.

"It's—it's private, sir!" he growled.

Hazell laughed.

"All right, my man," he said. "I was right, I think—hullo!—look out! Don't let him go!"

For the man had made a quick rush forward. But the Scotland Yard officer and Hazell were on him in a moment, and a few seconds later the handcuffs clicked on his wrists. Then they flung the door open, and there, lying in the corner, gagged and bound, was Horace Carr-Mathers.

An exclamation of joy broke forth from Wingrave, as he opened his knife to cut the cords. But Hazell stopped him.

"Just half a moment," he said: "I want to see how they've tied him up."

A peculiar method had been adopted in doing this. His wrists were fastened behind his back, a stout cord was round his body just under the armpits, and another cord above the knees. These were connected by a slack bit of rope.

"All right!" went on Hazell; "let's get the poor lad out of his troubles—there, that's better. How do you feel, my boy?"

"Awfully stiff!" said Horace, "but I'm not hurt. I say, sir," he continued to Wingrave, "how did you know I was here. I *am* glad you've come."

"The question is how did you *get* here?" replied Wingrave. "Mr. Hazell, here, seemed to know where you were, but it's a puzzle to me at present."

"If you'd come half an hour later you wouldn't have found him," growled the man who was handcuffed. "I ain't so much to blame as them as employed me."

"Oh, is that how the land lies?" exclaimed Hazell. "I see. You shall tell us presently, my boy, how it happened. Meanwhile, Mr. Mills, I think we can prepare a little trap—eh?"

In five minutes all was arranged. A couple of the navvies were brought up from the line, one stationed outside to guard against trains, and with certain other instructions, the other being inside the hut with the rest of them. A third navvy was also dispatched for the police.

"How are they coming?" asked Hazell of the handcuffed man.

"They were going to take a train down from London to Rockhampstead on the East-Northern, and drive over. It's about ten miles off."

"Good! they ought soon to be here," replied Hazell, as he munched some biscuits and washed them down with a draught of milk, after which he astonished them all by solemnly going through one of his "digestive exercises."

A little later they heard the sound of wheels on a road beside the line. Then the man on watch said, in gruff tones:

"The boy's inside!"

But they found more than the boy inside, and an hour later all three conspirators were safely lodged in Longmoor gaol.

"Oh, it was awfully nasty, I can tell you," said Horace Carr-Mathers, as he explained matters afterwards. "I went into the corridor, you know, and was looking about at things, when all of a sudden I felt my coat-collar grasped behind, and a hand was laid over my mouth. I tried to kick and shout, but it was no go. They got me into the compartment, stuffed a handkerchief into my mouth, and tied it in.

THE AFFAIR OF THE CORRIDOR EXPRESS

It was just beastly. Then they bound me hand and foot, and opened the window on the right-hand side—opposite the corridor. I was in a funk, for I thought they were going to throw me out, but one of them told me to keep my pecker up, as they weren't going to hurt me. Then they let me down out of the window by that slack rope, and made it fast to the handle of the door outside. It was pretty bad. There was I, hanging from the door-handle in a sort of doubled-up position, my back resting on the footboard of the carriage, and the train rushing along like mad. I felt sick and awful, and I had to shut my eyes. I seemed to hang there for ages."

"I told you you only examined the *inside* of the train," said Thorpe Hazell to Wingrave. "I had my suspicions that he was somewhere on the outside all the time, but I was puzzled to know where. It was a clever trick."

"Well," went on the boy, "I heard the window open above me after a bit. I looked up and saw one of the men taking the rope off the handle. The train was just beginning to slow down. Then he hung out of the window, dangling me with one hand. It was horrible. I was hanging below the footboard now. Then the train came almost to a stop, and someone caught me round the waist. I lost my senses for a minute or two, and then I found myself lying in the hut."

"Well, Mr. Hazell," said the assistant-superintendent, "you were perfectly right, and we all owe you a debt of gratitude."

"Oh!" said Hazell, "it was only a guess at the best. I presumed it was simply kidnapping, and the problem to be solved was how and where the boy was got off the train without injury. It was obvious that he had been disposed of before the train reached London. There was only one other inference. The man on duty was evidently the confederate, for, if not, his presence would have stopped the whole plan of action. I'm very glad to have been of any use. There are interesting points about the case, and it has been a pleasure to me to undertake it."

A little while afterwards Mr. Carr-Mathers himself called on Hazell to thank him.

"I should like," he said, "to express my deep gratitude substantially; but I understand you are not an ordinary detective. But is there any way in which I can serve you, Mr. Hazell?"

"Yes—two ways."

"Please name them."

"I should be sorry for Mr. Wingrave to get into trouble through this affair—or Dr. Spring either."

"I understand you, Mr. Hazell. They were both

to blame, in a way. But I will see that Dr. Spring's reputation does not suffer, and that Wingrave comes out of it harmlessly."

"Thank you very much."

"You said there was a second way in which I could serve you."

"So there is. At Dunn's sale last month you were the purchaser of two first editions of 'The New Bath Guide.' If you cared to dispose of one, I——"

"Say no more, Mr. Hazell. I shall be glad to give you one for your collection."

Hazell stiffened.

"You misunderstand me!" he exclaimed icily. "I was about to add that if you cared to dispose of a copy I would write you out a cheque."

"Oh, certainly," replied Mr. Carr-Mathers with a smile, "I shall be extremely pleased."

Whereupon the transaction was concluded.

MAURICE LEBLANC

The Mysterious Railway-Passenger

I had sent my motor-car to Rouen, by road, on the previous day. I was to meet it by train and go on to some friends who have a house on the Seine.

A few minutes before we left Paris, my compartment was invaded by seven gentlemen, five of whom were smoking. Short though the journey by the fast train is, I did not relish the prospect of taking it in such company, the more so as the old-fashioned carriage had no corridor. I therefore collected my overcoat, my newspapers and my railway-guide and sought refuge in one of the neighbouring compartments.

It was occupied by a lady. At the sight of me, she made a movement of vexation which did not escape my notice and leant towards a gentleman standing on the footboard: her husband, no doubt, who had come to see her off. The gentleman took stock of me and the examination seemed to conclude to my advantage, for he whispered to his wife and smiled, giving her the look with which we reassure a frightened child. She smiled, in her turn, and cast a friendly glance in my direction, as though she suddenly realised that I was one of those decent men with whom a woman can remain locked up for an hour or two, in a little box six feet square, without having anything to fear.

Her husband said to her:

'You mustn't mind, darling, but I have an important appointment and I can't wait.'

He kissed her affectionately and went away. His wife blew him some discreet little kisses through the window and waved her handkerchief.

Then the guard's whistle sounded and the train started.

At that moment and in spite of the warning shouts of the railway-officials, the door opened and a man burst into our carriage. My travelling-companion, who was standing up and arranging her things in the rack, uttered a cry of terror and dropped down upon the seat.

I am no coward, far from it, but I confess that these sudden incursions at the last minute are always annoying. They seem so ambiguous, so unnatural. There must be something behind them, else . . .

The appearance and bearing of the newcomer, however, were such as to correct the bad impression produced by the manner of his entrance. He was neatly, almost smartly dressed; his tie was in good taste, his gloves clean; he had a powerful face . . . But, speaking of his face, where on earth had I seen it before? For I had seen it: of that there was no doubt. Or, at least to be accurate, I found within myself that sort of recollection which is left by the sight of an oft-seen portrait of which one has never beheld the original. And at the same time, I felt the uselessness of any effort of memory that I might exert, so inconsistent and vague was that recollection.

But, when my eyes reverted to the lady, I sat astounded at the pallor and disorder of her features. She was staring at her neighbour – he was seated on the same side of the carriage – with an expression of genuine affright; and I saw one of her hands steal trembling towards a little wrist-bag that lay on the cushion a few inches from her lap. She ended by taking hold of it and nervously drawing it to her.

Our eyes met and I read in hers so great an amount of uneasiness and anxiety that I could not help saying:

'I hope you are not unwell, madame? . . . Shall I open the window?'

She made no reply, but, with a timid gesture, called my attention to the man. I smiled as her husband had done, shrugged my shoulders, and explained to her by signs that she had no cause for alarm, that I was there and that, besides, the gentleman seemed quite harmless.

Just then, he turned towards us, and after contemplating us, one after the other, from head to foot, huddled himself into his corner and made no further movement.

A silence ensued; but the lady, as though summoning all her energies to perform an act of despair, said to me, in a hardly intelligible tone:

'You know he is in our train?'

'Who?'

'Why, he . . . he himself . . . I assure you.'

'Whom do you mean?'

'Arsène Lupin!'

She had not removed her eyes from the passenger; and it was at him rather than at me that she flung the syllables of that dread name.

He pulled his hat down upon his nose. Was this to conceal his agitation, or was he merely preparing to go to sleep?

I objected:

'Arsène Lupin was sentenced yesterday, in his absence, to twenty years' penal servitude. It is not likely that he would commit the imprudence of showing himself in public today. Besides, the newspapers have discovered that he has been spending the winter in Turkey, ever since his famous escape from the Santé.'

'He is in this train,' repeated the lady, with the

more and more marked intention of being overheard by our companion. 'My husband is a deputy prison governor, and the station inspector himself told us that they were looking for Arsène Lupin.'

'That is no reason why . . .'

'He was seen at the booking-office. He took a ticket for Rouen.'

'It would have been easy to lay hands upon him.'

'He disappeared. The ticket collector at the door of the waiting-room did not see him; but they thought that he must have gone round by the suburban platforms and stepped into the express that leaves ten minutes after us.'

'In that case, they will have caught him there.'

'And supposing that, at the last moment, he jumped out of the express and entered this, our own train . . . as he probably . . . as he most certainly did?'

'In that case, they will catch him here. For the porters and the police cannot have failed to see him going from one train to the other and, when we reach Rouen, they will nab him finely.'

'Him? Never! He will find some means of escaping again.'

'In that case, I wish him a good journey.'

'But think of all that he may do in the meantime!'

'What?'

'How can I tell? One must be prepared for anything.'

She was greatly agitated; and, in point of fact, the situation, to a certain degree, warranted her nervous state of excitement. Almost in spite of myself, I said:

'There are such things as curious coincidences, it is true . . . But calm yourself. Admitting that Arsène Lupin is in one of these carriages, he is sure to keep quiet and, rather than bring fresh trouble upon himself, he will have no other idea than to avoid the danger that threatens him.'

My words failed to reassure her. However, she said no more, fearing, no doubt, lest I should think her troublesome.

As for myself, I opened my newspapers and read the reports of Arsène Lupin's trial. They contained nothing that was not already known and they interested me but slightly. Moreover, I was tired, I had had a poor night, I felt my eyelids growing heavy and my head began to nod.

'But, surely, sir, you are not going to sleep!'

The lady snatched my paper from my hands and looked at me with indignation.

'Certainly not,' I replied. 'I have no wish to.'

'It would be most imprudent,' she said.

'Most,' I repeated.

And I struggled hard, fixing my eyes on the landscape, on the clouds that streaked the sky, and soon all this became confused in space, the picture of the excited lady and the drowsy man was obliterated from my mind and I was filled with a great, deep silence of sleep.

It was soon made agreeable by light and incoherent dreams, in which a being who played the part and bore the name of Arsène Lupin occupied a certain place. He turned and shifted on the horizon, his back laden with valuables, clambering over walls and stripping country houses of their contents.

But the outline of this being, who had ceased to be Arsène Lupin, grew more distinct. He came towards me, grew bigger and bigger, leapt into the carriage with incredible agility and fell full upon my chest.

A sharp pain . . . a piercing scream . . . I awoke. The man, my fellow-traveller, with one knee on my chest, was clutching my throat.

I saw this very dimly, for my eyes were shot with blood. I also saw the lady, in a corner, writhing in a violent fit of hysterics. I did not even attempt to resist. I should not have had the strength for it, had I wished to: my temples were throbbing, I choked . . . my throat rattled . . . Another minute . . . and I should have been suffocated.

The man must have felt this. He loosened his grip. Without leaving hold of me, with his right hand he stretched a rope, in which he had prepared a slip-knot, and, with a quick turn, tied my wrists together. In a moment, I was bound, gagged, rendered motionless and helpless.

And he performed this task in the most natural manner in the world, with an ease that revealed the knowledge of a master, of an expert in theft and crime. Not a word, not a fevered movement. Sheer coolness and audacity. And there was I on the seat, tied up like a mummy, I, Arsène Lupin!

It was really ridiculous. And, notwithstanding the seriousness of the circumstances, I could not but appreciate and almost enjoy the irony of the situation. Arsène Lupin 'done' like a novice! Stripped like a first-comer—for of course the scoundrel relieved me of my pocket-book and purse! Arsène Lupin victimized in his turn, duped, defeated! What an adventure!

There remained the lady. He took no notice of her at all. He contented himself with picking up the wrist-bag that lay on the floor and extracting the jewels, the purse, the gold and silver knick-knacks which it contained. The lady opened her eyes, shuddered with fright, took off her rings and handed them to the man, as though she wished to spare him any superfluous exertion. He took the rings and looked at her: she fainted away.

Then, calm and silent as before, without troubling about us further, he resumed his seat, lit a cigarette, and abandoned himself to a careful scrutiny of the treasures which he had captured, the inspection of which seemed to satisfy him completely.

I was much less satisfied. I am not speaking of the twelve thousand francs of which I had been unduly plundered: this was a loss which I accepted only for the time; I had no doubt that those twelve thousand francs would return to my possession after a short interval, together with the exceedingly important papers which my pocket-book contained: plans, estimates, specifications, addresses, lists of correspondents, letters of a compromising character. But, for the moment, a more immediate and serious care was worrying me: what was to happen next?

As may be readily imagined, the excitement caused by my passing through the Gare Saint-Lazare had not escaped me. As I was going to stay with friends who knew me by the name of Guillaume Berlat and to whom my resemblance to Arsène Lupin was the occasion of many a friendly jest, I had not been able to disguise myself after my wont and my presence had been discovered. Moreover, a man, doubtless Arsène Lupin, had been seen to rush from the express into the other train. Hence it was inevitable and fated that the commissary of police at Rouen, warned by telegram, would await the arrival of the train, assisted by a respectable number of constables, question any suspicious passengers and proceed to make a minute inspection of the carriages.

All this I had foreseen and had not felt greatly excited about it; for I was certain that the Rouen police would display no greater perspicacity than the Paris police and that I should have been able to pass unperceived: was it not sufficient for me, at the wicket, carelessly to show my deputy's card, thanks to which I had already inspired the ticket-collector at Saint-Lazare with every confidence? But how things had changed since then! I was no longer free. It was impossible to attempt one of my usual moves. In one of the carriages the commissary would discover the Sieur Arsène Lupin, whom a propitious fate was sending to him bound hand and foot, gentle as a lamb, packed up complete. He had only to accept delivery, just as you receive a parcel addressed to you at a railway station, a hamper of game or a basket of vegetables and fruit.

And to avoid this annoying catastrophe what could I do, entangled as I was in my bonds?

The train was speeding towards Rouen, the next

and only stopping place; it rushed through Vernon, through Saint-Pierre . . .

I was puzzled also by another problem, in which I was not so directly interested, but the solution of which aroused my professional curiosity. What were my fellow-traveller's intentions?

If I had been alone, he would have had ample time to alight quite calmly at Rouen. But the lady? As soon as the carriage door was opened, the lady, meek and quiet as she sat at present, would scream and throw herself about and cry for assistance!

Hence my astonishment. Why did he not reduce her to the same state of helplessness as myself, which would have given him time to disappear before his two-fold misdemeanour was discovered?

He was still smoking, his eyes fixed on the view outside, which a hesitating rain was beginning to streak with long, slanting lines. Once, however, he turned round, took up my railway guide and consulted it.

As for the lady, she made every effort to continue fainting, so as to quiet her enemy. But a fit of coughing, produced by the smoke, gave the lie to her pretended swoon.

Myself, I was very uncomfortable and had pains all over my body. And I thought . . . I planned . . .

Pont-de-l'Arche . . . Oissell . . . The train was

hurrying on, glad drunk with speed . . . Saint-Etienne . . .

At that moment, the man rose and took two steps towards us, to which the lady hastened to reply with a new scream and a genuine fainting fit.

But what could his object be? He lowered the window on our side. The rain was now falling in torrents and he made a movement of annoyance at having neither umbrella nor overcoat. He looked up at the rack: the lady's *en-tout-cas* was there; he took it. He also took my overcoat and put it on.

We were crossing the Seine. He turned up his trousers and then, leaning out of the window, raised the outer latch.

Did he mean to fling himself on the permanent way? At the rate at which we were going, it would have been certain death. We plunged into the tunnel through the Côte Sainte-Catherine. The man opened the door and, with one foot, felt for the step. What madness! The darkness, the smoke, the din all combined to lend a fantastic appearance to any such attempt. But, suddenly, the train slowed up, the Westinghouse brakes counteracted the movement of the wheels. In a minute, the pace from fast became normal and decreased still more. Without a doubt, there was a gang at work repairing this part of the tunnel; this would necessitate a slower passage of the trains, for some days perhaps; and the man knew it.

He had only, therefore, to put his other foot on the step, climb down to the footboard and walk quietly away, not without first closing the door and throwing back the latch.

He had scarcely disappeared when the smoke showed whiter in the daylight. We emerged into a valley. One more tunnel and we should be at Rouen.

The lady at once recovered her wits and her first care was to bewail the loss of her jewels. I gave her a beseeching glance. She understood and relieved me of the gag which was stifling me. She wanted also to unfasten my bonds, but I stopped her:

'No, no: the police must see everything as it was. I want them to be fully informed as regards that blackguard's actions.'

'Shall I pull the alarm signal?'

'Too late: you should have thought of that while he was attacking me.'

'But he would have killed me! Ah, sir, didn't I tell you that he was travelling by this train? I knew him at once, by his portrait. And now he's taken my jewels.'

'They'll catch him, have no fear.'

'Catch Arsène Lupin! Never.'

'It all depends on you, madame. Listen. When we

arrive, be at the window, call out, make a noise. The police and porters will come up. Tell them what you have seen, in a few words: the assault of which I was the victim and the flight of Arsène Lupin. Give his description: a soft hat, an umbrella—yours—a grey frock overcoat . . .'

'Yours,' she said.

'Mine? No, his own. I didn't have one.'

'I thought that he had none either when he got in.'

'He must have had . . . unless it was a coat which some one had left behind in the rack. In any case, he had it when he got out and that is the essential thing . . . A grey frock overcoat, remember . . . Oh, I was forgetting . . . tell them your name to start with. Your husband's position will stimulate their zeal.'

We were arriving. She was already leaning out of the window. I resumed, in a louder, almost imperious voice, so that my words should sink into her brain:

'Give my name also, Guillaume Berlat. If necessary, say you know me . . . That will save time . . . we must hurry on the preliminary inquiries . . . the important thing is to catch Arsène Lupin . . . with your jewels . . . You quite understand, don't you? Guillaume Berlat, a friend of your husband's.'

'Quite . . . Guillaume Berlat.'

She was already calling out and gesticulating. Before the train had come to a standstill, a gentleman climbed in, followed by a number of other men. The critical hour was at hand.

Breathlessly, the lady exclaimed:

'Arsène Lupin . . . he attacked us . . . he has stolen my jewels . . . I am Madame Renaud . . . my husband is a deputy prison governor . . . Ah, here is my brother Georges Andelle, manager of the Crédit Rouennais . . . What I want to say is . . .'

She kissed a young man who had just come up and who exchanged greetings with the commissary of police. She continued, weeping:

'Yes, Arsène Lupin . . . He flew at this gentleman's throat in his sleep . . . Monsieur Berlat, a friend of my husband's.'

'But where is Arsène Lupin?'

'He jumped out of the train in the tunnel, after we had crossed the Seine.'

'Are you sure it was he?'

'Certain; I recognised him at once. Besides, he was seen at the Gare Saint-Lazare. He was wearing a soft hat . . .'

'No, a hard felt hat, like this,' said the commissary, pointing to my hat.

'A soft hat, I assure you,' repeated Madame Renaud, 'and a grey frock overcoat.'

'Yes,' muttered the commissary, 'the telegram mentions a grey frock overcoat with a black velvet collar.'

'A black velvet collar, that's it!' exclaimed Madame Renaud, triumphantly.

I breathed again. What a good, excellent friend I had found in her!

Meanwhile, the policeman had released me from my bonds. I bit my lips violently till the blood flowed. Bent in two, with my handkerchief to my mouth, as seems proper to a man who has long been sitting in a constrained position and who bears on his face the blood-stained marks of the gag, I said to the commissary, in a feeble voice:

'Sir, it was Arsène Lupin, there is no doubt of it . . . You can catch him, if you hurry . . . I think I may be of some use to you . . .'

The coach, which was needed for the inspection by the police, was slipped. The remainder of the train went on to Le Havre. We were taken to the station master's office through a crowd of onlookers who filled the platform.

Just then, I felt a hesitation. I must make some excuse to absent myself, find my motor-car and be off. It was dangerous to wait. If anything happened, if a telegram came from Paris, I was lost.

Yes, but what about my robber? Left to my own

resources, in a district with which I was not very familiar, I could never hope to come up with him.

'Bah!' I said to myself. 'Let us risk it and stay. It's a difficult hand to win, but a very amusing one to play. And the stakes are worth the trouble.'

And, as we were being asked provisionally to repeat our depositions, I exclaimed:

'Mr Commissary, Arsène Lupin is at this moment getting a start on us. My motor is waiting for me in the station yard. If you will do me the pleasure to accept a seat in it, we will try . . .'

The commissary gave a knowing smile:

'It's not a bad idea . . . such a good idea, in fact, that it's already being carried out.'

'Oh?'

'Yes, two of my officers started on bicycles . . . some time ago.'

'But where to?'

'To the entrance of the tunnel. There they will pick up the clues and the evidence and follow the track of Arsène Lupin.'

I could not help shrugging my shoulders:

'Your two officers will pick up no clues and no evidence.'

'Really!'

'Arsène Lupin will have arranged that no one

should see him leave the tunnel. He will have taken the nearest road and, from there . . .'

'From there made for Rouen, where we shall catch him.'

'He will not go to Rouen.'

'In that case, he will remain in the neighbourhood, where we shall be even more certain . . .'

'He will not remain in the neighbourhood.'

'Oh? Then where will he hide himself?'

I took out my watch:

'At the present moment Arsène Lupin is hanging about the station at Darnétal. At ten-fifty, that is to say, in twenty-two minutes from now, he will take the train which leaves Rouen, from the Gare du Nord, for Amiens.'

'Do you think so? And how do you know?'

'Oh, it's very simple. In the carriage, Arsène Lupin consulted my railway guide. What for? To see if there was another line near the place where he disappeared, a station on that line and a train which stopped at that station. I have just looked at the guide myself and learnt what I wanted to know.'

'Upon my word, sir,' said the commissary, 'you possess marvellous powers of deduction. What an expert you must be!'

Dragged on by my conviction, I had blundered into displaying too much cleverness. He looked at me in astonishment and I saw that a suspicion flickered through his mind. Only just, it is true, for the photographs dispatched in every direction were so unlike, represented an Arsène Lupin so different from the one that stood before him, that he could not possibly recognise the original in me. Nevertheless, he was troubled, restless, perplexed.

There was a moment of silence. A certain ambiguity and doubt seemed to interrupt our words. A shudder of anxiety passed through me. Was luck about to turn against me? Mastering myself, I began to laugh:

'Ah, well, there's nothing to sharpen one's wits like the loss of a pocket-book and the desire to find it again. And it seems to me, that, if you will give me two of your men, the three of us might, perhaps . . .'

'Oh, please, Mr Commissary,' exclaimed Madame Renaud, 'do what Monsieur Berlat suggests.'

My kind friend's intervention turned the scale. Uttered by her, the wife of an influential person, the name of Berlat became mine in reality and conferred upon me an identity which no suspicion could touch. The commissary rose:

'Believe me, Monsieur Berlat, I shall be only too pleased to see you succeed. I am as anxious as yourself to have Arsène Lupin arrested.'

He escorted me to my car. He introduced two of his men to me: Honoré Massol and Gaston Delivet. They took their seats. I placed myself at the wheel. My chauffeur started the engine. A few seconds later we had left the station. I was saved.

I confess that, as we dashed in my powerful 35-hp Moreau-Lepton along the boulevards that skirt the old Norman city, I was not without a certain sense of pride. The engine hummed harmoniously. The trees sped behind us to right and left. And now, free and out of danger, I had nothing to do but to settle my little private affairs, with the co-operation of those two worthy representatives of the law. Arsène Lupin was going in search of Arsène Lupin.

Ye humble mainstays of the social order of things, Gaston Delivet and Honoré Massol, how precious was your assistance to me! Where should I have been without you? But for you, at how many cross-roads should I have taken the wrong turning! But for you, Arsène Lupin would have gone astray and the other escaped!

But all was not over yet. Far from it. I had first to capture the fellow and next to take possession, myself, of the papers of which he had robbed me. At no cost must my two satellites be allowed to catch a sight of those documents, much less lay hands upon them. To make use of them and yet act independently of them was what I wanted to do; and it was no easy matter.

We reached Darnétal three minutes after the train had left. I had the consolation of learning that a man in a grey frock overcoat with a black velvet collar had got into a second-class carriage, with a ticket for Amiens. There was no doubt about it: my first appearance as a detective was a promising one.

Delivet said:

'The train is an express and does not stop before Montérolier-Buchy, in nineteen minutes from now. If we are not there before Arsène Lupin, he can go on towards Amiens, branch off to Clères, and, from there, make for Dieppe or Paris.'

'How far is Montérolier?'

'Fourteen and a half miles.'

'Fourteen and a half miles in nineteen minutes . . . We shall be there before him.'

It was a stirring race. Never had my trusty Moreau-Lepton responded to my impatience with greater ardour and regularity. It seemed to me as though I communicated my wishes to her directly, without the intermediary of levers or handles. She shared my desires. She approved of my determination. She understood my animosity against that blackguard Arsène Lupin. The scoundrel! The sneak! Should I get the better of him? Or would he once more baffle authority, that authority of which I was the embodiment?

'Right!' cried Delivet . . . 'Left! . . . Straight ahead! . . .'

We skimmed the ground. The milestones looked like little timid animals that fled at our approach.

And suddenly, at the turn of a road, a cloud of smoke, the north express!

For half a mile, it was a struggle, side by side, an unequal struggle, of which the issue was certain. We beat the train by twenty lengths.

In three seconds we were on the platform, in front of the second class. The doors were flung open. A few people stepped out. My thief was not among them. We examined the carriages. No Arsène Lupin.

'By jove!' I exclaimed. 'He must have recognized me in the motor, while we were going alongside, and jumped out!'

The guard of the train confirmed my supposition. He had seen a man scrambling down the embankment, at two hundred yards from the station.

'There he is! . . . Look! . . . At the level crossing!'

I darted in pursuit, followed by my two satellites, or rather by one of them, for the other, Massol, turned out to be an uncommonly fast sprinter, gifted with both speed and staying power. In a few seconds, the distance between him and the fugitive was greatly diminished. The man saw him, jumped a hedge and scampered off towards a slope, which he climbed. We saw him further still, entering a little wood.

When we reached the wood, we found Massol waiting for us. He had thought it wiser not to go on, lest he should lose us.

'You were quite right, my dear fellow,' I said. 'After a run like this, our friend must be exhausted. We've got him.'

I examined the skirts of the wood, while thinking how I could best proceed alone to arrest the fugitive, in order myself to effect certain recoveries which the law, no doubt, would only have allowed after a number of disagreeable inquiries. Then I returned to my companions.

'Look here, it's quite easy. You, Massol, take up your position on the left: you, Delivet, on the right. From there, you can watch the whole rear of the wood and he can't leave it, unseen by you, except by this hollow way, where I shall stand. If he does not come out, I'll go in and force him back towards one or the other. You have nothing to do, therefore, but wait. Oh, I was forgetting: in case of alarm, I'll fire a shot.'

Massol and Delivet moved off, each to his own side. As soon as they were out of sight, I made my way into the wood, with infinite precautions, so as to be neither seen nor heard. It consisted of close thickets, contrived for the shooting, and intersected by very narrow paths, in which it was only possible to walk by stooping, as though in a leafy tunnel.

One of these ended in a glade where the damp grass showed the marks of footsteps. I followed them, taking care to steal through the undergrowth. They led me to the bottom of a little mound, crowned by a rickety lath-and-plaster hovel.

'He must be there,' I thought. 'He has chosen a good post of observation.'

I crawled close up to the building. A slight sound warned me of his presence and, in fact, I caught sight of him through an opening, with his back turned towards me.

Two bounds brought me upon him. He tried to point the revolver which he held in his hand. I did not give him time, but pulled him to the ground, in such a way that his two arms were twisted and caught under him, while I held him pinned down with my knee upon his chest.

'Listen to me, old chap,' I whispered in his ear. 'I am Arsène Lupin. You've got to give me back my pocket-book and the lady's wrist-bag, this minute and without fuss . . . in return for which I'll save you from the clutches of the police and enrol you among my pals. Which is it to be: yes or no?'

'Yes,' he muttered.

'That's right. Your plan of this morning was cleverly thought out. We shall be good friends.'

I got up. He fumbled in his pocket, fetched out a great knife, and tried to strike me with it.

'You ass!' I cried.

With one hand I parried the attack. With the other, I caught him a violent blow on the carotid artery, the blow which is known as the 'carotid hook'. He fell back stunned.

In my pocket-book, I found my papers and bank notes. I took his own out of curiosity. On an envelope addressed to him I read his name: Pierre Onfrey.

I gave a start. Pierre Onfrey, the perpetrator of the murder in the Rue Lafontaine at Auteuil! Pierre Onfrey, the man who had cut the throats of Madame Delbois and her two daughters! I bent over him. Yes, that was the face which, in the railway carriage, had aroused in me the memory of features which I had seen before.

But time was passing. I placed two hundred-franc notes in an envelope, with a visiting-card bearing these words:

'Arsène Lupin to his worthy assistants, Honoré Massol and Gaston Delivet, with his best thanks.'

I laid this where it could be seen, in the middle of the room. Beside it I placed Madame Renaud's wrist-bag. Why should it not be restored to the kind friend who had rescued me? I confess, however that I took from it everything that seemed in any way interesting, leaving only a tortoise-shell comb, a stick of lip salve, and an empty purse. Business is business, when all is said and done! And, besides, her husband followed such a disreputable occupation! . . .

There remained the man. He was beginning to move. What was I to do? I was not qualified either to save or to condemn him.

I took away his weapons and fired my revolver in the air:

'That will bring the two others,' I thought. 'He must find a way out of his difficulties. Let fate take its course.'

And I went down the hollow way at a run.

Twenty minutes later, a cross-road, which I had noticed during our pursuit, brought me back to my car.

At four o'clock I telegraphed to my friends from Rouen that an unexpected incident compelled me to put off my visit. Between ourselves, I greatly fear that, in view of what they must now have learnt, I shall be obliged to postpone it indefinitely. It will be a cruel disappointment for them!

At six o'clock, I returned to Paris by L'Isle-Adam, Enghien and the Porte Bineau.

I gathered from the evening papers that the police had at last succeeded in capturing Pierre Onfrey.

The next morning—why should we despise the advantages of intelligent advertisement?—the *Echo de France* contained the following sensational paragraph:

> Yesterday, near Buchy, after a number of incidents, Arsène Lupin effected the arrest of Pierre Onfrey. The Autcuil murderer had robbed a lady of the name of Renaud, the wife of the deputy prison governor, in the train between Paris and Le Havre. Arsène Lupin has restored to Madame Renaud the wrist-bag which contained her jewels and has generously rewarded the two detectives who assisted him in the matter of this dramatic arrest.

Arthur Conan Doyle

The Man with the Watches

There are many who will still bear in mind the singular circumstances which, under the heading of the Rugby Mystery, filled many columns of the daily Press in the spring of the year 1892. Coming as it did at a period of exceptional dulness, it attracted perhaps rather more attention than it deserved, but it offered to the public that mixture of the whimsical and the tragic which is most stimulating to the popular imagination. Interest drooped, however, when, after weeks of fruitless investigation, it was found that no final explanation of the facts was forthcoming, and the tragedy seemed from that time to the present to have finally taken its place in the dark catalogue of inexplicable and unexpiated crimes. A recent communication (the authenticity of which appears to be above question) has, however, thrown some new and clear light upon the matter. Before laying it before the public it would be as well, perhaps, that I should refresh their memories as to the singular facts upon which this commentary is founded. These facts were briefly as follows:—

At five o'clock on the evening of the 18th of

March in the year already mentioned a train left Euston Station for Manchester. It was a rainy, squally day, which grew wilder as it progressed, so it was by no means the weather in which any one would travel who was not driven to do so by necessity. The train, however, is a favourite one among Manchester business men who are returning from town, for it does the journey in four hours and twenty minutes, with only three stoppages upon the way. In spite of the inclement evening it was, therefore, fairly well filled upon the occasion of which I speak. The guard of the train was a tried servant of the company—a man who had worked for twenty-two years without blemish or complaint. His name was John Palmer.

The station clock was upon the stroke of five, and the guard was about to give the customary signal to the engine-driver when he observed two belated passengers hurrying down the platform. The one was an exceptionally tall man, dressed in a long black overcoat with Astrakhan collar and cuffs. I have already said that the evening was an inclement one, and the tall traveller had the high, warm collar turned up to protect his throat against the bitter March wind. He appeared, as far as the guard could judge by so hurried an inspection, to be a man between fifty and sixty years of age, who had retained a good deal of the vigour and activity of his youth. In one hand he carried a brown leather Gladstone bag. His companion was a lady, tall and erect, walking with a vigorous step which outpaced the gentleman beside her. She wore a long, fawn-coloured dust-cloak, a black, close-fitting toque, and a dark veil which concealed the greater part of her face. The two might very well have passed as father and daughter. They walked swiftly down the line of carriages, glancing in at the windows, until the guard, John Palmer, overtook them.

"Now, then, sir, look sharp, the train is going," said he.

"First-class," the man answered.

The guard turned the handle of the nearest door. In the carriage, which he had opened, there sat a small man with a cigar in his mouth. His appearance seems to have impressed itself upon the guard's memory, for he was prepared, afterwards, to describe or to identify him. He was a man of thirty-four or thirty-five years of age, dressed in some grey material, sharp-nosed, alert, with a ruddy, weather-beaten face, and a small, closely cropped black beard. He glanced up as the door was opened. The tall man paused with his foot upon the step.

"This is a smoking compartment. The lady dislikes smoke," said he, looking round at the guard.

"All right! Here you are, sir!" said John Palmer. He slammed the door of the smoking carriage, opened that of the next one, which was empty, and thrust the two travellers in. At the same moment he sounded his whistle and the wheels of the train began to move. The man with the cigar was at the window of his carriage, and said something to the guard as he rolled past him, but the words were lost in the bustle of the departure. Palmer stepped into the guard's van, as it came up to him, and thought no more of the incident.

Twelve minutes after its departure the train reached Willesden Junction, where it stopped for a very short interval. An examination of the tickets has made it certain that no one either joined or left it at this time, and no passenger was seen to alight upon the platform. At 5.14 the journey to Manchester was resumed, and Rugby was reached at 6.50, the express being five minutes late.

At Rugby the attention of the station officials was drawn to the fact that the door of one of the first-class carriages was open. An examination of that compartment, and of its neighbour, disclosed a remarkable state of affairs.

The smoking carriage in which the short, red-faced man with the black beard had been seen was now empty. Save for a half-smoked cigar, there was no trace whatever of its recent occupant. The door of this carriage was fastened. In the next compartment, to which attention had been originally drawn, there was no sign either of the gentleman with the Astrakhan collar or of the young lady who accompanied him. All three passengers had disappeared. On the other hand, there was found upon the floor of this carriage—the one in which the tall traveller and the lady had been—a young man, fashionably dressed and of elegant appearance. He lay with his knees drawn up, and his head resting against the further door, an elbow upon either seat. A bullet had penetrated his heart and his death must have been instantaneous. No one had seen such a man enter the train, and no railway ticket was found in his pocket, neither were there any markings upon his linen, nor papers nor personal property which might help to identify him. Who he was, whence he had come, and how he had met his end were each as great a mystery as what had occurred to the three people who had started an hour and a half before from Willesden in those two compartments.

I have said that there was no personal property which might help to identify him, but it is true that there was one peculiarity about this unknown young man which was much commented upon at the time. In his pockets were found no fewer than six valuable gold watches, three in the various pockets of his waistcoat, one in his ticket-pocket, one in his breast-pocket, and one small one set in a leather strap and fastened round his left wrist. The obvious explanation that the man was a pickpocket, and that this was his plunder, was discounted by the fact that all six were of American make, and of a type which is rare in England. Three of them bore the mark of the Rochester Watchmaking Company; one was by Mason, of Elmira; one was unmarked; and the small one, which was highly jewelled and ornamented, was from Tiffany, of New York. The other contents of his pocket consisted of an ivory knife with a corkscrew by Rodgers, of Sheffield; a small circular mirror, one inch in diameter; a re-admission slip to the Lyceum theatre; a silver box full of vesta matches, and a brown leather cigar-case containing two cheroots—also two pounds fourteen shillings in money. It was clear, then, that whatever motives may have led to his death, robbery was not among them. As already mentioned, there were no markings upon the man's linen, which appeared to be new, and no tailor's name upon his coat. In appearance he was young, short, smooth-cheeked, and delicately featured. One of his front teeth was conspicuously stopped with gold.

On the discovery of the tragedy an examination

was instantly made of the tickets of all passengers, and the number of the passengers themselves was counted. It was found that only three tickets were unaccounted for, corresponding to the three travellers who were missing. The express was then allowed to proceed, but a new guard was sent with it, and John Palmer was detained as a witness at Rugby. The carriage which included the two compartments in question was uncoupled and side-tracked. Then, on the arrival of Inspector Vane, of Scotland Yard, and of Mr. Henderson, a detective in the service of the railway company, an exhaustive inquiry was made into all the circumstances.

That crime had been committed was certain. The bullet, which appeared to have come from a small pistol or revolver, had been fired from some little distance, as there was no scorching of the clothes. No weapon was found in the compartment (which finally disposed of the theory of suicide), nor was there any sign of the brown leather bag which the guard had seen in the hand of the tall gentleman. A lady's parasol was found upon the rack, but no other trace was to be seen of the travellers in either of the sections. Apart from the crime, the question of how or why three passengers (one of them a lady) could get out of the train, and one other get in during the unbroken run between Willesden and Rugby, was one which excited the utmost curiosity among the general public, and gave rise to much speculation in the London Press.

John Palmer, the guard, was able at the inquest to give some evidence which threw a little light upon the matter. There was a spot between Tring and Cheddington, according to his statement, where, on account of some repairs to the line, the train had for a few minutes slowed down to a pace not exceeding eight or ten miles an hour. At that place it might be possible for a man, or even for an exceptionally active woman, to have left the train without serious injury. It was true that a gang of platelayers was there, and that they had seen nothing, but it was their custom to stand in the middle between the metals, and the open carriage door was upon the far side, so that it was conceivable that someone might have alighted unseen, as the darkness would by that time be drawing in. A steep embankment would instantly screen anyone who sprang out from the observation of the navvies.

The guard also deposed that there was a good deal of movement upon the platform at Willesden Junction, and that though it was certain that no one had either joined or left the train there, it was still quite possible that some of the passengers might have changed unseen from one compartment to another. It was by no means uncommon for a gentleman to finish his cigar in a smoking carriage and then to change to a clearer atmosphere. Supposing that the man with the black beard had done so at Willesden (and the half-smoked cigar upon the floor seemed to favour the supposition), he would naturally go into the nearest section, which would bring him into the company of the two other actors in this drama. Thus the first stage of the affair might be surmised without any great breach of probability. But what the second stage had been, or how the final one had been arrived at, neither the guard nor the experienced detective officers could suggest.

A careful examination of the line between Willesden and Rugby resulted in one discovery which might or might not have a bearing upon the tragedy. Near Tring, at the very place where the train slowed down, there was found at the bottom of the embankment a small pocket Testament, very shabby and worn. It was printed by the Bible Society of London, and bore an inscription: "From John to Alice. Jan. 13th, 1856," upon the fly-leaf. Underneath was written: "James, July 4th, 1859," and beneath that again: "Edward. Nov. 1st, 1869," all the entries being in the same handwriting. This was the only clue, if it could be called a clue, which the police obtained, and the coroner's verdict of "Murder by a person or persons unknown" was the unsatisfactory ending of a singular case. Advertisement, rewards, and inquiries proved equally fruitless, and nothing could be found which was solid enough to form the basis for a profitable investigation.

It would be a mistake, however, to suppose that no theories were formed to account for the facts. On the contrary, the Press, both in England and in America, teemed with suggestions and suppositions, most of which were obviously absurd. The fact that the watches were of American make, and some peculiarities in connection with the gold stopping of his front tooth, appeared to indicate that the deceased was a citizen of the United States, though his linen, clothes, and boots were undoubtedly of British manufacture. It was surmised, by some, that he was concealed under the seat, and that, being discovered, he was for some reason, possibly because he had overheard their guilty secrets, put to death by his fellow-passengers. When coupled with generalities as to the ferocity and cunning of anarchical and other secret societies, this theory sounded as plausible as any.

The fact that he should be without a ticket would be consistent with the idea of concealment, and it was well known that women played a prominent part in the Nihilistic propaganda. On the other hand, it was clear, from the guard's statement, that the man must have been hidden there *before* the others arrived, and how unlikely the coincidence that conspirators should stray exactly into the very compartment in which a spy was already concealed! Besides, this explanation ignored the man in the smoking carriage, and gave no reason at all for his simultaneous disappearance. The police had little difficulty in showing that such a theory would not cover the facts, but they were unprepared in the absence of evidence to advance any alternative explanation.

There was a letter in the *Daily Gazette*, over the signature of a well-known criminal investigator, which gave rise to considerable discussion at the time. He had formed a hypothesis which had at least ingenuity to recommend it, and I cannot do better than append it in his own words.

"Whatever may be the truth," said he, "it must depend upon some bizarre and rare combination of events, so we need have no hesitation in postulating such events in our explanation. In the absence of data we must abandon the analytic or scientific method of investigation, and must approach it in the synthetic fashion. In a word, instead of taking known events and deducing from them what has occurred, we must build up a fanciful explanation if it will only be consistent with known events. We can then test this explanation by any fresh facts which may arise. If they all fit into their places, the probability is that we are upon the right track, and with each fresh fact this probability increases in a geometrical progression until the evidence becomes final and convincing.

"Now, there is one most remarkable and suggestive fact which has not met with the attention which it deserves. There is a local train running through Harrow and King's Langley, which is timed in such a way that the express must have overtaken it at or about the period when it eased down its speed to eight miles an hour on account of the repairs of the line. The two trains would at that time be travelling in the same direction at a similar rate of speed and upon parallel lines. It is within everyone's experience how, under such circumstances, the occupant of each carriage can see very plainly the passengers in the other carriages opposite to him. The lamps of the express had been lit at Willesden, so that each compartment was brightly illuminated, and most visible to an observer from outside.

"Now, the sequence of events as I reconstruct them would be after this fashion. This young man with the abnormal number of watches was alone in the carriage of the slow train. His ticket, with his papers and gloves and other things, was, we will suppose, on the seat beside him. He was probably an American, and also probably a man of weak intellect. The excessive wearing of jewellery is an early symptom in some forms of mania.

"As he sat watching the carriages of the express which were (on account of the state of the line) going at the same pace as himself, he suddenly saw some people in it whom he knew. We will suppose for the sake of our theory that these people were a woman whom he loved and a man whom he hated—and who in return hated him. The young man was excitable and impulsive. He opened the door of his carriage, stepped from the footboard of the local train to the footboard of the express, opened the other door, and made his way into the presence of these two people. The feat (on the supposition that the trains were going at the same pace) is by no means so perilous as it might appear.

"Having now got our young man without his ticket into the carriage in which the elder man and the young woman are travelling, it is not difficult to imagine that a violent scene ensued. It is possible that the pair were also Americans, which is the more probable as the man carried a weapon—an unusual thing in England. If our supposition of incipient mania is correct, the young man is likely to have assaulted the other. As the upshot of the quarrel the elder man shot the intruder, and then made his escape from the carriage, taking the young lady with him. We will suppose that all this happened very rapidly, and that the train was still going at so slow a pace that it was not difficult for them to leave it. A woman might leave a train going at eight miles an hour. As a matter of fact, we know that this woman *did* do so.

"And now we have to fit in the man in the smoking carriage. Presuming that we have, up to this point, reconstructed the tragedy correctly, we shall find nothing in this other man to cause us to reconsider our conclusions. According to my theory, this man saw the young fellow cross from one train to the other, saw him open the door, heard the pistol-shot, saw the two fugitives spring out on to the line, realized that murder had been done, and sprang out himself in pursuit. Why he has never been heard of since—whether he met his own death in the pursuit, or whether, as is more likely, he was made to realize that it was not a case for his interference—is a detail which we have at present no means of explaining. I acknowledge that there are some difficulties in the way. At first sight, it might seem improbable that at such a moment a murderer would burden himself in his flight with a brown leather bag. My answer is that he was well aware that if the bag were found his identity would be established. It was absolutely necessary for him to take it with him. My theory stands or falls upon one point, and I call upon the railway company to make strict inquiry as to whether a ticket was found unclaimed in the local train through Harrow and King's Langley upon the 18th of March. If such a ticket were found my case is proved. If not, my theory may still be the correct one, for it is conceivable either that he travelled without a ticket or that his ticket was lost."

To this elaborate and plausible hypothesis the answer of the police and of the company was, first, that no such ticket was found; secondly, that the slow train would never run parallel to the express; and, thirdly, that the local train had been stationary in King's Langley Station when the express, going at fifty miles an hour, had flashed past it. So perished the only satisfying explanation, and five years have elapsed without suppling a new one. Now, at last, there comes a statement which covers all the facts, and which must be regarded as authentic. It took the shape of a letter dated from New York, and addressed to the same criminal investigator whose theory I have quoted. It is given here in extenso, with the exception of the two opening paragraphs, which are personal in their nature:—

"You'll excuse me if I'm not very free with names. There's less reason now than there was five years ago when mother was still living. But for all that, I had rather cover up our tracks all I can. But I owe you an explanation, for if your idea of it was wrong, it was a mighty ingenious one all the same. I'll have to go back a little so as you may understand all about it.

"My people came from Bucks, England, and emigrated to the States in the early fifties. They settled in Rochester, in the State of New York, where my father ran a large dry goods store. There were only two sons: myself, James, and my brother, Edward. I was ten years older than my brother, and after my father died I sort of took the place of a father to him, as an elder brother would. He was a bright, spirited boy, and just one of the most beautiful creatures that ever lived. But there was always a soft spot in him, and it was like mould in cheese, for it spread and spread, and nothing that you could do would stop it. Mother saw it just as clearly as I did, but she went on spoiling him all the same, for he had such a way with him that you could refuse him nothing. I did all I could to hold him in, and he hated me for my pains.

"At last he fairly got his head, and nothing that we could do would stop him. He got off into New

York, and went rapidly from bad to worse. At first he was only fast, and then he was criminal; and then, at the end of a year or two, he was one of the most notorious young crooks in the city. He had formed a friendship with Sparrow MacCoy, who was at the head of his profession as a bunco-steerer, green goodsman, and general rascal. They took to card-sharping, and frequented some of the best hotels in New York. My brother was an excellent actor (he might have made an honest name for himself if he had chosen), and he would take the parts of a young Englishman of title, of a simple lad from the West, or of a college undergraduate, whichever suited Sparrow MacCoy's purpose. And then one day he dressed himself as a girl, and he carried it off so well, and made himself such a valuable decoy, that it was their favourite game afterwards. They had made it right with Tammany and with the police, so it seemed as if nothing could ever stop them, for those were in the days before the Lexow Commission, and if you only had a pull, you could do pretty nearly everything you wanted.

"And nothing would have stopped them if they had only stuck to cards and New York, but they must needs come up Rochester way, and forge a name upon a check. It was my brother that did it, though everyone knew that it was under the influence of Sparrow MacCoy. I bought up that check, and a pretty sum it cost me. Then I went to my brother, laid it before him on the table, and swore to him that I would prosecute if he did not clear out of the country. At first he simply laughed. I could not prosecute, he said, without breaking our mother's heart, and he knew that I would not do that. I made him understand, however, that our mother's heart was being broken in any case, and that I had set firm on the point that I would rather see him in a Rochester gaol than in a New York hotel. So at last he gave in, and he made me a solemn promise that he would see Sparrow MacCoy no more, that he would go to Europe, and that he would turn his hand to any honest trade that I helped him to get. I took him down right away to an old family friend, Joe Willson, who is an exporter of American watches and clocks, and I got him to give Edward an agency in London, with a small salary and a 15 per cent. commission on all business. His manner and appearance were so good that he won the old man over at once, and within a week he was sent off to London with a case full of samples.

"It seemed to me that this business of the check had really given my brother a fright, and that there was some chance of his settling down into an honest line of life. My mother had spoken with him, and what she said had touched him, for she had always been the best of mothers to him, and he had been the great sorrow of her life. But I knew that this man Sparrow MacCoy had a great influence over Edward, and my chance of keeping the lad straight lay in breaking the connection between them. I had a friend in the New York detective force, and through him I kept a watch upon MacCoy. When within a fortnight of my brother's sailing I heard that MacCoy had taken a berth in the *Etruria*, I was as certain as if he had told me that he was going over to England for the purpose of coaxing Edward back again into the ways that he had left. In an instant I had resolved to go also, and to put my influence against MacCoy's. I knew it was a losing fight, but I thought, and my mother thought, that it was my duty. We passed the last night together in prayer for my success, and she gave me her own Testament that my father had given her on the day of their marriage in the Old Country, so that I might always wear it next my heart.

"I was a fellow-traveller, on the steamship, with Sparrow MacCoy, and at least I had the satisfaction of spoiling his little game for the voyage. The very first night I went into the smoking-room, and found him at the head of a card table, with half-a-dozen young fellows who were carrying their full purses and their empty skulls over to Europe. He was settling down for his harvest, and a rich one it would have been. But I soon changed all that.

"'Gentlemen,' said I, 'are you aware whom you are playing with?'

"'What's that to you? You mind your own business!' said he, with an oath.

"'Who is it, anyway?' asked one of the dudes.

"'He's Sparrow MacCoy, the most notorious card-sharper in the States.'

"Up he jumped with a bottle in his hand, but he remembered that he was under the flag of the effete Old Country, where law and order run, and Tammany has no pull. Gaol and the gallows wait for violence and murder, and there's no slipping out by the back door on board an ocean liner.

"'Prove your words, you——!' said he.

"'I will!' said I. 'If you will turn up your right shirt-sleeve to the shoulder, I will either prove my words or I will eat them.'

"He turned white and said not a word. You see, I knew something of his ways, and I was aware that part of the mechanism which he and all such sharpers use consists of an elastic down the arm with a clip just above the wrist. It is by means of this clip that they withdraw from their hands the cards which they do not want, while they substitute other cards from another hiding-place. I reckoned on it being there, and it was. He cursed me, slunk out of the saloon, and was hardly seen again during the voyage. For once, at any rate, I got level with Mister Sparrow MacCoy.

"But he soon had his revenge upon me, for when it came to influencing my brother he outweighed me every time. Edward had kept himself straight in London for the first few weeks, and had done some business with his American watches, until this villain came across his path once more. I did my best, but the best was little enough. The next thing I heard there had been a scandal at one of the Northumberland Avenue hotels: a traveller had been fleeced of a large sum by two confederate card-sharpers, and the matter was in the hands of Scotland Yard. The first I learned of it was in the evening paper, and I was at once certain that my brother and MacCoy were back at their old games. I hurried at once to Edward's lodgings. They told me that he and a tall gentleman (whom I recognized as MacCoy) had gone off together, and that he had left the lodgings and taken his things with him. The landlady had heard them give several directions to the cabman, ending with Euston Station, and she had accidentally overheard the tall gentleman saying something about Manchester. She believed that that was their destination.

"A glance at the time-table showed me that the most likely train was at five, though there was another at 4.35 which they might have caught. I had only time to get the later one, but found no sign of them either at the depôt or in the train. They must have gone on by the earlier one, so I determined to follow them to Manchester and search for them in the hotels there. One last appeal to my brother by all that he owed to my mother might even now be the salvation of him. My nerves were overstrung, and I lit a cigar to steady them. At that moment, just as the train was moving off, the door of my compartment was flung open, and there were MacCoy and my brother on the platform.

"They were both disguised, and with good reason, for they knew that the London police were after them. MacCoy had a great Astrakhan collar drawn up, so that only his eyes and nose were showing. My brother was dressed like a woman, with a black veil half down his face, but of course it did not deceive me for an instant, nor would it have done so even if I had not known that he had often used such a dress before. I started up, and as I did so MacCoy recognized me. He said something, the conductor slammed the door, and they were shown into the next compartment. I tried to stop the train so as to follow them, but the wheels were already moving, and it was too late.

"When we stopped at Willesden, I instantly changed my carriage. It appears that I was not seen to do so, which is not surprising, as the station was crowded with people. MacCoy, of course, was expecting me, and he had spent the time between Euston and Willesden in saying all he could to harden my brother's heart and set him against me. That is what I fancy, for I had never found him so impossible to soften or to move. I tried this way and I tried that; I pictured his future in an English gaol; I described the sorrow of his mother when I came back with the news; I said everything to touch his heart, but all to no purpose. He sat there with a fixed sneer upon his handsome face, while every now and then Sparrow MacCoy would throw in a taunt at me, or some word of encouragement to hold my brother to his resolutions.

"'Why don't you run a Sunday-school?' he would say to me, and then, in the same breath: 'He thinks you have no will of your own. He thinks you are just the baby brother and that he can lead you where he likes. He's only just finding out that you are a man as well as he.'

"It was those words of his which set me talking

bitterly. We had left Willesden, you understand, for all this took some time. My temper got the better of me, and for the first time in my life I let my brother see the rough side of me. Perhaps it would have been better had I done so earlier and more often.

"'A man!' said I. 'Well, I'm glad to have your friend's assurance of it, for no one would suspect it to see you like a boarding-school missy. I don't suppose in all this country there is a more contemptible-looking creature than you are as you sit there with that Dolly pinafore upon you.' He coloured up at that, for he was a vain man, and he winced from ridicule.

"'It's only a dust-cloak,' said he, and he slipped it off. 'One has to throw the coppers off one's scent, and I had no other way to do it.' He took his toque off with the veil attached, and he put both it and the cloak into his brown bag. 'Anyway, I don't need to wear it until the conductor comes round,' said he.

"'Nor then, either,' said I, and taking the bag I slung it with all my force out of the window. 'Now,' said I, 'you'll never make a Mary Jane of yourself while I can help it. If nothing but that disguise stands between you and a gaol, then to gaol you shall go.'

"That was the way to manage him. I felt my advantage at once. His supple nature was one which yielded to roughness far more readily than to entreaty. He flushed with shame, and his eyes filled with tears. But MacCoy saw my advantage also, and was determined that I should not pursue it.

"'He's my pard, and you shall not bully him,' he cried.

"'He's my brother, and you shall not ruin him,' said I. 'I believe a spell of prison is the very best way of keeping you apart, and you shall have it, or it will be no fault of mine.'

"'Oh, you would squeal, would you?' he cried, and in an instant he whipped out his revolver. I sprang for his hand, but saw that I was too late, and jumped aside. At the same instant he fired, and the bullet which would have struck me passed through the heart of my unfortunate brother.

"He dropped without a groan upon the floor of the compartment, and MacCoy and I, equally horrified, knelt at each side of him, trying to bring back some signs of life. MacCoy still held the loaded revolver in his hand, but his anger against me and my resentment towards him had both for the moment been swallowed up in this sudden tragedy. It was he who first realized the situation. The train was for some reason going very slowly at the moment, and he saw his opportunity for escape. In an instant he had the door open, but I was as quick as he, and jumping upon him the two of us fell off the foot-board and rolled in each other's arms down a steep embankment. At the bottom I struck my head against a stone, and I remembered nothing more. When I came to myself I was lying among some low bushes, not far from the railroad track, and somebody was bathing my head with a wet handkerchief. It was Sparrow MacCoy.

"'I guess I couldn't leave you,' said he. 'I didn't want to have the blood of two of you on my hands in one day. You loved your brother, I've no doubt; but you didn't love him a cent more than I loved him, though you'll say that I took a queer way to show it. Anyhow, it seems a mighty empty world now that he is gone, and I don't care a continental whether you give me over to the hangman or not.'

"He had turned his ankle in the fall, and there we sat, he with his useless foot, and I with my throbbing head, and we talked and talked until gradually my bitterness began to soften and to turn into something like sympathy. What was the use of revenging his death upon a man who was as much stricken by that death as I was? And then, as my wits gradually returned, I began to realize also that I could do nothing against MacCoy which would not recoil upon my mother and myself. How could we convict him without a full account of my brother's career being made public—the very thing which of all others we wished to avoid? It was really as much our interest as his to cover the matter up, and from being an avenger of crime I found myself changed to a conspirator against Justice. The place in which we found ourselves was one of those pheasant preserves which are so common in the Old Country, and as we groped our way through it I found myself consulting the slayer of my brother as to how far it would be possible to hush it up.

"I soon realized from what he said that unless there were some papers of which we knew nothing in my brother's pockets, there was really no possible means by which the police could identify him or learn how he had got there. His ticket was in MacCoy's pocket, and so was the ticket for some baggage which they had left at the depôt. Like most Americans, he had found it cheaper and easier to buy an outfit in London than to bring one from New York, so that all his linen and clothes were new and unmarked. The bag, containing the dust cloak, which I had thrown out of the window, may have fallen among some bramble patch where it is still concealed, or may have been carried off by some tramp, or may have come into the possession of the police, who kept the incident to themselves. Anyhow, I have seen nothing about it in the London papers.

As to the watches, they were a selection from those which had been intrusted to him for business purposes. It may have been for the same business purposes that he was taking them to Manchester, but—well, it's too late to enter into that.

"I don't blame the police for being at fault. I don't see how it could have been otherwise. There was just one little clew that they might have followed up, but it was a small one. I mean that small circular mirror which was found in my brother's pocket. It isn't a very common thing for a young man to carry about with him, is it? But a gambler might have told you what such a mirror may mean to a card-sharper. If you sit back a little from the table, and lay the mirror, face upwards, upon your lap, you can see, as you deal, every card that you give to your adversary. It is not hard to say whether you see a man or raise him when you know his cards as well as your own. It was as much a part of a sharper's outfit as the elastic clip upon Sparrow MacCoy's arm. Taking that, in connection with the recent frauds at the hotels, the police might have got hold of one end of the string.

"I don't think there is much more for me to explain. We got to a village called Amersham that night in the character of two gentlemen upon a walking tour, and afterwards we made our way quietly to London, whence MacCoy went on to Cairo and I returned to New York. My mother died six months afterwards, and I am glad to say that to the day of her death she never knew what happened. She was always under the delusion that Edward was earning an honest living in London, and I never had the heart to tell her the truth. He never wrote; but, then, he never did write at any time, so that made no difference. His name was the last upon her lips.

"There's just one other thing that I have to ask you, sir, and I should take it as a kind return for all this explanation, if you could do it for me. You remember that Testament that was picked up. I always carried it in my inside pocket, and it must have come out in my fall. I value it very highly, for it was the family book with my birth and my brother's marked by my father in the beginning of it. I wish you would apply at the proper place and have it sent to me. It can be of no possible value to any one else. If you address it to X, Bassano's Library, Broadway, New York, it is sure to come to hand."

AMELIA B. EDWARDS

The Four-Fifteen Express

The events which I am about to relate took place between nine and ten years ago. Sebastopol had fallen in the early spring, the Peace of Paris had been concluded since March, our commercial relations with the Russian empire were but recently renewed; and I, returning home after my first northward journey since the war, was well pleased with the prospect of spending the month of December under the hospitable and thoroughly English roof of my excellent friend, Jonathan Jelf, Esquire, of Dumbleton Manor, Clayborough, East Anglia. Travelling in the interests of the well-known firm in which it is my lot to be a junior partner, I had been called upon to visit not only the capitals of Russia and Poland, but had found it also necessary to pass some weeks among the trading ports of the Baltic; whence it came that the year was already far spent before I again set foot on English soil, and that, instead of shooting pheasants with him, as I had hoped, in October, I came to be my friend's guest during the more genial Christmastide.

My voyage over, and a few days given up to

business in Liverpool and London, I hastened down to Clayborough with all the delight of a schoolboy whose holidays are at hand. My way lay by the Great East Anglian Line as far as Clayborough station, where I was to be met by one of the Dumbleton carriages and conveyed across the remaining nine miles of country. It was a foggy afternoon, singularly warm for the 4th of December, and I had arranged to leave London by the 4:15 express. The early darkness of winter had already closed in; the lamps were lighted in the carriages; a clinging damp dimmed the windows, adhered to the door-handles, and pervaded all the atmosphere; while the gas-jets at the neighbouring bookstand diffused a luminous haze that only served to make the gloom of the terminus more visible. Having arrived some seven minutes before the starting of the train, and, by the connivance of the guard, taken sole possession of an empty compartment, I lighted my travelling-lamp, made myself particularly snug, and settled down to the undisturbed enjoyment of a book and a cigar. Great, therefore, was my disappointment when, at the last moment, a gentleman came hurrying along the platform, glanced into my carriage, opened the locked door with a private key, and stepped in.

It struck me at the first glance that I had seen him before – a tall, spare man, thin-lipped, light-eyed, with an ungraceful stoop in the shoulders and scant grey hair worn somewhat long upon the collar. He carried a light waterproof coat, an umbrella and a large brown japanned deed-box, which last he placed under the seat. This done, he felt carefully in his breast-pocket, as if to make certain of the safety of his purse or pocketbook, laid his umbrella in the netting overhead, spread the waterproof across his knees, and exchanged his hat for a travelling-cap of some Scotch material. By this time the train was moving out of the station and into the faint grey of the wintry twilight beyond.

I now recognised my companion. I recognised him from the moment when he removed his hat and uncovered the lofty, furrowed and somewhat narrow brow beneath. I had met him, as I distinctly remembered, some three years before, at the very house for which, in all probability, he was now bound, like myself. His name was Dwerrihouse, he was a lawyer by profession, and, if I was not greatly mistaken, was first cousin to the wife of my host. I knew also that he was a man eminently 'well-to-do', both as regarded his professional and private means. The Jelfs entertained him with that sort of observant courtesy which falls to the lot of the rich relation, the children made much of him, and the old butler, albeit somewhat surly 'to the general', treated him with deference. I thought, observing him by the vague mixture of lamplight and twilight, that Mrs Jelf's cousin looked all the worse for the three years' wear and tear which had gone over his head since our last meeting. He was very pale, and had a restless light in his eye that I did not remember to have observed before. The anxious lines, too, about his mouth were deepened, and there was a cavernous, hollow look about his cheeks and temples which seemed to speak of sickness or sorrow. He had glanced at me as he came in, but without any gleam of recognition in his face. Now he glanced again, as I fancied, somewhat doubtfully. When he did so for the third or fourth time I ventured to address him.

'Mr John Dwerrihouse, I think?'

'That is my name,' he replied.

'I had the pleasure of meeting you at Dumbleton about three years ago.'

Mr Dwerrihouse bowed. 'I thought I knew your face,' he said; 'but your name, I regret to say—'

'Langford – William Langford. I have known Jonathan Jelf since we were boys together at Merchant Taylors', and I generally spend a few weeks at Dumbleton in the shooting season. I suppose we are bound for the same destination?'

'Not if you are on your way to the manor,' he replied. 'I am travelling upon business – rather troublesome business too – while you, doubtless, have only pleasure in view.'

'Just so. I am in the habit of looking forward to this visit as to the brightest three weeks in all the year.'

'It is a pleasant house,' said Mr Dwerrihouse.

'The pleasantest I know.'

'And Jelf is thoroughly hospitable.'

'The best and kindest fellow in the world!'

'They have invited me to spend Christmas week with them,' pursued Mr Dwerrihouse, after a moment's pause.

'And you are coming?'

'I cannot tell. It must depend on the issue of this business which I have in hand. You have heard perhaps that we are about to construct a branch line from Blackwater to Stockbridge.'

I explained that I had been for some months away from England, and had therefore heard nothing of the contemplated improvement. Mr Dwerrihouse smiled complacently.

'It *will* be an improvement,' he said, 'a great improvement. Stockbridge is a flourishing town, and needs but a more direct railway communication with the metropolis to become an important centre of commerce. This branch was my own idea. I brought the project before the board, and have myself super-intended the execution of it up to the present time.'

'You are an East Anglian director, I presume?'

'My interest in the company,' replied Mr Dwerrihouse, 'is threefold. I am a director, I am a considerable shareholder, and, as head of the firm of Dwerrihouse, Dwerrihouse & Craik, I am the company's principal solicitor.'

Loquacious, self-important, full of his pet project, and apparently unable to talk on any other subject, Mr Dwerrihouse then went on to tell of the opposition he had encountered and the obstacles he had overcome in the cause of the Stockbridge branch. I was entertained with a multitude of local details and local grievances. The rapacity of one squire, the impracticability of another, the indignation of the rector whose glebe was threatened, the culpable indifference of the Stockbridge townspeople, who could *not* be brought to see that their most vital interests hinged upon a junction with the Great East Anglian Line, the spite of the local newspaper, and the unheard-of difficulties attending the Common question, were each and all laid before me with a circumstantiality that possessed the deepest interest for my excellent fellow-traveller, but none whatever for myself. From these, to my despair, he went on to more intricate matters: to the approximate expenses of construction per mile; to the estimates sent in by different contractors, to the probable traffic returns of the new line; to the provisional clauses of the new act as enumerated in Schedule D of the company's last half-yearly report; and so on and on and on, till my head ached and my attention flagged and my eyes kept closing in spite of every effort that I made to keep them open. At length I was roused by these words: 'Seventy-five thousand pounds, cash down.'

'Seventy-five thousand pounds, cash down,' I repeated, in the liveliest tone I could assume. 'That is a heavy sum.'

'A heavy sum to carry here,' replied Mr Dwerrihouse, pointing significantly to his breast pocket, 'but a mere fraction of what we shall ultimately have to pay.'

'You do not mean to say that you have seventy-five thousand pounds at this moment upon your person?' I exclaimed.

'My good sir, have I not been telling you so for the last half-hour?' said Mr Dwerrihouse, testily. 'That money has to be paid over at half-past eight o'clock this evening, at the office of Sir Thomas's solicitors, on completion of the deed of sale.'

'But how will you get across by night from Blackwater to Stockbridge with seventy-five thousand pounds in your pocket?'

'To Stockbridge!' echoed the lawyer. 'I find I have made myself very imperfectly understood. I thought I had explained how this sum only carries us as far as Mallingford – the first stage, as it were, of our journey – and how our route from Blackwater to Mallingford lies entirely through Sir Thomas Liddell's property.'

'I beg your pardon,' I stammered. 'I fear my thoughts were wandering. So you only go as far as Mallingford tonight?'

'Precisely. I shall get a conveyance from the Blackwater Arms. And you?'

'Oh, Jelf sends a trap to meet me at Clayborough! Can I be the bearer of any message from you?'

'You may say, if you please. Mr Langford, that I wished I could have been your companion all the way, and that I will come over, if possible, before Christmas.'

'Nothing more?'

Mr Dwerrihouse smiled grimly. 'Well,' he said, 'you may tell my cousin that she need not burn the hall down in my honour this time, and that I shall be obliged if she will order the blue-room chimney to be swept before I arrive.'

'That sounds tragic. Had you a conflagration on the occasion of your last visit to Dumbleton?'

'Something like it. There had been no fire lighted

in my bedroom since the spring, the flue was foul and the jackdaws had built in it; so when I went up to dress for dinner I found the room full of smoke and the chimney on fire. Are we already at Blackwater?'

The train had gradually come to a pause while Mr Dwerrihouse was speaking, and, on putting my head out of the window, I could see the station some few hundred yards ahead. There was another train before us blocking the way, and the guard was making use of the delay to collect the Blackwater tickets. I had scarcely ascertained our position when the ruddy-faced official appeared at our carriage door.

'Tickets, sir!' said he.

'I am for Clayborough,' I replied, holding out the pink card.

He took it, glanced at it by the light of his little lantern, gave it back, looked, as I fancied, somewhat sharply at my fellow-traveller, and disappeared.

'He did not ask for yours,' I said, with some surprise.

'They never do,' replied Mr Dwerrihouse; 'they all know me, and of course I travel free.'

'Blackwater! Blackwater!' cried the porter, running along the platform beside us as we glided into the station.

Mr Dwerrihouse pulled out his deed-box, put his

travelling-cap in his pocket, resumed his hat, took down his umbrella, and prepared to be gone.

'Many thanks, Mr Langford, for your society,' he said, with old-fashioned courtesy. 'I wish you a good-evening.'

'Good-evening,' I replied, putting out my hand.

But he either did not see it or did not choose to see it, and, slightly lifting his hat, stepped out upon the platform. Having done this, he moved slowly away and mingled with the departing crowd.

Leaning forward to watch him out of sight, I trod upon something which proved to be a cigar-case. It had fallen, no doubt, from the pocket of his waterproof coat, and was made of dark morocco leather, with a silver monogram upon the side. I sprang out of the carriage just as the guard came up to lock me in.

'Is there a minute to spare?' I asked, eagerly. 'The gentleman who travelled down with me from town has dropped his cigar-case; he is not yet out of the station.'

'Just a minute and a half, sir,' replied the guard. 'You must be quick.'

I dashed along the platform as fast as my feet could carry me. It was a large station, and Mr Dwerrihouse had by this time got more than halfway to the farther end.

I, however, saw him distinctly, moving slowly with the stream. Then, as I drew nearer, I saw that he had met some friend, that they were talking as they walked, that they presently fell back somewhat from the crowd and stood aside in earnest conversation. I made straight for the spot where they were waiting. There was a vivid gas-jet just above their heads, and the light fell full upon their faces. I saw both distinctly – the face of Mr Dwerrihouse and the face of his companion. Running, breathless, eager as I was, getting in the way of porters and passengers, and fearful every instant lest I should see the train going on without me, I yet observed that the newcomer was considerably younger and shorter than the director, that he was sandy-haired, mustachioed, small-featured, and dressed in a close-cut suit of Scotch tweed. I was now within a few yards of them. I ran against a stout gentleman, I was nearly knocked down by a luggage-truck, I stumbled over a carpet-bag; I gained the spot just as the driver's whistle warned me to return.

To my utter stupefaction, they were no longer there. I had seen them but two seconds before – and they were gone! I stood still; I looked to right and left; I saw no sign of them in any direction. It was as if the platform had gaped and swallowed them.

'There were two gentlemen standing here a

moment ago,' I said to a porter at my elbow; 'which way can they have gone?'

'I saw no gentlemen, sir,' replied the man. The whistle shrilled out again. The guard, far up the platform, held up his arm, and shouted to me to 'come on!'

'If you're going on by this train, sir,' said the porter, 'you must run for it.'

I did run for it, just gained the carriage as the train began to move, was shoved in by the guard, and left, breathless and bewildered, with Mr Dwerrihouse's cigar-case still in my hand.

It was the strangest disappearance in the world; it was like a transformation trick in a pantomime. They were there one moment – palpably there, with the gaslight full upon their faces – and the next moment they were gone. There was no door near, no window, no staircase; it was a mere slip of barren platform, tapestried with big advertisements. Could anything be more mysterious?

It was not worth thinking about, and yet, for my life, I could not help pondering upon it – pondering, wondering, conjecturing, turning it over and over in my mind, and beating my brains for a solution of the enigma. I thought of it all the way from Blackwater to Clayborough. I thought of it all the way from Clayborough to Dumbleton, as I rattled along the smooth highway in a trim dog-cart, drawn by a splendid black mare and driven by the silentest and dapperest of East Anglian grooms.

We did the nine miles in something less than an hour, and pulled up before the lodge-gates just as the church clock was striking half-past seven. A couple of minutes more, and the warm glow of the lighted hall was flooding out upon the gravel, a hearty grasp was on my hand, and a clear jovial voice was bidding me 'welcome to Dumbleton'.

'And now, my dear fellow,' said my host, when the first greeting was over, 'you have no time to spare. We dine at eight, and there are people coming to meet you, so you must just get the dressing business over as quickly as may be. By the way, you will meet some acquaintances: the Biddulphs are coming, and Prendergast (Prendergast of the Skirmishers) is staying in the house. Adieu! Mrs Jelf will be expecting you in the drawing-room.'

I was ushered to my room – not the blue room, of which Mr Dwerrihouse had made disagreeable experience, but a pretty little bachelor's chamber, hung with a delicate chintz and made cheerful by a blazing fire. I unlocked my portmanteau. I tried to be expeditious, but the memory of my railway adventure haunted me. I could not get free of it; I could not shake it off. It impeded me, worried me, it tripped me up, it caused me to mislay my studs, to mis-tie my cravat, to wrench the buttons off my gloves. Worst of all, it made me so late that the party had all assembled before I reached the drawing-room. I had scarcely paid my respects to Mrs Jelf when dinner was announced, and we paired off, some eight or ten couples strong, into the dining-room.

I am not going to describe either the guests or the dinner. All provincial parties bear the strictest family resemblance, and I am not aware that an East Anglian banquet offers any exception to the rule. There was the usual country baronet and his wife; there were the usual country parsons and their wives; there was the sempiternal turkey and haunch of venison. *Vanitas vanitatum.* There is nothing new under the sun.

I was placed about midway down the table. I had taken one rector's wife down to dinner, and I had another at my left hand. They talked across me, and their talk was about babies; it was dreadfully dull. At length there came a pause. The entrées had just been removed, and the turkey had come upon the scene. The conversation had all along been of the languidest, but at this moment it happened to have stagnated altogether. Jelf was carving the turkey; Mrs Jelf looked as if she was trying to think of something to say; everybody else was silent. Moved by an unlucky impulse, I thought I would relate my adventure.

'By the way, Jelf,' I began, 'I came down part of the way today with a friend of yours.'

'Indeed!' said the master of the feast, slicing scientifically into the breast of the turkey. 'With whom, pray?'

'With one who bade me tell you that he should, if possible, pay you a visit before Christmas.'

'I cannot think who that could be,' said my friend, smiling.

'It must be Major Thorp,' suggested Mrs Jelf.

I shook my head. 'It was not Major Thorp,' I replied; 'it was a near relation of your own, Mrs Jelf.'

'Then I am more puzzled than ever,' replied my hostess. 'Pray tell me who it was.'

'It was no less a person than your cousin, Mr John Dwerrihouse.'

Jonathan Jelf laid down his knife and fork. Mrs Jelf looked at me in a strange, startled way, and said never a word.

'And he desired me to tell you, my dear madam, that you need not take the trouble to burn the hall down in his honour this time, but only to have the chimney of the blue room swept before his arrival.'

Before I had reached the end of my sentence I became aware of something ominous in the faces of the guests. I felt I had said something which I had better have left unsaid, and that for some unexplained reason my words had evoked a general consternation. I sat confounded, not daring to utter another syllable, and for at least two whole minutes there was dead silence round the table. Then Captain Prendergast came to the rescue.

'You have been abroad for some months, have you not, Mr Langford?' he said, with the desperation of one who flings himself into the breach. 'I heard you had been to Russia. Surely you have something to tell us of the state and temper of the country after the war?'

I was heartily grateful to the gallant Skirmisher for this diversion in my favour. I answered him, I fear, somewhat lamely; but he kept the conversation up, and presently one or two others joined in and so the difficulty, whatever it might have been, was bridged over – bridged over, but not repaired. A something, an awkwardness, a visible constraint remained. The guests hitherto had been simply dull, but now they were evidently uncomfortable and embarrassed.

The dessert had scarcely been placed upon the table when the ladies left the room. I seized the opportunity to select a vacant chair next Captain Prendergast.

'In heaven's name,' I whispered, 'what was the matter just now? What had I said?'

'You mentioned the name of John Dwerrihouse.'

'What of that? I had seen him not two hours before.'

'It is a most astounding circumstance that you should have seen him,' said Captain Prendergast. 'Are you sure it was he?'

'As sure as of my own identity. We were talking all the way between London and Blackwater. But why does that surprise you?'

'*Because*,' replied Captain Prendergast, dropping his voice to the lowest whisper – '*because John Dwerrihouse absconded three months ago with seventy-five thousand pounds of the company's money, and has never been heard of since.*'

John Dwerrihouse had absconded three months ago – and I had seen him only a few hours back! John Dwerrihouse had embezzled seventy-five thousand pounds of the company's money, yet told me that he carried that sum upon his person! Were ever facts so strangely incongruous, so difficult to reconcile? How should he have ventured again into the light of day? How dared he show himself along the line? Above all, what had he been doing throughout those mysterious three months of disappearance?

Perplexing questions these – questions which at

once suggested themselves to the minds of all concerned, but which admitted of no easy solution. I could find no reply to them. Captain Prendergast had not even a suggestion to offer, Jonathan Jelf, who seized the first opportunity of drawing me aside and learning all that I had to tell, was more amazed and bewildered than either of us. He came to my room that night, when all the guests were gone, and we talked the thing over from every point of view; without, it must be confessed, arriving at any kind of conclusion.

'I do not ask you,' he said, 'whether you can have mistaken your man. That is impossible.'

'As impossible as that I should mistake some stranger for yourself.'

'It is not a question of looks or voice, but of facts. That he should have alluded to the fire in the blue room is proof enough of John Dwerrihouse's identity. How did he look?'

'Older, I thought; considerably older, paler, and more anxious.'

'He has had enough to make him look anxious, anyhow,' said my friend, gloomily, 'be he innocent or guilty.'

'I am inclined to believe that he is innocent,' I replied. 'He showed no embarrassment when I addressed him, and no uneasiness when the guard came round. His conversation was open to a fault. I might almost say that he talked too freely of the business which he had in hand.'

'That is strange, for I know no one more reticent on such subjects. He actually told you that he had the seventy-five thousand pounds in his pocket?'

'He did.'

'Humph! My wife has an idea about it, and she may be right—'

'What idea?'

'Well, she fancies – women are so clever, you know, at putting themselves inside people's motives – she fancies that he was tempted, that he did actually take the money, and that he has been concealing himself these three months in some wild part of the country, struggling possibly with his conscience all the time, and daring neither to abscond with his booty nor to come back and restore it.'

'But now that he has come back?'

'That is the point. She conceives that he has probably thrown himself upon the company's mercy, made restitution of the money, and, being forgiven, is permitted to carry the business through as if nothing whatever had happened.'

'The last,' I replied, 'is an impossible case. Mrs Jelf thinks like a generous and delicate-minded woman, but not in the least like a board of railway directors. They would never carry forgiveness so far.'

'I fear not; and yet it is the only conjecture that bears a semblance of likelihood. However we can run over to Clayborough tomorrow and see if anything is to be learned. By the way Prendergast tells me you picked up his cigar-case.'

'I did so, and here it is.'

Jelf took the cigar-case, examined it by the light of the lamp, and said at once that it was beyond doubt Mr Dwerrihouse's property, and that he remembered to have seen him use it.

'Here, too, is his monogram on the side,' he added – 'a big J transfixing a capital D. He used to carry the same on his note-paper.'

'It offers, at all events, a proof that I was not dreaming.'

'Ay, but it is time you were asleep and dreaming now. I am ashamed to have kept you up so long. Good-night.'

'Good-night, and remember that I am more than ready to go with you to Clayborough or Blackwater or London or anywhere, if I can be of the least service.'

'Thanks! I know you mean it, old friend, and it may be that I shall put you to the test. Once more, good-night.'

So we parted for that night, and met again in the breakfast-room at half-past eight next morning. It was a hurried, silent, uncomfortable meal; none of us had slept well, and all were thinking of the same subject. Mrs Jelf had evidently been crying. Jelf was impatient to be off, and both Captain Prendergast and myself felt ourselves to be in the painful position of outsiders who are involuntarily brought into a domestic trouble. Within twenty minutes after we had left the breakfast-table the dog-cart was brought round and my friend and I were on the road to Clayborough.

'Tell you what it is, Langford,' he said, as we sped along between the wintry hedges, 'I do not much fancy to bring up Dwerrihouse's name at Clayborough. All the officials know that he is my wife's relation, and the subject just now is hardly a pleasant one. If you don't much mind, we will make the 11:10 to Blackwater. It's an important station, and we shall stand a far better chance of picking up information there than at Clayborough.'

So we took the 11:10, which happened to be an express, and, arriving at Blackwater about a quarter before twelve, proceeded at once to prosecute our enquiry.

We began by asking for the station-master, a big, blunt, businesslike person, who at once averred that he knew Mr John Dwerrihouse perfectly well, and that there was no director on the line whom he had seen and spoken to so frequently.

'He used to be down here two or three times a week about three months ago,' said he, 'when the new line was first set afoot; but since then, you know, gentlemen—'

He paused significantly.

Jelf flushed scarlet.

'Yes, yes,' he said, hurriedly; 'we know all about that. The point now to be ascertained is whether anything has been seen or heard of him lately.'

'Not to my knowledge,' replied the station-master.

'He is not known to have been down the line any time yesterday, for instance?'

The station-master shook his head. 'The East Anglian, sir,' said he, 'is about the last place where he would dare to show himself. Why, there isn't a station-master, there isn't a guard, there isn't a porter, who doesn't know Mr Dwerrihouse by sight as well as he knows his own face in the looking-glass, or who wouldn't telegraph for the police as soon as he had set eyes on him at any point along the line. Bless you, sir! there's been a standing order out against him ever since the 25th of September last.'

'And yet,' pursued my friend, 'a gentleman who

travelled down yesterday from London to Clayborough by the afternoon express testifies that he saw Mr Dwerrihouse in the train, and that Mr Dwerrihouse alighted at Blackwater station.'

'Quite impossible, sir,' replied the station-master promptly.

'Why impossible?'

'Because there is no station along the line where he is so well known or where he would run so great a risk. It would be just running his head into the lion's mouth; he would have been mad to come nigh Blackwater station; and if he had come he would have been arrested before he left the platform.'

'Can you tell me who took the Blackwater tickets of that train?'

'I can, sir. It was the guard, Benjamin Somers.'

'And where can I find him?'

'You can find him, sir, by staying here, if you please, till one o'clock. He will be coming through with the up express from Crampton, which stays in Blackwater for ten minutes.'

We waited for the up express, beguiling the time as best we could by strolling along the Blackwater road till we came almost to the outskirts of the town, from which the station was distant nearly a couple of miles. By one o'clock we were back again upon the platform and waiting for the train. It came punctually, and I at once recognised the ruddy-faced guard who had gone down with my train the evening before.

'The gentlemen want to ask you something about Mr Dwerrihouse, Somers,' said the station-master, by way of introduction.

The guard flashed a keen glance from my face to Jelf's and back again to mine. 'Mr John Dwerrihouse, the late director?' said he, interrogatively.

'The same,' replied my friend. 'Should you know him if you saw him?'

'Anywhere, sir.'

'Do you know if he was in the 4:15 express yesterday afternoon?'

'He was not, sir.'

'How can you answer so positively?'

'Because I looked into every carriage and saw every face in that train, and I could take my oath that Mr Dwerrihouse was not in it. This gentleman was,' he added, turning sharply upon me. 'I don't know that I ever saw him before in my life, but I remember *his* face perfectly. You nearly missed taking your seat in time at this station, sir, and you got out at Clayborough.'

'Quite true, guard,' I replied; 'but do you not remember the face of the gentleman who travelled down in the same carriage with me as far as here?'

'It was my impression, sir, that you travelled down alone,' said Somers, with a look of some surprise.

'By no means. I had a fellow-traveller as far as Blackwater, and it was in trying to restore him the cigar-case which he had dropped in the carriage that I nearly let you go on without me.'

'I remember your saying something about a cigar-case, certainly,' replied the guard; 'but—'

'You asked for my ticket just before we entered the station.'

'I did, sir.'

'Then you must have seen him. He sat in the corner next the very door to which you came.'

'No, indeed; I saw no one.'

I looked at Jelf. I began to think the guard was in the ex-director's confidence, and paid for his silence.

'If I had seen another traveller I should have asked for his ticket,' added Somers. 'Did you see me ask for his ticket, sir?'

'I observed that you did not ask for it, but he explained that by saying—' I hesitated. I feared I might be telling too much, and so broke off abruptly.

The guard and the station-master exchanged glances. The former looked impatiently at his watch.

'I am obliged to go on in four minutes more, sir,' he said.

'One last question, then,' interposed Jelf, with a sort of desperation. 'If this gentleman's fellow traveller had been Mr John Dwerrihouse, and he had been sitting in the corner next the door in which you took the tickets, could you have failed to see and recognise him?'

'No, sir; it would have been quite impossible!'

'And you are certain you did *not* see him?'

'As I said before, sir, I could take my oath, I did not see him. And if it wasn't that I don't like to contradict a gentleman, I would say I could also take my oath that this gentlemen was quite alone in the carriage the whole way from London to Clayborough. Why, sir,' he added dropping his voice so as to be inaudible to the station-master, who had been called away to speak to some person close by, 'you expressly asked me to give you a compartment to yourself, and I did so. I locked you in, and you were so good as to give me something for myself.'

'Yes; but Mr Dwerrihouse had a key of his own.'

'I never saw him, sir; I saw no one in that compartment but yourself. Beg pardon, sir; my time's up.'

And with this the ruddy guard touched his cap and was gone. In another minute the heavy panting of the engine began afresh, and the train glided slowly out of the station.

We looked at each other for some moments in silence. I was the first to speak. 'Mr Benjamin Somers knows more than he chooses to tell,' I said.

'Humph! do you think so?'

'It must be. He could not have come to the door without seeing him; it's impossible.'

'There is one thing not impossible, my dear fellow.'

'What is that?'

'That you may have fallen asleep and dreamed the whole thing.'

'Could I dream of a branch line that I had never heard of? Could I dream of a hundred and one business details that had no kind of interest for me? Could I dream of the seventy-five thousand pounds?'

'Perhaps you might have seen or heard some vague account of the affair while you were abroad. It might have made no impression upon you at the time, and might have come back to you in your dreams, recalled perhaps by the mere names of the stations on the line.'

'What about the fire in the chimney of the blue room – should I have heard of that during my journey?'

'Well, no; I admit there is a difficulty about that point.'

'And what about the cigar-case?'

'Ay, by Jove! there is the cigar-case. That *is* a stubborn fact. Well, it's a mysterious affair, and it will need a better detective than myself, I fancy, to clear it up. I suppose we may as well go home.'

A week had not gone by when I received a letter from the secretary of the East Anglian Railway Company, requesting the favour of my attendance at a special board meeting not then many days distant. No reasons were alleged and no apologies offered for this demand upon my time, but they had heard, it was clear, of my enquiries about the missing director, and had a mind to put me through some sort of official examination upon the subject. Being still a guest at Dumbleton Hall, I had to go up to London for the purpose and Jonathan Jelf accompanied me. I found the direction of the Great East Anglian Line represented by a party of some twelve or fourteen gentlemen seated in solemn conclave round a huge green-baize table, in a gloomy boardroom adjoining the London terminus.

Being courteously received by the chairman (who at once began by saying that certain statements of mine respecting Mr John Dwerrihouse had come to the knowledge of the direction, and that they in consequence desired to confer with me on those points),

I was placed at the table and the inquiry proceeded in due form.

I was first asked if I knew Mr John Dwerrihouse, how long I had been acquainted with him and whether I could identify him at sight. I was then asked when I had seen him last. To which I replied. 'On the 4th of this present month, December, 1856.' Then came the enquiry of where I had seen him on that fourth day of December; to which I replied that I met him in a first-class compartment of the 4:15 down express, that he got in just as the train was leaving the London terminus and that he alighted at Blackwater station. The chairman then enquired whether I had held any communication with my fellow-traveller; whereupon I related, as nearly as I could remember it, the whole bulk and substance of Mr John Dwerrihouse's diffuse information respecting the new branch line.

To all this the board listened with profound attention, while the chairman presided and the secretary took notes. I then produced the cigar-case. It was passed from hand to hand, and recognised by all. There was not a man present who did not remember that plain cigar-case with its silver monogram, or to whom it seemed anything less than entirely corroborative of my evidence. When at length I had told all that I had to tell, the chairman whispered something to the secretary; the secretary touched a silver handbell, and the guard, Benjamin Somers, was ushered into the room. He was then examined as carefully as myself. He declared that he knew Mr John Dwerrihouse perfectly well, that he could not be mistaken in him, that he remembered going down with the 4:15 express on the afternoon in question, that he remembered me, and that, there being one or two empty first-class compartments on that especial afternoon, he had, in compliance with my request, placed me in a carriage by myself. He was positive that I remained alone in that compartment all the way from London to Clayborough. He was ready to take his oath that Dwerrihouse was neither in that carriage with me nor in any other compartment of that train. He remembered distinctly to have examined my ticket to Blackwater; was certain that there was no one else at that time in the carriage; could not have failed to observe a second person, if there had been one; had that second person been Mr John Dwerrihouse, should have quietly double-locked the door of the carriage and have at once given information to the Blackwater station-master. So clear, so decisive, so ready, was Somers with this testimony that the board looked fairly puzzled.

'You hear this person's statement, Mr Langford,'

said the chairman. 'It contradicts yours in every particular. What have you to say in reply?'

'I can only repeat what I said before. I am quite as positive of the truth of my own assertions as Mr Somers can be of the truth of his.'

'You say that Mr Dwerrihouse alighted in Blackwater, and that he was in possession of a private key. Are you sure that he had not alighted by means of that key before the guard came round for the tickets?'

'I am quite positive that he did not leave the carriage till the train had fairly entered the station, and the other Blackwater passengers alighted. I even saw that he was met there by a friend.'

'Indeed! Did you see that person distinctly?'

'Quite distinctly.'

'Can you describe his appearance?'

'I think so. He was short and very slight, sandy-haired, with a bushy moustache and beard, and he wore a closely fitting suit of grey tweed. His age I should take to be about thirty-eight or forty.'

'Did Mr Dwerrihouse leave the station in this person's company?'

'I cannot tell. I saw them walking together down the platform, and then I saw them standing inside under a gas-jet, talking earnestly. After that I lost sight of them quite suddenly, and just then my train went on, and I with it.'

The chairman and secretary conferred together in an undertone. The directors whispered to one another. One or two looked suspiciously at the guard. I could see that my evidence remained unshaken, and that, like myself, they suspected some complicity between the guard and the defaulter.

'How far did you conduct that 4:15 express on the day in question, Somers?' asked the chairman.

'All through, sir,' replied the guard, 'from London to Crampton.'

'How was it that you were not relieved at Clayborough? I thought there was always a change of guards at Clayborough.'

'There used to be, sir, till the new regulations came in force last midsummer, since when the guards in charge of express trains go the whole way through.'

The chairman turned to the secretary.

'I think it would be as well,' he said, 'if we had the daybook to refer to upon this point.'

Again the secretary touched the silver handbell, and desired the porter in attendance to summon Mr Raikes. From a word or two dropped by another of the directors I gathered that Mr Raikes was one of the under-secretaries.

He came, a small, slight, sandy-haired, keen-eyed man, with an eager, nervous manner, and a forest of light beard and moustache. He just showed himself at the door of the board-room, and, being requested to bring a certain daybook from a certain shelf in a certain room, bowed and vanished.

He was there such a moment, and the surprise of seeing him was so great and sudden, that it was not till the door had closed upon him that I found voice to speak. He was no sooner gone, however, than I sprang to my feet.

'That person,' I said, 'is the same who met Mr Dwerrihouse upon the platform at Blackwater!'

There was a general movement of surprise. The chairman looked grave and somewhat agitated.

'Take care, Mr Langford,' he said; 'take care what you say.'

'I am as positive of his identity as of my own.'

'Do you consider the consequences of your words? Do you consider that you are bringing a charge of the gravest character against one of the company's servants?'

'I am willing to be put upon my oath, if necessary. The man who came to that door a minute since is the same whom I saw talking with Mr Dwerrihouse on the Blackwater platform. Were he twenty times the company's servant, I could say neither more nor less.'

The chairman turned again to the guard.

'Did you see Mr Raikes in the train or on the platform?' he asked.

Somers shook his head. 'I am confident Mr Raikes was not in the train,' he said, 'and I certainly did not see him on the platform.'

The chairman turned next to the secretary.

'Mr Raikes is in your office, Mr Hunter,' he said. 'Can you remember if he was absent on the 4th instant?'

'I do not think he was,' replied the secretary, 'but I am not prepared to speak positively. I have been away most afternoons myself lately, and Mr Raikes might easily have absented himself if he had been disposed.'

At this moment the under-secretary returned with the daybook under his arm.

'Be pleased to refer, Mr Raikes,' said the chairman, 'to the entries of the 4th instant, and see what Benjamin Somers's duties were on that day.'

Mr Raikes threw open the cumbrous volume, and ran a practised eye and finger down some three or four successive columns of entries. Stopping suddenly at the foot of a page, he then read aloud that Benjamin Somers had on that day conducted the 4:15 express from London to Crampton.

The chairman leaned forward in his seat, looked the under-secretary full in the face, and said, quite sharply and suddenly: 'Where were you, Mr Raikes, on the same afternoon?'

'*I*, sir?'

'You, Mr Raikes. Where were you on the afternoon and evening of the 4th of the present month?'

'Here, sir, in Mr Hunter's office. Where else should I be?'

There was a dash of trepidation in the under-secretary's voice as he said this, but his look of surprise was natural enough.

'We have some reason for believing, Mr Raikes, that you were absent that afternoon without leave. Was this the case?'

'Certainly not, sir. I have not had a day's holiday since September. Mr Hunter will bear me out in this.'

Mr Hunter repeated what he had previously said on the subject, but added that the clerks in the adjoining office would be certain to know. Whereupon the senior clerk, a grave, middle-aged person in green glasses, was summoned and interrogated.

His testimony cleared the under-secretary at once. He declared that Mr Raikes had in no instance, to his knowledge, been absent during office hours since his return from his annual holiday in September.

I was confounded. The chairman turned to me

with a smile, in which a shade of covert annoyance was scarcely apparent.

'You hear, Mr Langford?' he said.

'I hear, sir; but my conviction remains unshaken.'

'I fear, Mr Langford, that your convictions are very insufficiently based,' replied the chairman, with a doubtful cough. 'I fear that you "dream dreams", and mistake them for actual occurrences. It is a dangerous habit of mind, and might lead to dangerous results. Mr Raikes here would have found himself in an unpleasant position had he not proved so satisfactory an abbi.'

I was about to reply, but he gave me no time.

'I think, gentlemen,' he went on to say, addressing the board, 'that we should be wasting time to push this inquiry further. Mr Langford's evidence would seem to be of an equal value throughout. The testimony of Benjamin Somers disproves his first statement, and the testimony of the last witness disproves his second. I think we may conclude that Mr Langford fell asleep in the train on the occasion of his journey to Clayborough, and dreamed an unusually vivid and circumstantial dream, of which, however, we have now heard quite enough.'

There are few things more annoying than to find one's positive convictions met with incredulity. I could not help feeling impatience at the turn that affairs had taken. I was not proof against the civil sarcasm of the chairman's manner. Most intolerable of all, however, was the quiet smile lurking about the corners of Benjamin Somers's mouth, and the half-triumphant, half-malicious gleam in the eyes of the under-secretary. The man was evidently puzzled and somewhat alarmed. His looks seemed furtively to interrogate me. Who was I? What did I want? Why had I come there to do him an ill turn with his employers? What was it to me whether or no he was absent without leave?

Seeing all this, and perhaps more irritated by it than the thing deserved, I begged leave to detain the attention of the board for a moment longer. Jelf plucked me impatiently by the sleeve.

'Better let the thing drop,' he whispered. 'The chairman's right enough; you dreamed it, and the less said now the better.'

I was not to be silenced, however, in this fashion. I had yet something to say, and I would say it. It was to this effect: that dreams were not usually productive of tangible results, and that I requested to know in what way the chairman conceived I had evolved from my dream so substantial and well-made a delusion as the cigar-case which I had had the honour to place before him at the commencement of our interview.

'The cigar-case, I admit, Mr Langford,' the chairman replied, 'is a very strong point in your evidence. It is your *only* strong point, however, and there is just a possibility that we may all be misled by a mere accidental resemblance. Will you permit me to see the case again?'

'It is unlikely,' I said, as I handed it to him, 'that any other should bear precisely this monogram, and also be in all other particulars exactly similar.'

The chairman examined it for a moment in silence, and then passed it to Mr Hunter. Mr Hunter turned it over and over, and shook his head.

'This is no mere resemblance,' he said. 'It is John Dwerrihouse's cigar-case to a certainty. I remember it perfectly; I have seen it a hundred times.'

'I believe I may say the same,' added the chairman; 'yet how account for the way in which Mr Langford asserts that it came into his possession?'

'I can only repeat,' I replied, 'that I found it on the floor of the carriage after Mr Dwerrihouse had alighted. It was in leaning out to look after him that I trod upon it, and it was in running after him for the purpose of restoring it that I saw, or believed I saw, Mr Raikes standing aside with him in earnest conversation.'

Again I felt Jonathan Jelf plucking at my sleeve.

'Look at Raikes,' he whispered; 'look at Raikes!'

I turned to where the under-secretary had been standing a moment before, and saw him, white as death, with lips trembling and livid, stealing towards the door.

To conceive a sudden, strange and indefinite suspicion, to fling myself in his way, to take him by the shoulders as if he were a child, and turn his craven face, perforce, towards the board, were with me the work of an instant.

'Look at him!' I exclaimed. 'Look at his face! I ask no better witness to the truth of my words.'

The chairman's brow darkened.

'Mr Raikes,' he said, sternly, 'if you know anything you had better speak.'

Vainly trying to wrench himself from my grasp, the under-secretary stammered out an incoherent denial.

'Let me go,' he said. 'I know nothing – you have no right to detain me – let me go!'

'Did you, or did you not, meet Mr John Dwerrihouse at Blackwater station? The charge brought against you is either true or false. If true, you will do well to throw yourself upon the mercy of the board and make full confession of all that you know.'

The under-secretary wrung his hands in an agony of helpless terror. 'I was away!' he cried. 'I was two hundred miles away at the time! I know nothing about it – I have nothing to confess – I am innocent – I call God to witness I am innocent!'

'Two hundred miles away!' echoed the chairman. 'What do you mean?'

'I was in Devonshire. I had three weeks' leave of absence – I appeal to Mr Hunter – Mr Hunter knows I had three weeks' leave of absence! I was in Devonshire all the time; I can prove I was in Devonshire!'

Seeing him so abject, so incoherent, so wild with apprehension, the directors began to whisper gravely among themselves, while one got quietly up and called the porter to guard the door.

'What has your being in Devonshire to do with the matter?' said the chairman. 'When were you in Devonshire?'

'Mr Raikes took his leave in September,' said the secretary, 'about the time when Mr Dwerrihouse disappeared.'

'I never even heard that he had disappeared till I came back!'

'That must remain to be proved,' said the chairman. 'I shall at once put this matter in the hands of the police. In the meanwhile, Mr Raikes, being myself a magistrate and used to dealing with these cases, I advise you to offer no resistance but to confess while confession may yet do you service. As for your accomplice—'

The frightened wretch fell upon his knees.

'I had no accomplice!' he cried. 'Only have mercy upon me – only spare my life, and I will confess all! I didn't mean to harm him! I didn't mean to hurt a hair of his head! Only have mercy upon me, and let me go!'

The chairman rose in his place, pale and agitated.

'Good heavens!' he exclaimed, 'what horrible mystery is this? What does it mean?'

'As sure as there is a God in heaven,' said Jonathan Jelf, 'it means that murder has been done.'

'No! no! no!' shrieked Raikes, still upon his knees, and cowering like a beaten hound, 'not murder! No jury that ever sat could bring it in murder. I thought I had only stunned him – I never meant to do more than stun him! Manslaughter – manslaughter – not murder!'

Overcome by the horror of this unexpected revelation, the chairman covered his face with his hand and for a moment or two remained silent.

'Miserable man,' he said at length, 'you have betrayed yourself.'

'You bade me confess! You urged me to throw myself upon the mercy of the board!'

'You have confessed to a crime which no one suspected you of having committed,' replied the chairman, 'and which this board has no power either to punish or forgive. All that I can do for you is to advise you to submit to the law, to plead guilty, and to conceal nothing. When did you do this deed?'

The guilty man rose to his feet, and leaned heavily against the table. His answer came reluctantly, like the speech of one dreaming.

'On the 22nd of September!'

On the 22nd of September! I looked in Jonathan Jelf's face, and he in mine. I felt my own smiling with a strange sense of wonder and dread. I saw his blanch suddenly, even to the lips.

'Merciful Heaven!' he whispered. '*What was it, then, that you saw in the train?*'

What was it that I saw in the train? That question remains unanswered to this day. I have never been able to reply to it. I only know that it bore the living likeness of the murdered man, whose body had then been lying some ten weeks under a rough pile of branches and brambles and rotting leaves at the bottom of a deserted chalk-pit about halfway between Blackwater and Mallingford. I know that it spoke and moved and looked as that man spoke and moved and looked in life; that I heard, or seemed to hear, things revealed which I could never otherwise have learned; that I was guided, as it were, by that vision on the platform to the identification of the murderer; and that, a passive instrument myself, I was destined, by means of these mysterious teachings to bring about the ends of justice. For these things I have never been able to account.

As for that matter of the cigar-case, it proved, on enquiry, that the carriage in which I travelled down that afternoon to Clayborough had not been in use for several weeks, and was, in point of fact, the same in which poor John Dwerrihouse had performed his last journey. The case had doubtless been dropped by him, and had lain unnoticed till I found it.

Upon the details of the murder I have no need to dwell. Those who desire more ample particulars may find them, and the written confession of Augustus Raikes, in the files of *The Times* for 1856. Enough that the under-secretary, knowing the history of the new line, and following the negotiation step by step through all its stages, determined to waylay Mr Dwerrihouse, rob him of the seventy-five thousand pounds and escape to America with his booty.

In order to effect these ends he obtained leave of absence a few days before the time appointed for the payment of the money, secured his passage across the Atlantic in a steamer advertised to start on the 23rd, provided himself with a heavily loaded 'life-preserver', and went down to Blackwater to await the arrival of his victim. How he met him on the platform with a pretended message from the board, how he offered to conduct him by a short cut across the fields to Mallingford, how, having brought him to a lonely place, he struck him down with the life-preserver, and so killed him, and how, finding what he had done, he dragged the body to the verge of an out-of-the-way chalk-pit, and there flung it in and piled it over with branches and brambles, are facts still fresh in the memories of those who, like the connoisseurs in De Quincey's famous essay, regard murder as a fine art. Strangely enough, the murderer having done his work, was afraid to leave the country. He declared that he had not intended to take the director's life, but only to stun and rob him and that, finding the blow had killed, he dared not fly for fear of drawing down suspicion upon his head. As a mere robber he would have been safe in the States, but as a murderer he would inevitably have been pursued and given up to justice. So he forfeited his passage, returned to the office as usual at the end of his leave, and locked up his ill-gotten thousands till a more convenient opportunity. In the meanwhile he had the satisfaction of finding that Mr Dwerrihouse was universally believed to have absconded with the money, no one knew how or whither.

Whether he meant murder or not, however, Mr Augustus Raikes paid the full penalty of his crime, and was hanged at the Old Bailey in the second week of January 1857. Those who desire to make his further acquaintance may see him any day (admirably done in wax) in the Chamber of Horrors at Madame Tussaud's exhibition in Baker Street. He is there to be found in the midst of a select society of ladies and gentlemen of atrocious memory, dressed in the close-cut tweed suit which he wore on the evening of the murder and holding in his hand the identical life-preserver with which he committed it.

DIVERSIONS

Sir Arthur Quiller-Couch

Cuckoo Valley Railway

This century was still young and ardent when ruin fell upon Cuckoo Valley. Its head rested on the slope of a high and sombre moorland scattered with granite and china-clay; and by the small town of Ponteglos, where it widened out into arable and grey pasture-land, the Cuckoo River grew deep enough to float up vessels of small tonnage from the coast at the spring tides. I have seen there the boom of a trading schooner brush the grasses on the river-bank as she came before a westerly wind, and the haymakers stop and almost crick their necks staring up at her top-sails. But between the moors and Ponteglos the valley wound for fourteen miles or so between secular woods, so steeply converging that for the most part no more room was left at the bottom of the V than the river itself filled. The fisherman beside it trampled on pimpernels, sundew, watermint, and asphodels, or pushed between clumps of *Osmunda regalis* that overtopped him by a couple of feet. If he took to wading, there was much ado to stand against the current. Only here and there it spread into a still black pool, greased with eddies;

and beside such a pool, it was odds that he found a diminutive meadow, green and flat as a billiard-table, and edged with clumps of fern. To think of Cuckoo Valley is to call up the smell of that fern as it wrapped at the bottom of the creel the day's catch of salmon-peal and trout.

The town of Tregarrick (which possessed a gaol, a workhouse, and a lunatic asylum, and called itself the centre of the Duchy) stood three miles back from the lip of this happy valley, whither on summer evenings its burghers rambled to eat cream and junket at the Dairy Farm by the river bank, and afterwards sit to watch the fish rise, while the youngsters and maidens played at hide-and-seek in the woods. But there came a day when the names of Watt and Stephenson waxed great in the land, and these slow citizens caught the railway frenzy. They took it, however, in their own fashion. They never dreamed of connecting themselves with other towns and a larger world, but of aggrandisement by means of a railway that should run from Tregarrick to nowhere in particular, and bring the intervening wealth to their doors. They planned a railway that should join Tregarrick with Cuckoo Valley, and there divide into two branches, the one bringing ore and clay from the moors, the other fetching up sand and coal from the sea.

Surveyors and engineers descended upon the woods; then a cloud of navvies. The days were filled with the crash of falling timber and the rush of emptied trucks. The stream was polluted, the fish died, the fairies were evicted from their rings beneath the oak, the morals of the junketing houses underwent change. The vale knew itself no longer; its smoke went up week by week with the noise of pick-axes and oaths.

On August 13th, 1834, the Mayor of Tregarrick declared the new line open, and a locomotive was run along its rails to Dunford Bridge, at the foot of the moors. The engine was christened *The Wonder of the Age*; and I have before me a handbill of the festivities of that proud day, which tells me that the mayor himself rode in an open truck, "embellished with Union Jacks, lions and unicorns, and other loyal devices." And then Nature settled down to heal her wounds, and the Cuckoo Valley Railway to pay no dividend to its promoters.

It is now two years and more since, on an August day, I wound up my line by Dunford Bridge, and sauntered towards the Light Horseman Inn, two gunshots up the road. The time was four o'clock, or thereabouts, and a young couple sat on a bench by the inn-door, drinking cocoa out of one cup. Above their heads and along the house-front a vine-tree straggled, but its foliage was too thin to afford a speck of shade as they sat there in the eye of the westering sun. The man (aged about one-and-twenty) wore the uncomfortable Sunday-best of a mechanic, with a shrivelled, but still enormous, bunch of Sweet-William in his buttonhole. The girl was dressed in a bright green gown and a white bonnet. Both were flushed and perspiring, and I still think they must have ordered hot cocoa in haste, and were repenting it at leisure. They lifted their eyes, and blushed with a yet warmer red as I passed into the porch.

Two men were seated in the cool tap-room, each with a pasty and a mug of beer. A composition of sweat and coal-dust had caked their faces, and so deftly smoothed all distinction out of their features that it seemed at the moment natural and proper to take them for twins. Perhaps this was an error: perhaps, too, their appearance of extreme age was produced by the dark grey dust that overlaid so much of them as showed above the table. As twins, however, I remember them, and cannot shake off the impression that they had remained twins for an unusual number of years.

One addressed me. "Parties outside pretty comfortable?" he asked.

"They were drinking out of the same cup," I answered.

He nodded. "Made man and wife this mornin'. I don't fairly know what's best to do. Lord knows I wouldn' hurry their soft looks and dilly-dallyin'; but did 'ee notice how much beverage was left in the cup?"

"They was mated at Tregarrick, half-after-nine this mornin'," observed the other twin, pulling out a great watch, "and we brought 'em down here in a truck for their honeymoon. The agreement was for an afternoon in the woods; but by crum! sir, they've sat there and held one another's hand for up'ards of an hour after the stated time to start. And we ha'nt the heart to tell 'em so."

He walked across to the window and peered over the blind.

"There's a mort of grounds in the cocoa that's sold here," he went on, after a look, "and 'tisn't the sort that does the stomach good, neither. For their own sakes, I'll give the word to start, and chance their thankin' me some day later when they learn what things be made of."

The other twin arose, shook the crumbs off his trousers, and stretched himself. I guessed now that this newly-married pair had delayed traffic at the Dunford terminus of the Cuckoo Valley Railway for almost an hour and a half; and I determined to travel into Tregarrick by the same train.

So we strolled out of the inn towards the line, the lovers following, arm-in-arm, some fifty paces behind.

"How far is it to the station?" I inquired.

The twins stared at me.

Presently we turned down a lane scored with dry ruts, passed an oak plantation, and came on a clearing where the train stood ready. The line did not finish: it ended in a heap of sand. There were eight trucks, seven of them laden with granite, and an engine, with a prodigiously long funnel, bearing the name *The Wonder of the Age* in brass letters along its boiler.

"Now," said one of the twins, while the other raked up the furnace, "you can ride in the empty truck with the lovers, or on the engine along with us—which you like."

I chose the engine. We climbed on board, gave a loud whistle, and jolted off. Far down, on our right, the river shone between the trees, and these trees, encroaching on the track, almost joined their branches above us. Ahead, the moss that grew upon the sleepers gave the line the appearance of a green glade, and the grasses, starred with golden-rod and mallow, grew tall to the very edge of the rails. It seemed that in a few more years Nature would cover this scar of 1834, and score the return match against man. Rails, engine, officials, were already no better than ghosts: youth and progress lay in the pushing trees, the salmon leaping against the dam below, the young man and maid sitting with clasped hands and amatory looks in the hindmost truck.

At the end of three miles or so we gave an alarming whistle, and slowed down a bit. The trees were thinner here, and I saw that a highroad came down the hill, and cut across our track some fifty yards ahead. We prepared to cross it cautiously.

"Ho—o—oy! Stop!"

The brake was applied, and as we came to a standstill a party of men and women descended the hill towards us.

"'Tis Susan Warne's seventh goin' to be christen'd, by the look of it," said the engine-driver beside me; "an', by crum! we've got the Kimbly."

The procession advanced. In the midst walked a stout woman, carrying a baby in long clothes, and in front a man bearing in both hands a plate covered with a white cloth. He stepped up beside the train, and, almost before I had time to be astonished, a large yellow cake was thrust into my hands. Engine-driver and stoker were also presented with a cake a-piece, and then the newly-married pair, who took and ate with some shyness and giggling.

"Is it a boy or a girl?" asked the stoker, with his mouth full.

"A boy," the man answered; "and I count it good luck that you men of modern ways should be the first we meet on our way to church. The child 'll be a go-ahead if there's truth in omens."

"You're right, naybour. We're the speediest men in this part of the universe, I d' believe. Here's luck to 'ee, Susan Warne!" he piped out, addressing one of the women; "an' if you want a name for your seventh, you may christen 'en after the engine here, *The Wonder of the Age*."

We waved our hats and jolted off again towards Tregarrick. At the end of the journey the railway officials declined to charge for the pleasure of my company. But after some dispute, they agreed to compromise by adjourning to the Railway Inn, and drinking prosperity to Susan Warne's seventh.

Amelia B. Edwards

The Engineer

His name, Sir, was Matthew Price; mine is Benjamin Hardy. We were born within a few days of each other; bred up in the same village; taught at the same school. I cannot remember the time when we were not close friends. Even as boys, we never knew what it was to quarrel. We had not a thought, we had not a possession, that was not in common. We would have stood by each other, fearlessly, to the death. It was such a friendship as one reads about sometimes in books; fast and firm as the great Tors upon our native moorlands, true as the sun in the heavens.

The name of our village was Chadleigh. Lifted high above the pasture flats which stretched away at our feet like a measureless green lake and melted into mist on the furthest horizon, it nestled, a tiny stone-built hamlet, in a sheltered hollow about midway between the plain and the plateau. Above us, rising ridge beyond ridge, slope beyond slope, spread the mountainous moor-country, bare and bleak for the most part, with here and there a patch of cultivated field or hardy plantation, and crowned highest of all with masses of huge grey crag, abrupt, isolated, hoary, and older than the deluge. These were the Tors—Druids' Tor, King's Tor, Castle Tor, and the like; sacred places, as I have heard, in the ancient time, where crownings, burnings, human sacrifices, and all kinds of bloody heathen rites were performed. Bones, too, have been found there, and arrow-heads, and ornaments of gold and glass. I had a vague awe of the Tors in those boyish days, and would not have gone near them after dark for the heaviest bribe.

I have said that we were born in the same village. He was the son of a small farmer, named William Price, and the eldest of a family of seven; I was the only child of Ephraim Hardy, the Chadleigh blacksmith—a well-known man in those parts, whose memory is not forgotten to this day. Just so far as a farmer is supposed to be a bigger man than a blacksmith, Mat's father might be said to have a better standing than mine; but William Price with his small holding and his seven boys, was, in fact, as poor as many a day-labourer; whilst, the blacksmith, well-to-do, bustling, popular, and open-handed, was a person of some importance in the place.

All this, however, had nothing to do with Mat and myself. It never occurred to either of us that his jacket was out at elbows, or that our mutual funds came altogether from my pocket. It was enough for us that we sat on the same school-bench, conned our tasks from the same primer, fought each other's battles, screened each other's faults, fished, nutted, played truant, robbed orchards and birds' nests together, and spent every half-hour, authorised or stolen, in each others' society. It was a happy time; but it could not go on for ever. My father, being prosperous, resolved to put me forward in the world. I must know more, and do better, than himself. The forge was not good enough, the little world of Chadleigh not wide enough, for me. Thus it happened that I was still swinging the satchel when Mat was whistling at the plough, and that at last, when my future course was shaped out, we were separated, as it then seemed to us, for life. For, blacksmith's son as I was, furnace and forge, in some form or other, pleased me best, and I chose to be a working engineer. So my father by-and-by apprenticed me to a Birmingham iron-master; and, having bidden farewell to Mat, and Chadleigh, and the grey old Tors in the shadow of which I had spent all the days of my life, I turned my face northward, and went over into 'the Black Country'.

I am not going to dwell on this part of my story. How I worked out the term of my apprenticeship; how, when I had served my full time and become a skilled workman, I took Mat from the plough and brought him over to the Black Country, sharing with him lodging, wages, experience—all, in short, that I had to give; how he, naturally quick to learn and brimful of quiet energy, worked his way up a step at a time, and came by-and-by to be a 'first hand' in his own department; how, during all these years of change, and trial, and effort, the old boyish affection never wavered or weakened, but went on, growing with our growth and strengthening with our strength—are facts which I need do no more than outline in this place.

About this time—it will be remembered that I speak of the days when Mat and I were on the bright side of thirty—it happened that our firm contracted to supply six first-class locomotives to run on the new line, then in process of construction, between Turin and Genoa. It was the first Italian order we had taken. We had had dealings with France, Holland, Belgium, Germany; but never with Italy. The connection, therefore, was new and valuable—all the more valuable because our Transalpine neighbours had but lately begun to lay down the iron roads, and would be safe to need more of our good English work as they went on. So the Birmingham firm set themselves to the contract with a will, lengthened our working hours, increased our wages, took on fresh hands, and determined, if energy and promptitude could do it, to place themselves at the head of the Italian labour-market, and stay there. They deserved and achieved success. The six locomotives were not only turned out to time, but were shipped, dispatched and delivered with a promptitude that fairly amazed our Piedmontese consignee. I was not a little proud, you may be sure, when I found myself appointed to superintend the transport of the engines. Being allowed a couple of assistants, I contrived that Mat should be one of them; and thus we enjoyed together the first great holiday of our lives.

It was a wonderful change for two Birmingham operatives fresh from the Black Country. The fairy city, with its crescent background of Alps; the port crowded with strange shipping; the marvellous blue sky and the bluer sea; the painted houses on the quays; the quaint cathedral, faced with black and white marble; the street of jewellers, like an Arabian Nights' bazaar; the street of palaces, with its Moorish courtyards, its fountains and orange trees; the women veiled like brides; the galley-slaves chained two and two; the processions of priests and friars; the everlasting clangour of bells; the babble of a strange tongue; the singular lightness and brightness of the climate—made, altogether such a combination of wonders that we wandered about, the first day, in a kind of bewildered dream, like children at a fair. Before that week was ended, being tempted by the beauty of the place and the liberality of the pay, we had agreed to take service with the Turin and Genoa Railway Company, and to turn our backs upon Birmingham for ever.

Then began a new life—a life so active and healthy, so steeped in fresh air and sunshine, that we sometimes marvelled how we could have endured the gloom of the Black Country. We were constantly up and down the line; now at Genoa, now at Turin, taking trial trips with the locomotives, and placing our old experiences at the service of our new employers.

In the meanwhile we made Genoa our headquarters, and hired a couple of rooms over a small shop in a bystreet sloping down to the quays. Such a busy little street—so steep and winding that no vehicles could pass through it, and so narrow that the sky looked like a mere strip of deep blue ribbon overhead! Every house in it, however, was a shop, where the goods encroached on the footway, or were piled about the door, or hung like tapestry from the balconies; and all day long, from dawn to dusk, an incessant stream of passers-by poured up and down between the port and the upper quarter of the city.

THE ENGINEER

Our landlady was the widow of a silver-worker, and lived by the sale of filigree ornaments, cheap jewellery, combs, fans and toys in ivory and jet. She had an only daughter named Gianetta, who served in the shop, and was simply the most beautiful woman I ever beheld. Looking back across this weary chasm of years, and bringing her image before me (as I can and do) with all the vividness of life, I am unable, even now, to detect a flaw in her beauty. I do not attempt to describe her. I do not believe there is a poet living who could find the words to do it; but I once saw a picture that was somewhat like her (not half so lovely, but still like her), and, for aught I know, that picture is still hanging where I last looked at it—upon the walls of the Louvre. It represented a woman with brown eyes and golden hair, looking over her shoulder into a circular mirror held by a bearded man in the background. In this man, as I then understood, the artist had painted his own portrait; in her, the portrait of the woman he loved. No picture that I ever saw was half so beautiful, and yet it was not worthy to be named in the same breath with Gianetta Coneglia.

You may be certain the widow's shop did not want for customers. All Genoa knew how fair a face was to be seen behind that dingy little counter; and Gianetta, flirt as she was, had more lovers than she cared to remember, even by name. Gentle and simple, rich and poor, from the red-capped sailor buying his ear-rings or his amulet, to the nobleman carelessly purchasing half the filigrees in the window, she treated them all alike—encouraged them, laughed at them, led them on and turned them off at her pleasure. She had no more heart than a marble statue; as Mat and I discovered by-and-by, to our bitter cost.

I cannot tell to this day how it came about, or what first led me to suspect how things were going with us both; but long before the waning of that autumn a coldness had sprung up between my friend and myself. It was nothing that could have been put into words. It was nothing that either of us could have explained or justified, to save his life. We lodged together, ate together, worked together, exactly as before; we even took our long evening's walk together, when the day's labour was ended; and except, perhaps, that we were more silent than of old, no mere looker-on could have detected a shadow of change. Yet there it was, silent and subtle, widening the gulf between us every day.

It was not his fault. He was too true and gentle-hearted to have willingly brought about such a state of things between us. Neither do I believe—fiery as my nature is—that it was mine. It was all hers—hers from first to last—the sin, and the shame, and the sorrow.

If she had shown a fair and open preference for either of us, no real harm could have come of it. I would have put any constraint upon myself, and, Heaven knows! have borne any suffering, to see Mat really happy. I know that he would have done the same, and more if he could, for me. But Gianetta cared not one sou for either. She never meant to choose between us. It gratified her vanity to divide us; it amused her to play with us. It would pass my power to tell how, by a thousand imperceptible shades of coquetry—by the lingering of a glance, the substitution of a word, the flitting of a smile—she contrived to turn our heads, and torture our hearts, and lead us on to love her. She deceived us both. She buoyed us both up with hope; she maddened us with jealousy; she crushed us with despair. For my part, when I seemed to wake to a sudden sense of the ruin that was about our path and I saw how the truest friendship that ever bound two lives together was drifting on to wreck and ruin, I asked myself whether any woman in the world was worth what Mat had been to me and I to him. But this was not often. I was readier to shut my eyes upon the truth than to face it; and so lived on; wilfully, in a dream.

Thus the autumn passed away, and winter

came—the strange treacherous Genoese winter, green with olive and flex, brilliant with sunshine, and bitter with storm. Still, rivals at heart and friends on the surface, Mat and I lingered on in our lodgings in the Vicolo Balba. Still Gianetta held us with her fatal wiles and her still more fatal beauty. At length there came a day when I felt I could bear the horrible misery and suspense of it no longer. The sun, I vowed, should not go down before I knew my sentence. She must choose between us. She must either take me or let me go. I was reckless. I was desperate. I was determined to know the worst, or the best. If the worst, I would at once turn by back upon Genoa, upon her, upon all the pursuits and purposes of my past life, and begin the world anew. This I told her, passionately and sternly, standing before her in the little parlour at the back of the shop, one bleak December morning.

'If it's Mat whom you care for most,' I said, 'tell me so in one word, and I will never trouble you again. He is better worth your love. I am jealous and exacting; he is as trusting and unselfish as a woman. Speak, Gianetta; am I to bid you good-bye for ever and ever, or am I to write home to my mother in England, bidding her pray to God to bless the woman who has promised to be my wife?'

'You plead your friend's cause well,' she replied,

haughtily. 'Matteo ought to be grateful. This is more than he ever did for you.'

'Give me my answer, for pity's sake,' I exclaimed, 'and let me go!'

'You are free to go or stay, Signor Inglese,' she replied. 'I am not your jailor.'

'Do you bid me leave you?'

'Beata Madre! Not I.'

'Will you marry me, if I stay?'

She laughed aloud—such a merry, mocking, musical laugh, like a chime of silver bells!

'You ask too much,' she said.

'Only what you have led me to hope these five or six months past!'

'That is just what Matteo says. How tiresome you both are!'

'O, Gianetta,' I said passionately, 'be serious for one moment! I am a rough fellow, it is true—not half good enough or clever enough for you; but I love you with my whole heart, and an Emperor could do no more.'

'I am glad of it,' she replied, 'I do not want you to love me less.'

'Then you cannot wish to make me wretched! Will you promise me?'

'I promise nothing,' said she, with another burst of laughter; 'except that I will not marry Matteo!'

Except that she would not marry Matteo! Only that. Not a word of hope for myself. Nothing but my friend's condemnation. I might get comfort, and selfish triumph, and some sort of base assurance out of that, if I could. And so, to my shame, I did. I grasped at the vain encouragement, and, fool that I was, let her put me off again unanswered. From that day, I gave up all effort at self-control, and let myself drift blindly on—to destruction.

At length things became so bad between Mat and myself that it seemed as if an open rupture must be at hand. We avoided each other, scarcely exchanged a dozen sentences in a day, and fell away from all our old familiar habits. At this time—I shudder to remember it—there were moments when I felt that I hated him.

Thus, with the trouble deepening and widening between us day by day, another month or five weeks went by; and February came; and, with February, the Carnival. They said in Genoa that it was a particularly dull carnival; and so it must have been; for, save a flag or two hung out in some of the principal streets, and a sort of fiesta look about the women, there were no special indications of the season. It was, I think, the second day when, having been on the line all the morning. I returned to Genoa at dusk, and, to my surprise, found Mat Price on the platform. He came up to me, and laid his hand on my arm.

'You are in late,' he said, 'I have been waiting for you three-quarters of an hour. Shall we dine together today?'

Impulsive as I am, this evidence of returning goodwill at once called up my better feelings.

'With all my heart, Mat,' I replied, 'shall we go to Gozzoli's?'

'No, no,' he said, hurriedly. 'Some quieter place—some place where we can talk. I have something to say to you.'

I noticed now that he looked pale and agitated, and an uneasy sense of apprehension stole upon me. We decided on the 'Pescatore,' a little out-of-the-way trattoria, down near the Malo Vecchio. There, in a dingy salon, frequented chiefly by seamen, and redolent of tobacco, we ordered our simple dinner. Mat scarcely swallowed a morsel; but, calling presently for a bottle of Sicilian wine, drank eagerly.

'Well, Mat,' I said, as the last dish was placed on the table, 'what news have you?'

'Bad.'

'I guessed that from your face.'

'Bad for you—bad for me, Gianetta.'

'What of Gianetta?'

He passed his hand nervously across his lips.

'Gianetta is false—worse than false,' he said, in a hoarse voice. 'She values an honest man's heart just as she values a flower for her half—wears it for a day, then throws it aside for ever. She has cruelly wronged us both.'

'In what way? Good Heavens, speak out!'

'In the worst way that a woman can wrong those who love her. She has sold herself to the Marchese Loredano.'

The blood rushed to my head and face in a burning torrent. I could scarcely see, and dared not trust myself to speak.

'I saw her going towards the cathedral,' he went on, hurriedly. 'It was about three hours ago. I thought she might be going to confession, so I hung back and followed her at a distance. When she got inside, however, she went straight to the back of the pulpit, where this man was waiting for her. You remember him—an old man who used to haunt the shop a month or two back. Well, seeing how deep in conversation they were, and how they stood close under the pulpit with their backs towards the church. I fell into a passion of anger and went straight up the aisle, intending to say or do something; I scarcely knew what; but at all events, to draw her arm through mine, and take her home. When I came within a few feet, however, and found only a big pillar between myself and them, I paused. They could not see me, nor I them; but I could hear their voices distinctly, and—I listened.'

'Well, and you heard—.'

'The terms of a shameful bargain—beauty on the one side, gold on the other; so many thousand francs a year; a villa near Naples—Pah! it makes me sick to repeat it.'

And, with a shudder, he poured out another glass of wine and drank it at a draught.

'After that,' he said, presently, 'I made no effort to bring her away. The whole thing was so cold-blooded, so deliberate, so shameful, that I felt I had only to wipe her out of my memory, and leave her to her fate. I stole out of the cathedral, and walked about here by the sea for ever so long, trying to get my thoughts straight. Then I remembered you, Ben; and the recollection of how this wanton had come between us and broken up our lives drove me wild. So I went up to the station and waited for you. I felt you ought to know it all; and I thought, perhaps, that we might go back to England together.'

'The Marchese Loredano!'

It was all that I could say; all that I could think. As Mat had just said of himself, I felt 'like one stunned'.

'There is one other thing I may as well tell you,' he added, reluctantly, 'if only to show you how false a woman can be. We—we were to have been married next month.'

'We? Who? What do you mean?'

'I mean that we were to have been married—Gianetta and I.'

A sudden storm of rage, of scorn, of incredulity, swept over me at this, and seemed to carry my senses away.

'You!' I cried out. 'Gianetta marry you! I don't believe it.'

'I wish I had not believed it,' he replied, looking up as if puzzled by my vehemence. 'But she promised me; and I thought, when she promised it, she meant it.'

'She told me, weeks ago, that she would never be your wife!'

His colour rose, his brow darkened; but when his answer came, it was as calm as the last.

'Indeed!' he said. 'Then it is only one baseness more. She told me that she had refused you; and that was why we kept our engagement secret.'

'Tell the truth, Mat Price,' I said, well-nigh beside myself with suspicion. 'Confess that every word of this is false! Confess that Gianetta will not listen to you, and that you are afraid I may succeed where you have failed. As perhaps I shall—as perhaps I shall, after all!'

'Are you mad?' he exlaimed. 'What do you mean?'

'That I believe it's just a trick to get me away to England—that I don't credit a syllable of your story. You're a liar, and I hate you!'

He rose, and, lying one hand on the back of his chair, looked me sternly in the face.

'If you were not Benjamin Hardy,' he said, deliberately, 'I would thrash you within an inch of your life.'

The words had no sooner passed his lips than I sprang at him. I have never been able distinctly to remember what followed. A curse—a blow—a struggle—a moment of blind fury—a cry—a confusion of tongues—a circle of strange faces. Then I see Mat lying back in the arms of a bystander; myself trembling and bewildered—the knife dropping from my grasp; blood upon the floor; blood upon my hands; blood upon his shirt. And then I hear those dreadful words:

'O, Ben, you have murdered me!'

He did not die—at least, not there and then. He was carried to the nearest hospital, and lay for some weeks between life and death. His case, they said, was difficult and dangerous. The knife had gone in just below the collar-bone, and pierced down into the lungs. He was not allowed to speak or turn—scarcely to breathe with freedom. He might not even lift his head to drink. I sat by him day and night all through that sorrowful time. I gave up my situation on the railway; I quitted my lodging in the Vicolo Balba; I tried to forget that such a woman as Gianetta Coneglia had ever drawn breath. I lived only for Mat; and he tried to live more, I believe, for my sake than his own. Thus, in the bitter silent hours of pain and penitence, when no hand but mine approached his lips or smoothed his pillow, the old friendship came back with even more than its old trust and faithfulness. He forgave me, fully and freely; and I would thankfully have given my life for him.

At length there came one bright spring morning, when, dismissed as convalescent, he tottered out through the hospital gates, leaning on my arm, and feeble as an infant. He was not cured; neither, as I then learned to my horror and anguish, was it possible that he ever could be cured. He might live, with care, for some years; but the lungs were injured beyond hope of remedy, and a strong or healthy man he could never be again. These, spoken aside to me, were the parting words of the chief physician, who advised me to take him further south without delay.

I took him to a little coast-town called Rocca,

some thirty miles beyond Genoa—a sheltered lonely place along the Riviera, where the sea was even bluer than the sky, and the cliffs were green with strange tropical plants, cacti, and aloes, and Egyptian palms. Here we lodged in the house of a small tradesman; and Mat, to use his own words, 'set to work at getting well in good earnest'. But, alas! it was a work which no earnestness could forward. Day after day he went down to the beach, and sat for hours drinking the sea air and watching the sails that came and went in the offing.

By-and-by he could go no further than the garden of the house in which we lived. A little later, and he spent his days on a couch beside the open window, waiting patiently for the end. Ay, for the end! It had come to that. He was fading fast, waning with the waning summer, and conscious that the Reaper was at hand. His whole aim now was to soften the agony of my remorse, and prepare me for what must shortly come.

'I would not live longer, if I could,' he said, lying on his couch one summer evening, and looking up to the stars. 'If I had my choice at this moment, I would ask to go. I should like Gianetta to know that I forgave her.'

'She shall know it,' I said, trembling suddenly from head to foot.

He pressed my hand.

'And you'll write to father?'

'I will.'

I had drawn a little back, that he might not see the tears raining down my cheeks; but he raised himself on his elbow, and looked round.

'Don't fret, Ben,' he whispered; laid his head back wearily upon the pillow—and so died.

And this was the end of it. This was the end of all that made life life to me. I buried him there, in hearing of the wash of a strange sea on a strange shore. I stayed by the grave till the priest and the bystanders were gone. I saw the earth filled in to the last sod, and the gravedigger stamped it down with his feet. Then, and not till then, I felt that I had lost him for ever—the friend I had loved, and hated, and slain. Then, and not till then, I knew that all rest, and joy, and hope were over for me. From that moment my heart hardened within me, and my life was filled with loathing. Day and night, land and sea, labour and rest, food and sleep, were alike hateful to me. It was the curse of Cain, and that my brother had pardoned me made it lie none the lighter. Peace on earth was for me no more, and goodwill towards men was dead in my heart for ever. Remorse softens some natures; but it poisoned mine. I hated all mankind; but above all mankind I hated the woman who had come between us two, and ruined both our lives.

He had bidden me seek her out, and be the messenger of his forgiveness. I had sooner have gone down to the port of Genoa and taken upon me the serge cap and shotted chain of any galley-slave at his toil in the public works; but for all that I did my best to obey him. I went back, alone and on foot. I went back, intending to say to her, 'Gianetta Coneglia, he forgave you; but God never will.' But she was gone. The little shop was let to a fresh occupant; and the neighbours only knew that mother and daughter had left the place quite suddenly, and that Gianetta was supposed to be under the 'protection' of the Marchese Loredano. How I made inquiries here and there—how I heard that they had gone to Naples—and how, being restless and reckless of my time, I worked my passage in a French steamer, and followed her—how, having found the sumptuous villa that was now hers, I learned that she had left there some ten days and gone to Paris, where the Marchese was ambassador for the Two Sicilies—how, working my passage back again to Marseilles, and thence, in part by the river and in part by the rail, I made my way to Paris—how, day after day, I paced the streets and the parks, watched at the ambassador's gates, followed his carriage, and at last, after weeks of waiting, discovered her address—how, having written to request an interview, her servants spurned me from her door and flung my letter in my face—how, looking up at her windows, I then, instead of forgiving, solemnly cursed her with the bitterest curses my tongue could devise—and how, this done. I shook the dust of Paris from my feet, and became a wanderer upon the face of the earth, are facts which I have now no space to tell.

The next six or eight years of my life were shifting and unsettled enough. A morose and restless man, I took employment here and there, as opportunity offered, turning my hand to many things, and caring little what I earned, so long as the work was hard and the change incessant. First of all I engaged myself as chief engineer in one of the French steamers plying between Marseilles and Constantinople. At Constantinople I changed to one of the Austrian Lloyd's boats, and worked for some time to and from Alexandria, Jaffa, and those parts. After that, I fell in with a party of Mr Layard's men at Cairo, and so went up the Nile and took a turn at the excavations of the mound of Nimroud.

Then I became a working engineer on the new desert line between Alexandria and Suez; and by-and-by I worked my passage out to Bombay, and took service as an engine fitter on one of the great Indian railways. I stayed a long time in India; that is to say, I stayed nearly two years, which was a long time for me; and I might not even have left so soon, but for the war that was declared just then with Russia. That tempted me. For I loved danger and hardship as other men love safety and ease; and as for my life. I had sooner have parted from it than kept it, any day. So I came straight back to England; betook myself to Portsmouth, where my testimonials at once procured me the sort of berth I wanted. I went out to the Crimea in the engine-room of one of her Majesty's war steamers.

I served with the fleet, of course, while the war lasted; and when it was over, went wandering off again, rejoicing in my liberty. This time I went to Canada, and after working on a railway then in progress near the American frontier, I presently passed over into the States; journeyed from north to south; crossed the Rocky Mountains; tried a month or two of life in the gold country; and then, being seized with a sudden, aching, unaccountable longing to revisit that solitary grave so far away on the Italian coast, I turned my face once more towards Europe.

Poor little grave! I found it rank with weeds, the cross half shattered, the inscription half effaced. It was as if no one had loved him, or remembered him.

I went back to the house in which we had lodged together. The same people were still living there, and made me kindly welcome. I stayed with them for some weeks. I weeded, and planted, and trimmed the grave with my own hands, and set up a fresh cross in pure white marble. It was the first season of rest that I had known since I laid him there; and when at last I shouldered my knapsack and set forth again to battle with the world, I promised myself that, God willing, I would creep back to Rocca, when my days drew near to ending, and be buried by his side.

From hence, being, perhaps, a little less inclined than formerly for very distant parts, and willing to keep within reach of that grave, I went no further than Mantua, where I engaged myself as an engine-driver on the line, then not long completed, between that city and Venice. Somehow, although I had been trained to the working of engineering, I preferred in these days to earn my bread by driving. I liked the excitement of it, the sense of power, the rush of the air, the roar of the fire, the flitting of the landscape. Above all, I enjoyed to drive a night express. The worse the weather, the better it suited my sullen temper. For I was as hard, and harder than ever. The years had done nothing to soften me. They had only confirmed all that was blackest and bitterest in my heart.

THE ENGINEER

I continued pretty faithful to the Mantua line, and had been working on it steadily for more than seven months when that which I am now about to relate took place.

It was in the month of March. The weather had been unsettled for some days past, and the nights stormy; and at one point along the line, near Ponte di Brenta, the waters had risen and swept away some seventy yards of embankment. Since this accident, the trains had all been obliged to stop at a certain spot between Padua and Ponte di Brenta, and the passengers, with their luggage, had thence to be transported in all kinds of vehicles, by a circuitous country road, to the nearest station on the other side of the gap, where another train and engine awaited them. This, of course, caused great confusion and annoyance, put all our time-tables wrong and subjected the public to a large amount of inconvenience. In the meanwhile an army of navvies was drafted to the spot, and worked day and night to repair the damage. At this time I was driving two through trains each day; namely, one from Mantua to Venice in the early morning, and a return train from Venice to Mantua in the afternoon—a tolerably full days' work, covering about one hundred and ninety miles of ground, and occupying between ten and eleven hours. I was therefore not best pleased when, on the third or fourth day after the accident, I was informed that, in addition to my regular allowance of work, I should that evening be required to drive a special train to Venice. This special train, consisting of an engine, a single carriage, and a break-van, was to leave the Mantua platform at eleven; at Padua the passengers were to alight and find post-chaises waiting to convey them to Ponte di Brenta; at Ponte di Brenta another engine, carriage, and break-van were to be in readiness; I was charged to accompany them throughout.

'Corpo di Bacco,' said the clerk who gave me my orders, 'you need not look so black, man. You are certain of a handsome gratuity. Do you know who goes with you?'

'Not I.'

'Not you, indeed! Why, it's the Duca Loredano, the Neapolitan ambassador.'

'Loredano!' I stammered. 'What Loredano? There was a Marchese —.'

'Certo. He was the Marchese Loredano some years ago; but he has come into his dukedom since then.'

'He must be a very old man by this time.'

'Yes, he is old; but what of that? He is as hale, and bright, and stately as ever. You have seen him before?'

'Yes,' I said, turning away; 'I have seen him—years ago.'

'You have heard of his marriage?'

I shook my head.

The clerk chuckled, rubbed his hands, and shrugged his shoulders.

'An extraordinary affair,' he said. 'Made a tremendous esclandre at the time. He married his mistress—quite a common, vulgar girl—a Genoese—very handsome; but not received, of course. Nobody visits her.'

'Married her!' I exclaimed. 'Impossible.'

'True, I assure you.'

I put my hand to my head. I felt as if I had had a fall or a blow.

'Does she—does she go to-night?' I faltered.

'O dear, yes—she goes everywhere with him—never lets him out of her sight. You'll see her—la bella Duchessa!'

With this my informant laughed, and rubbed his hands again, and went back to his office.

The day went by, I scarcely know how, except that my whole soul was in a tumult of rage and bitterness. I returned from my afternoon's work about 7.25, and at 10.30 I was once again at the station. I had examined the engine; given instructions to the Fochista, or stoker, about the fire; seen to the supply of oil; and got all in readiness, when just as I was about to compare my watch with the clock in the ticket-office, a hand was laid upon my arm, and a voice in my ear said:

'Are you the engine-driver who is going on with this special train?'

I had never seen the speaker before. He was a small, dark man, muffled up about the throat, with blue glasses, a large black beard, and his hat drawn low upon his eyes.

'You are a poor man, I suppose,' he said, in a quick, eager whisper, 'and, like other poor men, would not object to be better off. Would you like to earn a couple of thousand florins?'

'In what way?'

'Hush! You are to stop at Padua, are you not, and to go on again at Ponte di Brenta?'

I nodded.

'Suppose you did nothing of the kind. Suppose, instead of turning off the steam, you jump off the engine, and let the train run on?'

'Impossible. There are seventy yards of embankment gone, and —.'

'Basta! I know that. Save yourself, and let the train run on. It would be nothing but an accident.'

I turned hot and cold; I trembled; my heart beat fast, and my breath failed.

'Why do you tempt me?' I faltered.

'For Italy's sake,' he whispered; 'for liberty's sake. I know you are no Italian; but, for all that, you may be a friend. This Loredano is one of his country's bitterest enemies. Stay, here are the two thousand florins.'

I thrust his hand back fiercely.

'No—no,' I said. 'No blood-money. If I do it, I do it neither for Italy nor for money; but for vengeance.'

'For vengeance!' he repeated.

At this moment the signal was given for backing up to the platform. I sprang to my place upon the engine without another word. When I again looked towards the spot where he had been standing, the stranger was gone.

I saw them take their places— Duke and Duchess, secretary and priest, valet and maid. I saw the station-master bow them into the carriage, and stand, bareheaded, beside the door. I could not distinguish their faces; the platform was too dusk, and the glare from the engine fire too strong; but I recognised her stately figure, and the poise of her head. Had I not been told who she was, I should have known her by those traits alone. Then the guard's whistle shrilled out, and the stationmaster made his last bow; I turned the steam on; and we started.

My blood was on fire. I no longer trembled or hesitated. I felt as if every nerve was iron, and every pulse instinct with deadly purpose. She was in my power, and I would be avenged. She should die—she, for whom I had stained my soul with my friend's blood! She should die, in the plentitude of her wealth and her beauty, and no power upon earth should save her!

The stations flew past. I put on more steam; I bade the fireman heap in the coke, and stir the blazing mass. I would have out-stripped the wind, had it been possible. Faster and faster—hedges and trees, bridges and stations, flashing past—villages no sooner seen than gone—telegraph wires twisting, and dipping, and twining themselves in one, with the awful swiftness of our pace! Faster and faster, till the fireman at my side looks white and scared, and refuses to add more fuel to the furnace. Faster and faster, till the wind rushes in our faces and drives the breath back upon our lips.

I would have scorned to save myself. I meant to die with the rest. Mad as I was—and believe from my very soul that I was utterly mad for the time—I felt a passing pang of pity for the old man and his suite. I would have spared the poor fellow at my side, too, if I could; but the pace at which we were going made escape impossible.

Vicenza was passed—a mere confused vision of lights. Pojana flew by. At Padua, but nine miles distant, our passengers were to alight. I saw the fireman's face turned upon me in remonstrance; I saw his lips move, though I could not hear a word; I saw his expression change suddenly from remonstrance to a deadly terror, and then—merciful Heaven! then, for the first time. I saw that he and I were no longer alone upon the engine.

There was a third man—a third man standing on my right hand, as the fireman was standing on my left—a tall, stalwart man, with short curling hair, and a flat Scotch cap upon his head. As I fell back in the first shock of surprise, he stepped nearer; took my place at the engine, and turned the steam off. I opened my lips to speak to him; he turned his head slowly, and looked me in the face.

Matthew Price!

I uttered one long wild cry, flung my arms wildly up above my head, and fell as if I had been smitten with an axe.

I am prepared for the objections that may be made to my story. I expect, as a matter of course, to be told that this was an optical illusion, or that I was suffering from pressure on the brain, or even that I laboured under an attack of temporary insanity. I have heard all these arguments before, and, if I may be forgiven for saying so, I have no desire to hear them again. My own mind has been made up upon this subject for many a year. All that I can say—all that I know is—that Matthew Price came back from the dead, to save my soul and the lives of those whom I, in my guilty rage, would have hurried to destruction. I believe this as I believe in the mercy of Heaven and the forgiveness of repentant sinners.

O. Henry

Holding Up a Train

NOTE. The man who told me these things was for several years an outlaw in the Southwest and a follower of the pursuit he so frankly describes. His description of the *modus operandi* should prove interesting, his counsel of value to the potential passenger in some future "hold-up," while his estimate of the pleasures of train robbing will hardly induce any one to adopt it as a profession. I give the story in almost exactly his own words.   O. H.

Most people would say, if their opinion was asked for, that holding up a train would be a hard job. Well, it isn't; it's easy. I have contributed some to the uneasiness of railroads and the insomnia of express companies, and the most trouble I ever had about a hold-up was in being swindled by unscrupulous people while spending the money I got. The danger wasn't anything to speak of, and we didn't mind the trouble.

One man has come pretty near robbing a train by himself; two have succeeded a few times; three can do it if they are hustlers, but five is about the right number. The time to do it and the place depend upon several things.

The first "stick-up" I was ever in happened in 1890. Maybe the way I got into it will explain how most train robbers start in the business. Five out of six Western outlaws are just cowboys out of a job and gone wrong. The sixth is a tough from the East who dresses up like a bad man and plays some low-down trick that gives the boys a bad name. Wire fences and "nesters" made five of them; a bad heart made the sixth.

Jim S—— and I were working on the 101 Ranch in Colorado. The nesters had the cowman on the go. They had taken up the land and elected officers who were hard to get along with. Jim and I rode into La Junta one day, going south from a round-up. We were having a little fun without malice toward anybody when a farmer administration cut in and tried to harvest us. Jim shot a deputy marshal, and I kind of corroborated his side of the argument. We skirmished up and down the main street, the boomers having bad luck all the time. After a while we leaned forward and shoved for the ranch down on the Ceriso. We were riding a couple of horses that couldn't fly, but they could catch birds.

A few days after that, a gang of the La Junta boomers came to the ranch and wanted us to go back with them. Naturally, we declined. We had the house on them, and before we were done refusing, that old 'dobe was plumb full of lead. When dark came we fagged 'em a batch of bullets and shoved out the back door for the rocks. They sure smoked us as we went. We had to drift, which we did, and rounded up down in Oklahoma.

Well, there wasn't anything we could get there, and, being mighty hard up, we decided to transact a little business with the railroads. Jim and I joined forces with Tom and Ike Moore — two brothers who had plenty of sand they were willing to convert into dust. I can call their names, for both of them are dead. Tom was shot while robbing a bank in Arkansas; Ike was killed during the more dangerous pastime of attending a dance in the Creek Nation.

We selected a place on the Santa Fé where there was a bridge across a deep creek surrounded by heavy timber. All passenger trains took water at the tank close to one end of the bridge. It was a quiet place, the nearest house being five miles away. The day before it happened, we rested our horses and "made medicine" as to how we should get about it. Our plans were not at all elaborate, as none of us had ever engaged in a hold-up before.

The Santa Fé flyer was due at the tank at 11.15 p. m. At eleven, Tom and I lay down on one side of the track, and Jim and Ike took the other. As the train rolled up, the headlight flashing far down the track and the steam hissing from the engine, I turned weak all over. I would have worked a whole year on the ranch for nothing to have been out of that affair right then. Some of the nerviest men in the business have told me that they felt the same way the first time.

The engine had hardly stopped when I jumped on the running-board on one side, while Jim mounted the other. As soon as the engineer and fireman saw our guns they threw up their hands without being told, and begged us not to shoot, saying they would do anything we wanted them to.

"Hit the ground," I ordered, and they both jumped off. We drove them before us down the side of the train. While this was happening, Tom and Ike had been blazing away, one on each side of the train, yelling like Apaches, so as to keep the passengers herded in the cars. Some fellow stuck a little twenty-two calibre out one of the coach windows and fired it straight up in the air. I let drive and smashed the glass just over his head. That settled everything like resistance from that direction.

By this time all my nervousness was gone. I felt a kind of pleasant excitement as if I were at a dance or a frolic of some sort. The lights were all out in the coaches, and, as Tom and Ike gradually quit firing and yelling, it got to be almost as still as a graveyard. I remember hearing a little bird chirping in a bush at the side of the track, as if it were complaining at being waked up.

I made the fireman get a lantern, and then I went to the express car and yelled to the messenger to open up or get perforated. He slid the door open and stood in it with his hands up. "Jump overboard, son," I said, and he hit the dirt like a lump of lead. There were two safes in the car — a big one and a little one. By the way, I first located the messenger's arsenal — a double-barrelled shot-gun with buckshot cartridges and a thirty-eight in a drawer. I drew the cartridges from the shot-gun, pocketed the pistol, and called the messenger inside. I shoved my gun against his nose and put him to work. He couldn't open the big one, but he did the little one. There was only nine hundred dollars in it. That was mighty small winnings for our trouble, so we decided to go through the passengers. We took our prisoners to the smoking-car, and from there sent the engineer through the train to light up the coaches. Beginning with the first one, we placed a man at each door and ordered the passengers to stand between the seats with their hands up.

If you want to find out what cowards the majority of men are, all you have to do is rob a passenger train. I don't mean because they don't resist — I'll tell you later on why they can't do that — but it makes a man feel sorry for them the way they lose their heads. Big, burly drummers and farmers and ex-soldiers and high-collared dudes and sports that, a few moments before, were filling the car with noise and bragging, get so scared that their ears flop.

There were very few people in the day coaches at that time of night, so we made a slim haul until we got to the sleeper. The Pullman conductor met me at one door while Jim was going round to the other one. He very politely informed me that I could not go into that car, as it did not belong to the railroad company, and, besides, the passengers had already been greatly disturbed by the shouting and firing. Never in all my life have I met with a finer instance of official dignity and reliance upon the power of Mr. Pullman's great name. I jabbed my six-shooter so hard against Mr. Conductor's front that I afterward found one of his vest buttons so firmly wedged in the end of the barrel that I had to shoot it out. He just shut up like a weak-springed knife and rolled down the car steps.

I opened the door of the sleeper and stepped inside. A big, fat old man came wabbling up to me, puffing and blowing. He had one coat-sleeve on and was trying to put his vest on over that. I don't know who he thought I was.

"Young man, young man," says he, "you must keep cool and not get excited. Above everything, keep cool."

"I can't," says I. "Excitement's just eating me up." And then I let out a yell and turned loose my forty-five through the skylight.

That old man tried to dive into one of the lower berths, but a screech came out of it and a bare foot that took him in the bread-basket and landed him on the floor. I saw Jim coming in the other door, and I hollered for everybody to climb out and line up.

They commenced to scramble down, and for a while we had a three-ringed circus. The men looked as frightened and tame as a lot of rabbits in a deep snow. They had on, on an average, about a quarter of a suit of clothes and one shoe apiece. One chap was sitting on the floor of the aisle, looking as if he were working a hard sum in arithmetic. He was trying, very solemn, to pull a lady's number two shoe on his number nine foot.

The ladies didn't stop to dress. They were so curious to see a real, live train robber, bless 'em, that they just wrapped blankets and sheets around themselves and came out, squeaky and fidgety looking.

They always show more curiosity and sand than the men do.

We got them all lined up and pretty quiet, and I went through the bunch. I found very little on them — I mean in the way of valuables. One man in the line was a sight. He was one of those big, overgrown, solemn snoozers that sit on the platform at lectures and look wise. Before crawling out he had managed to put on his long, frocktailed coat and his high silk hat. The rest of him was nothing but pajamas and bunions. When I dug into that Prince Albert, I expected to drag out at least a block of gold mine stock or an armful of Government bonds, but all I found was a little boy's French harp about four inches long. What it was there for, I don't know. I felt a little mad because he had fooled me so. I stuck the harp up against his mouth.

"If you can't pay — play," I says.

"I can't play," says he.

"Then learn right off quick," says I, letting him smell the end of my gun-barrel.

He caught hold of the harp, turned red as a beet, and commenced to blow. He blew a dinky little tune I remembered hearing when I was a kid:

> Prettiest little gal in the country — oh!
> Mammy and Daddy told me so.

I made him keep on playing it all the time we were in the car. Now and then he'd get weak and off the key, and I'd turn my gun on him and ask what was the matter with that little gal, and whether he had any intention of going back on her, which would make him start up again like sixty. I think that old boy standing there in his silk hat and bare feet, playing his little French harp, was the funniest sight I ever saw. One little red-headed woman in the line broke out laughing at him. You could have heard her in the next car.

Then Jim held them steady while I searched the berths. I grappled around in those beds and filled a pillow-case with the strangest assortment of stuff you ever saw. Now and then I'd come across a little pop-gun pistol, just about right for plugging teeth with, which I'd throw out the window. When I finished with the collection, I dumped the pillow-case load in the middle of the aisle. There were a good many watches, bracelets, rings, and pocket-books, with a sprinkling of false teeth, whiskey flasks, face-powder boxes, chocolate caramels, and heads of hair of various colours and lengths. There were also about a dozen ladies' stockings into which jewellery, watches, and rolls of bills had been stuffed and then wadded up tight and stuck under the mattresses. I offered to return what I called the "scalps," saying that we were not Indians on the warpath, but none of the ladies seemed to know to whom the hair belonged.

One of the women — and a good-looker she was — wrapped in a striped blanket, saw me pick up one of the stockings that was pretty chunky and heavy about the toe, and she snapped out:

"That's mine, sir. You're not in the business of robbing women, are you?"

Now, as this was our first hold-up, we hadn't agreed upon any code of ethics, so I hardly knew what to answer. But, anyway, I replied: "Well, not as a specialty. If this contains your personal property you can have it back."

"It just does," she declared eagerly, and reached out her hand for it.

"You'll excuse my taking a look at the contents," I said, holding the stocking up by the toe. Out dumped a big gent's gold watch, worth two hundred, a gent's leather pocket-book that we afterward found to contain six hundred dollars, a 32-calibre revolver; and the only thing of the lot that could have been a lady's personal property was a silver bracelet worth about fifty cents.

I said: "Madame, here's your property," and handed her the bracelet. "Now," I went on, "how can you expect us to act square with you when you try to deceive us in this manner? I'm surprised at such conduct."

The young woman flushed up as if she had been caught doing something dishonest. Some other woman down the line called out: "The mean thing!" I never knew whether she meant the other lady or me.

When we finished our job we ordered everybody back to bed, told 'em good night very politely at the door, and left. We rode forty miles before daylight and then divided the stuff. Each one of us got $1,752.85 in money. We lumped the jewellery around. Then we scattered, each man for himself.

That was my first train robbery, and it was about as easily done as any of the ones that followed. But that was the last and only time I ever went through the passengers. I don't like that part of the business. Afterward I stuck strictly to the express car. During the next eight years I handled a good deal of money.

The best haul I made was just seven years after the first one. We found out about a train that was going to bring out a lot of money to pay off the soldiers at a Government post. We stuck that train up in broad daylight. Five of us lay in the sand hills near a little station. Ten soldiers were guarding the money on the train, but they might just as well have been at home on a furlough. We didn't even allow them to stick their heads out the windows to see the fun. We had no trouble at all in getting the money, which was all in gold. Of course, a big howl was raised at the time about the robbery. It was Government stuff, and the Government got sarcastic and wanted to know what the convoy of soldiers went along for. The only excuse given was that nobody was expecting an attack among those bare sand hills in daytime. I don't know what the Government thought about the excuse, but I know that it was a good one. The surprise — that is the keynote of the train-robbing business. The papers published all kinds of stories about the loss, finally agreeing that it was between nine thousand and ten thousand dollars. The Government sawed wood. Here are the correct figures, printed for the first time — forty-eight thousand dollars. If anybody will take the trouble to look over Uncle Sam's private accounts for that little debit to profit and loss, he will find that I am right to a cent.

By that time we were expert enough to know what to do. We rode due west twenty miles, making a trail that a Broadway policeman could have followed, and then we doubled back, hiding our tracks. On the second night after the hold-up, while posses were scouring the country in every direction, Jim and I were eating supper in the second story of a friend's house in the town where the alarm started from. Our friend pointed out to us, in an office across the street, a printing press at work striking off handbills offering a reward for our capture.

I have been asked what we do with the money we get. Well, I never could account for a tenth part of it after it was spent. It goes fast and freely. An outlaw has to have a good many friends. A highly respected citizen may, and often does, get along with very few, but a man on the dodge has got to have "side-kickers." With angry posses and reward-hungry officers cutting out a hot trail for him, he must have a few places scattered about the country where he can stop and feed himself and his horse and get a few hours' sleep without having to keep both eyes open. When he makes a haul he feels like dropping some of the coin with these friends, and he does it liberally. Sometimes I have, at the end of a hasty visit at one of these havens of refuge, flung a handful of gold and bills into the laps of the kids playing on the floor, without knowing whether my contribution was a hundred dollars or a thousand.

When old-timers make a big haul they generally go far away to one of the big cities to spend their money. Green hands, however successful a hold-up they make, nearly always give themselves away by showing too much money near the place where they got it.

I was in a job in '94 where we got twenty

thousand dollars. We followed our favourite plan for a getaway — that is, doubled on our trail — and laid low for a time near the scene of the train's back luck. One morning I picked up a newspaper and read an article with big headlines stating that the marshal, with eight deputies and a posse of thirty armed citizens, had the train robbers surrounded in a mesquite thicket on the Cimarron, and that it was a question of only a few hours when they would be dead men or prisoners. While I was reading that article I was sitting at breakfast in one of the most elegant private residences in Washington City, with a flunky in knee pants standing behind my chair. Jim was sitting across the table talking to his half-uncle, a retired naval officer, whose name you have often seen in the accounts of doings in the capital. We had gone there and bought rattling outfits of good clothes, and were resting from our labours among the nabobs. We must have been killed in that mesquite thicket, for I can make an affidavit that we didn't surrender.

Now I propose to tell why it is easy to hold up a train, and, then, why no one should ever do it.

In the first place, the attacking party has all the advantage. That is, of course, supposing that they are old-timers with the necessary experience and courage. They have the outside and are protected by the darkness, while the others are in the light, hemmed into a small space, and exposed, the moment they show a head at a window or door, to the aim of a man who is a dead shot and who won't hesitate to shoot.

But, in my opinion, the main condition that makes train robbing easy is the element of *surprise* in connection with the imagination of the passengers. If you have ever seen a horse that has eaten loco weed you will understand what I mean when I say that the passengers get locoed. That horse gets the awfullest imagination on him in the world. You can't coax him to cross a little branch stream two feet wide. It looks as big to him as the Mississippi River. That's just the way with the passenger. He thinks there are a hundred men yelling and shooting outside, when maybe there are only two or three. And the muzzle of a forty-five looks like the entrance to a tunnel. The passenger is all right, although he may do mean little tricks, like hiding a wad of money in his shoe and forgetting to dig-up until you jostle his ribs some with the end of your six-shooter; but there's no harm in him.

As to the train crew, we never had any more trouble with them than if they had been so many sheep. I don't mean that they are cowards; I mean that they have got sense. They know they're not up against a bluff. It's the same way with the officers.

I've seen secret service men, marshals, and railroad detectives fork over their change as meek as Moses. I saw one of the bravest marshals I ever knew hide his gun under his seat and dig up along with the rest while I was taking toll. He wasn't afraid; he simply knew that we had the drop on the whole outfit. Besides, many of those officers have families and they feel that they oughtn't to take chances; whereas death has no terrors for the man who holds up a train. He expects to get killed some day, and he generally does. My advice to you, if you should ever be in a hold-up, is to line up with the cowards and save your bravery for an occasion when it may be of some benefit to you. Another reason why officers are backward about mixing things with a train robber is a financial one. Every time there is a scrimmage and somebody gets killed, the officers lose money. If the train robber gets away they swear out a warrant against John Doe et al, and travel hundreds of miles and sign vouchers for thousands on the trail of the fugitives, and the Government foots the bills. So, with them, it is a question of mileage rather than courage.

I will give one instance to support my statement that the surprise is the best card in playing for a hold-up.

Along in '92 the Daltons were cutting out a hot

trail for the officers down in the Cherokee Nation. Those were their lucky days, and they got so reckless and sandy, that they used to announce before hand what job they were going to undertake. Once they gave it out that they were going to hold up the M. K. & T. flyer on a certain night at the station of Pryor Creek, in Indian Territory.

That night the railroad company got fifteen deputy marshals in Muscogee and put them on the train. Beside them they had fifty armed men hid in the depot at Pryor Creek.

When the Katy Flyer pulled in not a Dalton showed up. The next station was Adair, six miles away. When the train reached there, and the deputies were having a good time explaining what they would have done to the Dalton gang if they had turned up, all at once it sounded like an army firing outside. The conductor and brakeman came running into the car yelling, "Train robbers!"

Some of those deputies lit out of the door, hit the ground, and kept on running. Some of them hid their Winchesters under the seats. Two of them made a fight and were both killed.

It took the Daltons just ten minutes to capture the train and whip the escort. In twenty minutes more they robbed the express car of twenty-seven thousand dollars and made a clean get-away.

My opinion is that those deputies would have put up a stiff fight at Pryor Creek, where they were expecting trouble, but they were taken by surprise and "locoed" at Adair, just as the Daltons, who knew their business, expected they would.

I don't think I ought to close without giving some deductions from my experience of eight years "on the dodge." It doesn't pay to rob trains. Leaving out the question of right and morals, which I don't think I ought to tackle, there is very little to envy in the life of an outlaw. After a while money ceases to have any value in his eyes. He gets to looking upon the railroads and express companies as his bankers, and his six-shooters as a cheque book good for any amount. He throws away money right and left. Most of the time he is on the jump, riding day and night, and he lives so hard between times that he doesn't enjoy the taste of high life when he gets it. He knows that his time is bound to come to lose his life or liberty, and that the accuracy of his aim, the speed of his horse, and the fidelity of his "sider," are all that postpone the inevitable.

It isn't that he loses any sleep over danger from the officers of the law. In all my experience I never knew officers to attack a band of outlaws unless they outnumbered them at least three to one.

But the outlaw carries one thought constantly in

his mind — and that is what makes him so sore against life, more than anything else — he knows where the marshals get their recruits of deputies. He knows that the majority of these upholders of the law were once lawbreakers, horse thieves, rustlers, highwaymen, and outlaws like himself, and that they gained their positions and immunity by turning state's evidence, by turning traitor and delivering up their comrades to imprisonment and death. He knows that some day — unless he is shot first — his Judas will set to work, the trap will be laid, and he will be the surprised instead of a surpriser at a stick-up.

That is why the man who holds up trains picks his company with a thousand times the care with which a careful girl chooses a sweetheart. That is why he raises himself from his blanket of nights and listens to the tread of every horse's hoofs on the distant road. That is why he broods suspiciously for days upon a jesting remark or an unusual movement of a tried comrade, or the broken mutterings of his closest friend, sleeping by his side.

And it is one of the reasons why the train-robbing profession is not so pleasant a one as either of its collateral branches — politics or cornering the market.

Margaret Oliphant

A Story of a Wedding Tour

CHAPTER I

They had been married exactly a week when this incident occurred.

It was not a love marriage. The man, indeed, had been universally described as "very much in love," but the girl was not by any one supposed to be in that desirable condition. She was a very lonely little girl, without parents, almost without relations. Her guardian was a man who had been engaged in business relations with her father, and who had accepted the charge of the little orphan as his duty. But neither he nor his wife had any love to expend upon her, and they did not feel that such visionary sentiments came within the line of duty. He was a very honourable man, and took charge of her small—very small—property with unimpeachable care.

If anything, he wronged himself rather than Janey, charging her nothing for the transfers which he made of her farthing's worth of stock from time to time, to get a scarcely appreciable rise of interest and income for her. The whole thing was scarcely appreciable, and to a large-handed man like Mr Midhurst, dealing with hundreds of thousands, it was almost ridiculous to give a moment's attention to what a few hundreds might produce. But he did so; and if there is any angel who has to do with trade affairs, I hope it was carefully put to his account to balance some of the occasions on which he was not perhaps so particular. Nor did Mrs Midhurst shrink from her duty in all substantial and real good offices to the girl. She, who spent hundreds at the dressmaker's every year on account of her many daughters, did not disdain to get Janey's serge frocks at a cheaper shop, and to have them made by an inexpensive workwoman, so that the girl should have the very utmost she could get for her poor little money.

Was not this real goodness, real honesty, and devotion to their duty? But to love a little thing like that with no real claim upon them, and nothing that could be called specially attractive about her, who could be expected to do it? They had plenty—almost more than enough—of children of their own. These children were big boys and girls, gradually growing, in relays, into manhood and womanhood, when this child came upon their hands. There was no room for her in the full and noisy house. When she was grown up most of the Midhurst children were married, but there was one son at home, who, in the well-known contradictiousness of young people—it being a very wrong and, indeed, impossible thing—was quite capable of falling in love with Janey—and one daughter, with whom it was also possible that Janey might come into competition.

The young Midhursts were nice-looking young people enough; but Janey was very pretty. If Providence did but fully consider all the circumstances, it cannot but be felt that Providence would not carry out, as often is done, such ridiculous arrangements. Janey was very pretty. Could anything more inconvenient, more inappropriate, be conceived?

The poor little girl had, accordingly, spent most of her life at school, where she had, let it not be doubted, made many friendships and little loves; but these were broken up by holidays, by the returning home of the other pupils, while she stayed for ever at school: and not at one school, but several—for in his extreme conscientiousness her guardian desired to do her "every justice," as he said, and prepare her fully for the life—probably that of a governess—which lay before her. Therefore, when she had become proficient in one part of her education she was carried on to another, with the highest devotion to her commercial value no doubt, but a sublime indifference to her little feelings. Thus, she had been in France for two years, and in Germany for two years, so as to be able to state that French and

German acquired in these countries were among the list of her accomplishments. English, of course, was the foundation of all; and Janey had spent some time at a famous academy of music,—her guardian adding something out of his own pocket to her scanty means, that she might be fully equipped for her profession. And then she was brought, I will not say home: Janey fondly said home, but she knew very well it did not mean home. And it was while Mrs Midhurst was actually writing out the advertisement for 'The Times,' and the 'Morning Post,' and 'The Guardian,' which was to announce to all the world that a young lady desired an engagement as governess, that her husband burst in with the extraordinary news that Mr Rosendale, who had chanced to travel with Janey from Flushing, on her return, and who had afterwards, by a still greater chance, met her when asked to lunch at the Midhursts', and stared very much at her, as they all remarked—had fallen in love with, and wanted to marry, this humble little girl.

"Fallen in love with Janey!" Mrs Midhurst cried. "Fallen in love with you, Janey!" said Agnes Midhurst, with a little emphasis on the pronoun. He was not, indeed, quite good enough to have permitted himself the luxury of falling in love with Mr Midhurst's daughter, but he was an astonishing match for Janey. He was a man who was very well off: he could afford himself such a caprice as that. He was not handsome. There was a strain of Jewish blood in him. He was a thick-set little man, and did not dress or talk in perfect taste; but—in love! These two words made all the difference. Nobody had ever loved her, much less been "in love" with her. Janey consented willingly enough for the magic of these two words. She felt that she was going to be like the best of women at last—to have some one who loved her, some one who was in love with her. He might not be "joli, joli," as they say in France. She might not feel any very strong impulse on her own part towards him; but if he was in love with her—in love! Romeo was no more than that with Juliet. The thought went to Janey's head. She married him quite willingly for the sake of this.

I am afraid that Janey, being young, and shy, and strange, was a good deal frightened, horrified, and even revolted, by her first discoveries of what it meant to be in love. She had made tremendous discoveries in the course of a week. She had found out that Mr Rosendale, her husband, was in love with her beauty, but as indifferent to herself as any of the persons she had quitted to give herself to him. He did not care at all what she thought, how she felt, what she liked or disliked. He did not care even for her comfort, or that she should be pleased and happy, which, in the first moment even of such a union, and out of pure self-regard to make a woman more agreeable to himself, a man—even the most brutal—generally regards more or less. He was, perhaps, not aware that he did not regard it. He took it for granted that, being his wife, she would naturally be pleased with what pleased him, and his mind went no further than this.

Therefore, as far as Janey liked the things he liked, all went well enough. She had these, but no other. Her wishes were not consulted further, nor did he know that he failed in any way towards her. He had little to say to her, except expressions of admiration. When he was not telling her that she was a little beauty, or admiring her pretty hair, her pretty eyes, the softness of her skin, and the smallness of her waist, he had nothing to say. He read his paper, disappearing behind it in the morning; he went to sleep after his midday meal (for the weather was warm); he played billiards in the evening in the hotels to which he took her on their wedding journey; or he overwhelmed her with caresses from which she shrank in disgust, almost in terror. That was all that being in love meant, she found; and to say that she was disappointed cruelly was to express in the very mildest way the dreadful downfall of all her expectations and hopes which happened to Janey before she had been seven days a wife. It is not disagreeable to be told that you are a little beauty, prettier than any one else. Janey would have been very well pleased to put up with that; but to be petted like a little lapdog and then left as a lapdog is—to be quiet and not to trouble in the intervals of petting—was to the poor little girl, unaccustomed to love and athirst for it, who had hoped to be loved, and to find a companion to whom she would be truly dear, a disenchantment and disappointment which was almost more than flesh and blood could bear.

She was in the full bitterness of these discoveries when the strange incident occurred which was of so much importance in her life. They were travelling through France in one of those long night journeys to which we are all accustomed nowadays; and Janey, pale and tired, had been contemplating for some time the figure of her husband thrown back in the corner opposite, snoring complacently with his mouth open, and looking the worst that a middle-aged man can look in the utter abandonment of self-indulgence and rude comfort, when the train began to slacken its speed, and to prepare to enter one of those large stations which look so ghastly in the desertion of the night.

Rosendale jumped up instinctively, only half awake, as the train stopped. The other people in the carriage were leaving it, having attained the end of their journey, but he pushed through them and their baggage to get out, with the impatience which some men show at any pause of the kind, and determination to stretch their legs, or get something to drink, which mark the breaks in the journey. He did not even say anything to Janey as he forced his way out, but she was so familiar with his ways by this time that she took no notice. She did take notice, however when, her fellow-passengers and their packages having all been cleared away, she suddenly became sensible that the train was getting slowly into motion again without any sign of her husband.

She thought she caught a glimpse of him strolling about on the opposite platform before she was quite sure of what was happening. And then there was a scurry of hurrying feet, a slamming of doors, and as she rose and ran to the window bewildered, she saw him, along with some other men, running at full speed, but quite hopelessly, to catch the train. The last she saw was his face, fully revealed by the light of the lamp, convulsed with rage and astonishment, evidently with a yell of denunciation on the lips. Janey trembled at the sight. There was that in him, too, though as yet in her submissiveness she had never called it forth, a temper as unrestrained as his love-making, and as little touched by any thought save that of his own gratification. Her first sensation was fright, a terror that she was in fault and was about to be crushed to pieces in his rage: and then Janey sank back in her corner, and a flood of feeling of quite another kind took possession of her breast.

Was it possible that she was alone? Was it possible that for the first time since that terrible moment of her marriage she was more safely by herself than any locked door or even watchful guardian could keep her, quite unapproachable in the isolation of the train? Alone!

"Safe!" Janey ventured to say to herself, clasping her hands together with a mingled sensation of excitement and terror and tremulous delight which words could not tell.

She did not know what to think at first. The sound of the train plunging along through the darkness, through the unknown country, filled her mind as if some one was talking to her. And she was fluttered by the strangeness of the incident and disturbed by alarms. There was a fearful joy in thus being alone, in having a few hours, perhaps a whole long tranquil night, to herself: whatever came of it, that was always so much gained. But then she seemed to see him in the morning coming in upon her heated and angry. She had always felt that the moment would come when he would be angry, and more terrible to confront than any governess, or even principal of a ladies' college. He would come in furious, accusing her of being the cause of the accident, of doing something to set the train in motion; or else he would come in fatigued and dusty, claiming her services as if she were his valet— a thing which had, more or less, happened already, and against which Janey's pride and her sense of what was fit had risen in arms. She thought of this for a little time with trouble, and of the difficulties she would have in arriving, and where she would go to, and what she would say. It was an absurd story to tell, not to his advantage, "I lost my husband at Montbard." How could she say it? The hotel people would think she was a deceiver. Perhaps they would not take her in. And how would he know where to find her when he arrived? He would feel that he had lost her, as much as she had lost him.

Just as this idea rose in her mind, like a new thing full of strange suggestions, the train began to shorten speed again, and presently stopped once more. She felt it to do so with a pang of horror. No doubt he had climbed up somewhere, at the end or upon the engine, and was now to be restored to his legitimate place, to fall upon her either in fondness or in rage, delighted to get back to her, or angry with her for leaving him behind: she did not know which would be the worst. Her heart began to beat with fright and anticipation. But to her great relief it was only the guard who came to the door. He wanted to know if madame was the lady whose husband had been left behind; and to offer a hundred apologies and explanations. One of those fools at Montbard had proclaimed twenty minutes' pause when there were but five. If he had but heard he would have put it right, but he was at the other end of the train. But madame must not be too much distressed; a few hours would put it all right.

"Then there is another train?" said Janey, her poor little head buzzing between excitement and relief. "Not for some hours," said the guard. "Madame will understand that there is not more than one *rapide* in the middle of the night; but in the morning quite early there is the train omnibus. Oh, very early, at five o'clock. Before madame is ready for her dinner monsieur will be at her side."

"Not till evening, then?" said Janey, with again a sudden acceleration of the movement of her heart.

The guard was desolated. "Not before evening. But if madame will remain quietly in the carriage when the train arrives at the station, I will find the omnibus of the hotel for her—I will see to everything! Madame, no doubt, knows which hotel to go to?"

Janey, as a matter of fact, did not know. Her husband had told her none of the details of the journey; but she said with a quick breath of excitement—

"I will go to the one that is nearest, the one at the Gare. There will be no need, for any omnibus."

"And the baggage? Madame has her ticket?"

"I have nothing," cried Janey, "except my travelling-bag. You must explain that for me. But otherwise—otherwise, I think I can manage."

"Madame speaks French so well," the man said, with admiration. It was, indeed, a piece of good fortune that she had been made to acquire the language in the country: that she was not frightened to find herself in a foreign place, and surrounded by people speaking a strange tongue, as many a young English bride would have been. There was a moment of tremendous excitement and noise at the station while all was explained to a serious *chef de Gare*, and a gesticulating band of porters and attendants, whose loud voices, as they all spoke together, would have frightened an ordinary English girl out of her wits. But Janey, in the strange excitement which had taken possession of her, and in her fortunate acquaintance with the language, stood still as a little rock amid all the confusion. "I will wait at the hotel till my husband comes," she said, taking out the travelling-bag and her wraps, and maintaining a composure worthy of all admiration. Not a tear, not an outcry. How astonishing are these English, cried the little crowd, with that swift classification which the Frenchman loves.

Janey walked into the hotel with her little belongings, not knowing whether she was indeed walking upon her feet or floating upon wings. She was quite composed. But if any one could only have seen the commotion within that youthful bosom! She locked the door of the little delightful solitary room in which she was placed. It was not delightful at all; but to Janey it was a haven of peace, as sweet, as secluded from everything alarming and terrible, as any bower. Not till evening could he by any possibility arrive—the man who had caused such a revolution in her life. She had some ten hours of divine quiet before her, of blessed solitude, of thought. She did not refuse to take the little meal that was brought to her, the breakfast of which she stood in need; and she was glad to be able to bathe her face, to take off her dusty dress, and put on the soft and fresh one, which, happily, had folded into very small space, and therefore could be put into her bag. Her head still buzzed with the strangeness of the position, yet began to settle a little. When she had made all these little arrangements she sat down to consider. Perhaps you will think there was very little to consider, nothing but how to wait till the next train brought him, which, after all, was not a very great thing to do. Appalling, perhaps, to a little inexperienced bride; but not to Janey, who had travelled alone so often, and knew the language, and all that.

But whoever had been able to look into Janey's mind would have seen that something more was there,—a very, very different thing from the question of how best to await his coming back. Oh, if he had loved her, Janey would have put up with many things! She would have schooled herself out of all her private repugnances; she would have been so grateful to him, so touched by the affection which nobody had ever bestowed upon her before! But he did not love her. He cared nothing about herself, Janey; did not even know her, or want to know her, or take into consideration her ways or her wishes. He was in love with her pretty face, her fresh little beauty, her power of pleasing him. If ever that power ceased, which it was sure to do, sooner or later, she would be to him less than nothing, the dreary little wife whom everybody has seen attached to a careless man: Janey felt that this was what was in store for her. She felt the horror of him, and his kind of loving, which had been such a miserable revelation to her. She felt the relief, the happiness, ah, the bliss, of having lost him for a moment, of being alone.

She took out her purse from her pocket, which was full of the change she had got in Paris of one of the ten-pound notes which her guardian had given her when she left his house on her wedding morning. She took out the clumsy pocket-book, an old one, in which there were still nine ten-pound notes. It was all her fortune, except a very, very small investment which brought her in some seven pounds a-year. This was the remainder of another small investment which had been withdrawn in order to provide her with her simple trousseau, leaving this sum of a hundred pounds which her guardian had given her, advising her to place it at once for security in her husband's hands. Janey had not done this, she scarcely could tell why. She spread them on the table—the nine notes, the twelve napoleons of shining French money. A hundred pounds: she had still the twelve francs which made up the sum. She had spent nothing. There were even the few coppers over for the *agio*. She spread them all out, and counted them from right to left, and again from left to right. Nine ten-pound notes, twelve and a-half French napoleons—or louis, as people call them nowadays—making a hundred pounds. A hundred pounds is a large sum in the eyes of a girl. It may not be much to you and me, who know that it means only ten times ten pounds, and that ten pounds goes like the wind as soon as you begin to spend it. But to Janey! Why, she could live upon a hundred pounds for—certainly for two years: for two long delightful years, with nobody to trouble her, nobody to scold, nobody to interfere. Something mounted to her head like the fumes of wine. Everything began to buzz again, to turn round, to sweep her away as on a rapidly mounting current. She put back all the money in the pocket-book—her fortune, the great sum that made her independent; and she put back her things into the bag. A sudden energy of resolution seized her. She put on her hat again, and as she looked at herself in the glass encountered the vision of a little face which was new to her. It was not that of Janey, the little governess-pupil; it was not young Mrs Rosendale. It was full of life, and meaning, and energy, and strength. Who was it? Janey? Janey herself, the real woman, whom nobody had ever seen before.

CHAPTER II

It is astonishing how many things can be done in sudden excitement and passion which could not be possible under any other circumstances. Janey was by nature a shy girl and easily frightened, accustomed indeed to do many things for herself, and to move quietly without attracting observation through the midst of a crowd; but she had never taken any initiative, and since her marriage had been reduced to such a state of complete dependence on her husband's wishes and plans that she had not attempted the smallest step on her own impulse.

Now, however, she moved about with a quiet assurance and decision which astonished herself. She carried her few possessions back again to the railway station, leaving the small gold piece of ten francs to pay, and much overpay, her hour's shelter and entertainment at the hotel.

Nobody noticed her as she went through the bustle of the place and back to the crowded station, where a little leisurely local train was about starting—a slow train occupied by peasants and country folk, and which stopped at every station along the line. English people abound in that place at all hours, except at this particular moment, when the *rapide* going towards Italy had but newly left and the little country train was preparing in peace. Nobody seemed to notice Janey as she moved about with her bag on her arm. She took her ticket in her irreproachable French "acquired in the country," which attracted no attention. She got into a second-class carriage in which there were already various country people, and especially a young mother with a baby, and its nurse in a white round cap with long streaming ribbons. Janey's heart went out to these people. She wondered if the young woman was happy, if her husband loved her, if it was not very sweet to have a child—a child must love you; it would not mind whether your cheeks were rosy or pale, whether you were pretty or not, whether you had accomplishments or languages acquired in the country.

Looking at this baby, Janey almost forgot that she was going out upon the world alone, and did not know where. It is a tremendous thing to do this, to separate from all the world you are acquainted with, to plunge into the unknown. Men do it often enough, though seldom without some clue, some link of connection with the past and way of return. Janey was about to cut herself off as by the Fury's shears from everything. She would never join her husband again. She would never fear her guardian again. She must drop out of sight like a stone into the sea. There was no longing love to search for her, no pardon to be offered, no one who would be heart-struck at the thought of the little girl lost and unhappy. Only anger would be excited by her running away, and a desire to punish, to shake her little fragile person to pieces, to make her suffer. She knew that if she did it at all, it must be final. But this did not overwhelm her. What troubled Janey a great deal more than the act of severance which she was about to accomplish, was the inevitable fib or fibs she must tell in order to account for her appearance in the unknown. She did not like to tell a fib, even a justifiable one. It was against all her traditions, against her nature. She felt that she could never do it anything but badly, never without exciting suspicions; and she must needs have some story, some way of accounting for herself.

This occupied her mind while the slow train crawled from station to station. It was the most friendly, idle, gossiping little train. It seemed to stop at the merest signal-box to have a talk, to drink as it were a social glass administered through that black hose, with a friend; it stopped wherever there were a few houses, it carried little parcels, it took up a leisurely passenger going next door, and the little electric bell went on tingling, and the guard cried "En voiture!" and the little bugle sounded. Janey was amused by all these little sounds and sights, and the country all flooded with sunshine, and the flowers everywhere, though it was only March, and dark black weather when she had left home.

Left home! and she had no home now, anywhere, no place to take refuge in, nobody to write to, to appeal to, to tell if she was happy or unhappy. But Janey did not care! She felt a strange elation of ease and relief. All alone, but everybody smiling upon her, the young mother opposite beginning to chatter, the baby to crow to her, the nurse to smile and approve of the *bonne petite* dame who took so much notice of the child. Her head was swimming, but with pleasure, and the blessed sensation of freedom—pleasure tinctured with the exhilaration of escape, and the thrill of fright which added to the excitement. Yet at that moment she was certainly in no danger. He was toiling along, no doubt, fuming and perhaps swearing, on another slow train on the other side of Marseilles. Janey laughed to herself a little guiltily at the thought.

And she had escaped! It was not her doing primarily. She might have gone on all her life till she had died, but for that accident which was none of her doing. It was destiny that had done it, fate. The cage door had been opened and the bird had flown away. And how nice it would be to settle down, with this little mother, just about her own age, for a neighbour, and to help to bring the baby up! The kind, sweet faces they all had, mother and baby and *bonne* all smiling upon her! When Janey looked out on the other side she saw the sea flashing in the sunshine, the red porphyry rocks reflecting themselves in the brilliant blue, and village after village perched upon a promontory or in the hollow of a bay. She had never in all her life before felt that sensation of blessedness, of being able to do what she liked, of having no one to call her to account. She did not know where she was going, but that was part of the pleasure. She did not want to know where she was going.

Then suddenly this sentiment changed, and she saw in a moment a place that smiled at her like the smiling of the mother and baby. It was one of those villages in a bay: a range of blue mountains threw forth a protecting arm into the sea to shield it: the roofs were red, the houses were white, they were all blazing in the sun. Soft olives and palms fringed the deep green of the pines that rolled back in waves of verdure over the country behind, and strayed down in groups and scattered files to the shore below. Oh, what a cheerful, delightsome place! and this was where the little group with the baby were preparing to get out. "I will go too," said Janey to herself; and her heart gave a little bound of pleasure. She was delighted to reach the place where she was going to stay—just as she had been delighted to go on in the little pottering train, not knowing where she was going, and not wishing to know.

This was how Janey settled herself on the day of

her flight from the world. She scarcely knew what story it was she told to the young woman whose face had so charmed her, and whom she asked whether she would be likely to find lodgings anywhere, lodgings that would not be too expensive.

"My husband is—at sea," Janey heard herself saying. She could scarcely tell what it was that put those words into her head.

"Oh, but yes," the other young woman cried with rapture. Nothing was more easy to get than a lodging in St Honorat, which was beginning to try to be a winter resort, and was eager to attract strangers. Janey had dreamed of a cottage and a garden, but she was not dissatisfied when she found herself in a sunbright room on the second floor of a tall white house facing the sea. It had a little balcony all to itself. The water rippled on the shore just over the road, the curve of the blue mountains was before her eyes.

I do not say that when she had settled down, when the thrill of movement was no longer in her brain, Janey was not without a shiver at the thought of what she had done. When the sun set, and that little chill which comes into the air of the south at the moment of its setting breathed a momentary cold about her, and when the woman of the house carefully closed the shutters and shut out the shining of the bay, and she was left alone with her candle, something sank in Janey's heart—something of the unreasonable elation, the fantastic happiness, of the day. She thought of "Mr Rosendale" (she had never got so near her husband as to call him by any other name) arriving, of the fuss there would be about her and the inquiries.

Was it rash to have come to a place so near as this—within an hour or two of where he was? Was there a danger that some one might have seen her? that it might be found out that she had taken her ticket? But then she had taken her ticket for a place much farther along the coast. She thought she could see him arrive all flaming with anger and eagerness, and the group that would gather round him, and how he would be betrayed by his bad French, and the rage he would get into! Again she laughed guiltily; but then got very grave again trying to count up all the chances—how some porter might have noticed and might betray her, how he might yet come down upon her furiously, to wreak upon her all the fury of his discomfiture. Janey knew by instinct that though it was in no way her fault, her husband would wreak his vengeance upon her even for being left behind by the train. She became desperate as she sat and thought it all over. It would be better for her to leap from the window, to throw herself into the sea, than to fall into his hands. There would be no forgiveness for her if he once laid hands upon her. Now that she had taken this desperate step, she must stand by it to the death.

CHAPTER III

Ten years had passed away since the time of that wedding tour.

Ten years! It is a very long time in a life. It makes a young man middle-aged, and a middle-aged man old. It takes away the bloom of youth, and the ignorance of the most inexperienced; and yet what a little while it is!—no more than a day when you look back upon it. The train from Marseilles to Nice, which is called the *rapide*, goes every day, and most people one time or another have travelled by it.

One day last winter one of the passengers in this train, established very comfortably in the best corner of a sleeping carriage in which he had passed the night luxuriously, and from which he was now looking out upon the shining sea, the red rocks, the many bays and headlands of the coast, suddenly received such a shock and sensation as seldom occurs to any one. He was a man of middle-age and not of engaging aspect. His face was red, and his eyes were dull yet fiery. He had the air of a man who had indulged himself much and all his inclinations, had loved good living and all the joys of the flesh, had denied himself nothing—and was now paying the penalties. Such men, to tell the truth, are not at all unusual apparitions on that beautiful coast or in the train *rapide*. No doubt appearances are deceitful, and it is not always a bad man who bears that aspect or who pays those penalties: but in this case few people would have doubted.

His eyes were bloodshot, he had a scowl upon his brow, his foot was supported upon a cushion. He had a servant with him to whom he rarely spoke but with an insult. Not an agreeable man—and the life he was now leading, whatever it had been, was not an agreeable life. He was staring out at the window upon the curves of the coast, sometimes putting up the collar of his fur coat over his ears, though it was a warm morning, and the sun had all the force of April. What he was thinking of it would be difficult to divine—perhaps of the good dinner that awaited him at Monte Carlo when he got there, perhaps of his good luck in being out of England when the east winds began to blow, perhaps of something quite different—some recollection of his past. The *rapide* does not stop at such small places as St Honorat, which indeed had not succeeded in making itself a winter resort. It was still a very small place. There were a few people on the platform when the train rushed through. It seemed to pass like a whirlwind, yet notwithstanding, in that moment two things happened. The gentleman in the corner of the carriage started in his seat, and flung himself half out of the window, with a sudden roar which lost itself in the tunnel into which the train plunged. There was an awful minute in that tunnel: for the servant thought his master had taken a fit, and there was no light to see what convulsions he might have fallen into, while at the same time he fought furiously against the man's efforts to loose his wrappings and place him in a recumbent position, exclaiming furiously all the time. He had not taken a fit, but when the train emerged into the light he was as near to it as possible—purple-red in his face, and shouting with rage and pain.

"Stop the train! stop the train!" he shouted. "Do you hear, you fool? stop the train! Ring the bell or whatever it is! break the —— thing! Stop the train!"

"Sir, sir! if you will only be quiet, I will get your medicine in a moment!"

"Medicine, indeed!" cried the master, indignantly, and every furious name that he could think of mounted to his lips—fool, idiot, ass, swine—there was no end to his epithets. "I tell you I saw her, I saw her!" he shouted. "Stop the train! Stop the train!"

On the other hand, among the few insignificant persons, peasants and others, who had been standing on the platform at St Honorat when the *rapide* dashed past, there had been a woman and a child. The woman was not a peasant: she was very simply dressed in black, with one of the small bonnets which were a few years ago so distinctively English, and with an air which corresponded to that simple coiffure. She was young, and yet had the air of responsibility and motherhood which marks a woman who is no longer in the first chapter of life. The child, a boy of nine or ten, standing close by her side, had seized her hand just as the train appeared impatiently to call her attention to something else; but, by some strange spell of attraction or coincidence, her eyes fixed upon that window out of which the gouty traveller was looking. She saw him as he saw her, and fell back dragging the boy with her as if she would have sunk into the ground. It was only a moment and the *rapide* was gone, screaming and roaring into the tunnel, making too much noise with the rush and sweep of its going to permit the shout of the passenger to be heard.

Ten years, ten long years, during which life had undergone so many changes! They all seemed to fly away in a moment, and the girl who had arrived at the little station of St Honorat alone, a fugitive, elated and intoxicated with her freedom, suddenly felt herself again the little Janey who had emancipated herself so strangely,—though she had for a long time been frightened by every train that passed and every stranger who came near.

In the course of these long years all this had changed. Her baby had been born, her forlorn state had called forth great pity, great remark and criticism, in the village where she had found refuge,— great censure also, for the fact of her marriage was not believed by everybody. But she was so lonely, so modest, and so friendly, that the poor little English stranger was soon forgiven. Perhaps her simple neighbours were glad to find that a prim Englishwoman, supposed to stand so fierce on her virtue, was in reality so fallible—or perhaps pity put all other sentiments out of court. She told her real story to the priest when the boy was baptised, and though he tried to persuade her to return to her husband, he only half believed in that husband, since the story was told not under any seal of confession. Janey never became absolutely one of his flock. She was a prim little Protestant in her heart, standing strong against the saints, but devoutly attending church, believing with simple religiousness that to go to church was better than not to go to church, whatever the rites might be, and reading her little English service steadily through all the prayers of the Mass, which she never learned to follow. But her boy was like the other children of St Honorat, and learned his catechism and said his lessons with the rest.

There were various things which she did to get a living, and got it very innocently and sufficiently, though in the humblest way. She taught English to the children of some of the richer people in the village: she taught them music. She had so much credit in this latter branch, that she often held the organ in church on a holiday and pleased everybody. Then she worked very well with her needle, and would help on an emergency at first for pure kindness, and then, as her faculties and her powers of service became known, for pay, with diligence and readiness. She found a niche in the little place which she filled perfectly, though only accident seemed to have made it for her. She had fifty pounds of her little fortune laid by for the boy. She had a share of a cottage in a garden—not an English cottage indeed, but the upper floor of a two-storeyed French house; and she and her boy did much in the garden, cultivating prettinesses which do not commend themselves much to the villagers of St Honorat. Whether she ever regretted the step she had taken nobody ever knew. She might have been a lady with a larger house than any in St Honorat, and servants at her call. Perhaps she sometimes thought of that; perhaps she felt herself happier as she was; sometimes, I think, she felt that if she had known the boy was coming she might have possessed her soul in patience, and borne even with Mr Rosendale. But then at the time the decisive step was taken she did not know.

She hurried home in a great fright, not knowing what to do; then calmed herself with the thought that even if he had recognised her, there were many chances against his following her, or at least finding her, with no clue, and after so many years. And then a dreadful panic seized her at the thought that he might take her boy from her. He had known nothing about the boy: but if he discovered that fact it would make a great difference. He could not compel Janey to return to him, but he could take the boy. When this occurred to her she started up again, having just sat down, and put on her bonnet and called the child.

"Are you going out again, mother?" he cried.

"Yes, directly, directly: come, John, come, come!" she said, putting his cap upon his head and seizing him by the hand. She led him straight to the presbytery, and asked for the *cure*, and went in to the good priest in great agitation, leaving the boy with his housekeeper.

"M. l'Abbe," she said, with what the village called her English directness, "I have just seen my husband go past in the train!"

"Not possible!" said M. l'Abbe, who only half believed there was a husband at all.

"And he saw me. He will come back, and I am afraid he will find me. I want you to do something for me."

"With pleasure," said the priest; "I will come and meet Monsieur your husband, and I will explain——"

"That is not what I want you to do. I want you to let John stay with you, to keep him here till—till——He will want to take him away from me!" she cried.

"He will want to take you both away, *chere petite dame*. He has a right to do so."

"No, no! but I do not ask you what is his right. I ask you to keep John safe; to keep him here—till the danger has passed away!"

The priest tried to reason, to entreat, to persuade her that a father, not to say a husband, had his rights. But Janey would hear no reason: had she heard reason either from herself or another, she would not have been at St Honorat now. And he gave at last a reluctant consent. There was perhaps no harm in it after all. If a man came to claim his rights, he would not certainly go away again without some appeal to the authorities—which was a thing it must come to sooner or later,—if there was indeed a husband at all, and the story was true.

Janey then went back to her home. She thought she could await him there and defy him. "I will not go with you," she would say. "I may be your wife, but I am not your slave. You have left me alone for ten years. I will not go with you now!" She repeated this to herself many times, but it did not subdue the commotion in her being. She went out again when it became too much for her, locking her door with a strange sense that she might never come back again. She walked along the sea shore, repeating these words to herself, and then she walked up and down the streets, and went into the church and made the round of it, passing all the altars and wondering if the saints did pay any attention to the poor women who were there, as always, telling St Joseph or the Blessed Mary all about it. She sank down in a dark corner, and said—

"Oh, my God! oh, my God!"

She could not tell Him about it in her agitation, with her heart beating so, but only call His attention, as the woman in the Bible touched the Redeemer's robe. And then she went out and walked up and down again. I cannot tell what drew her back to the station—what fascination, what dreadful spell.

A STORY OF A WEDDING TOUR

Before she knew what she was doing she found herself there, walking up and down, up and down.

As if she were waiting for some one! "You have come to meet a friend?" some one said to her, with an air of suspicion. And she first nodded and then shook her head; but still continued in spite of herself to walk up and down. Then she said to herself that it was best so—that to get it over would be a great thing, now John was out of the way; he would be sure to find her sooner or later—far better to get it over! When the train came in, the slow local train, coming from the side of Italy, she drew herself back a little to watch. There was a great commotion when it drew up at the platform. A man got out and called all the loungers about to help to lift out a gentleman who was ill,—who had had a bad attack in the train.

"Is there anywhere here we can take him to? Is there any decent hotel? Is there a room fit to put my master in?" he cried.

He was English with not much French at his command, and in great distress. Janey, forgetting herself and her terrors, and strong in the relief of the moment that he whom she feared had not come, went up to offer her help. She answered the man's questions; she called the right people to help him; she summoned the *chef de Gare* to make some provision for carrying the stricken man to the hotel.

"I will go with you," she said to the servant, who felt as if an angel speaking English had suddenly come to his help. She stood by full of pity, as they lifted that great inert mass out of the carriage. Then she gave a great cry and fell back against the wall.

It was a dreadful sight the men said afterwards, enough to overcome the tender heart of any lady, especially of one so kind as Madame Jeanne. A huge man, helpless, unconscious, with a purple countenance, staring eyes, breathing so that you could hear him a mile off. No wonder that she covered her eyes with her hands not to see him; and then covered her ears with her hands not to hear him: but finally she hurried away to the hotel to prepare for him, and to call the doctor, that no time should be lost. Janey felt as if she was restored for the moment to life when there was something she could do. The questions were all postponed. She did not think of flight or concealment, or even of John at the presbytery. "He is my husband," she said, with awe in her heart.

This was how the train brought back to Janey the man whom the train had separated from her ten years before. The whole tragedy was of the railway, the noisy carriages, the snorting locomotives. He was taken to the hotel, but he never came to himself again, and died there next day, without being able to say what his object was, or why he had got out of the *rapide*, though unable to walk, and insisted on returning to St Honorat. It cost him his life; but then his life was not worth a day's purchase, all the doctors said, in the condition in which he was.

Friends had to be summoned, and men of business, and it was impossible but that Janey's secret should be made known. When she found herself and her son recognised, and that there could be no doubt that the boy was his father's heir, she was struck with a great horror which she never quite got over all her life. She had not blamed herself before; but now seemed to herself no less than the murderer of her husband: and could not forgive herself, nor get out of her eyes the face she had seen, nor out of her ears the dreadful sound of that labouring breath.

MACMILLAN COLLECTOR'S LIBRARY

Own the world's great works of literature in one beautiful collectible library

Designed and curated to appeal to book lovers everywhere, Macmillan Collector's Library editions are small enough to travel with you and striking enough to take pride of place on your bookshelf. These much-loved literary classics also make the perfect gift.

Beautifully made, every Macmillan Collector's Library book adheres to the same high production values. Each hardback features gilt edges, a ribbon marker and cloth binding, and every paperback has a bespoke illustrated cover.

Discover a new and exciting anthology or cherish your favourite classic stories with this elegant collection.

**Macmillan Collector's Library:
own, collect, and treasure**

Discover the full range at
panmacmillan.com/mcl